SKYLA GRAY

A Matter of Taste

a Vampire Romance

Contents

Chapter One

My copy of *Fangs* falls out of my hands as someone bangs on the bathroom door. I scramble for the magazine, face heating even though there's no one here to witness my embarrassment. It feels like getting caught watching porn—though it's not! It's *tastefully erotic* photographs of vampires living their luxurious lifestyles, which is very different. But my roommates would never let me live it down if they caught me with something so ridiculous. Fantasizing about undead aristocrats is one of my few self-indulgences.

"Nora! *Nora!* Nora Rivers!"

"What?" I yell, shoving the magazine to the bottom of the stack atop the toilet. They all fall over, scattering across the tile, and I hiss out a curse as I bend to gather them again. "Christ's sake, can I not have a *minute* to myself?"

"It's an emergency," my roommate shouts back.

I roll my eyes, stacking the magazines. In Sophie's world, an emergency could mean anything from "she ran out of liquid eyeliner" to "she saw a spider on the wall."

I flush the toilet to keep up the facade I was using this bathroom like a normal person instead of hiding from the world with my spicy magazine. This is the only place I can get any privacy, and as Sophie's interruption proved, even that privacy is limited. At least I fixed the lock last week, so she can't barge in during my showers anymore.

I open the door and falter. Sophie is standing barely a foot away, hands clasped in front of her chest and eyes teary. Her face is splotchy, her poorly dyed blue hair in more disarray than usual. She looks genuinely distressed, which makes me feel bad for assuming this was another "I found a dead fly on the windowsill" type of emergency.

"Sophie," I say, softening. "What's wrong?"

"You have to come and see." She grabs my wrist and tugs me along, giving me no choice but to follow. She half drags me through our messy little studio apartment, which is cramped and chaotic with only thin divider screens to section off our three separate living areas. We barely make it through without knocking anything over, and then it's out into the hallway with its mysterious stains, down the creaking stairs, to the front door of the apartment building.

When I see the bright orange notice waiting there, my stomach drops. Other tenants are already gathering around, murmuring to each other, but I push through to read what it says.

The first line, in bold, damning letters, hits me like a fist: CONDEMNED.

I lean in, the words blurring as panic takes hold. The main details sink in: unfit for human occupancy or use. Effective immediately.

"We're being evicted," I whisper, straightening. This can't be happening. It just can't. I mean, we always knew this place was unsafe. There are the cockroaches, the broken carbon monoxide detectors, the lack of hot water… that one incident with the black mold…

But there's a reason we've stuck around despite all of that: we can't afford to live anywhere else in this goddamn city. Los Angeles is the most beautiful place in the world, in my opinion. Unfortunately, a lot of people seem to agree, thus the skyrocketing prices. Despite the problems, this apartment complex was an incredible find because of how affordable it was. That's why my roommates and I have hung on for years, especially as rent all around us climbed steadily upward. The landlord is a scumbag, but at least he didn't raise the prices too much. Speaking of which…

"Where's Mr. Wilson?" I ask aloud. I barge back into the building, Sophie following in my wake with her hands fluttering like distressed birds. I head to the landlord's office, but I'm unsurprised to find it locked and dark. Empty. I jiggle the handle and peer through the window, but it confirms what I've already suspected: that piece of shit is long gone. He's always proved difficult to find whenever there was an issue. He's likely halfway across the country by now to avoid the fallout from this. Probably sipping margaritas on a beach somewhere.

"Nora?" Sophie asks in a small voice from behind me. "What are we going to do?"

I've always been the levelheaded one. The mom friend. The one with all of the answers.

But as I stare at the landlord's locked door, that orange notice burning bright in my mind, my stomach sinks. I pride myself on being prepared and practical, ready for anything, an anchor in the chaos that always surrounds me. But right now, I'm at a loss.

The pressure weighs on me, pushing me down until I feel small and helpless.

"I…" I swallow with a dry click. The words *I don't know* are on the tip of my tongue, but I can't bring myself to voice them aloud and face her disappointment. I'm supposed to be the person my friends can rely on. I *need* to be that person for them now. "I need a minute," I say, and rush back up the stairs to our apartment. I head back into the bathroom, lock the door behind me, and try not to panic.

Chapter Two

After ten minutes of hyperventilating into the towels, I swallow both my panic and my pride, and call my mom.

My heart drums in my ears as it rings… and rings… and goes to voicemail.

I don't bother leaving a message. It was a long shot. Mom is doubtlessly off galivanting around the country in her home-slash-van, selling her stupid paintings, forgetting about my existence. I've always had to take care of myself, and this is no exception.

When I finally emerge from the bathroom, Sophie is on the couch in our tiny sectioned-off "living room." So is our other roommate Elaine, who must've just gotten home; she's still in her work clothes, radiating a powerful aroma of coffee. They look even more contrasting than usual, with Elaine in her black barista outfit and Sophie in her fuzzy pajamas. Elaine has dark skin, cat-eye glasses, and immaculate braids, while Sophie is chalky white with fading blue hair dye and last night's eyeliner.

Then there's me: tall and angular and awkward, with dirty blond hair piled in a messy bun and wire-rimmed glasses.

But despite our differences, we're a united trio—especially now, in our time of need. Sophie is on her phone, Elaine clicking away determinedly on her laptop. Without a word, I grab my own computer from my sectioned-off space and plop down in my armchair to join them in researching.

We start by looking at legal options. Of course we're supposed to be due financial compensation for this situation, but given that the landlord is MIA, I don't have much hope for that. Even if we eventually get a payout, it could take months or years for the legal system to catch up, and we need someplace to live *now*.

Which brings us to option two: finding a new place to rent. But we hit a wall quickly. That wall being *money*, of course. This building has always been a dumpster heap, but that meant it was *cheap*.

"Oh my God," Sophie groans, wincing as she scrolls through listings on her phone. "These numbers make me want to hurl. Like, who can afford this?"

"People with real jobs?" Elaine suggests, deadpan.

"Girl, you do realize I make more money than you—"

"*Barely*, and only since you started—"

"Ladies," I snap. "Focus."

They fall silent and continue scrolling. But even after hours of research and depressing discussions about where we can cut our already-paltry budgets, the numbers won't add up.

Our roommate situation has always sounded like the start of a bad joke. *A blogger, a barista, and a tutor-slash-college-student walk into a bar, and...*

And walk out again, probably, because they can't afford to buy a drink in this economy.

I shut my eyes, fingers stilling on my laptop as I fight back a wave of despair. I thought I was being responsible these last few years. I've scraped and clawed my way through life, working myself to the bone in dead-end jobs. A college degree in a practical field would change everything for me. Most people I went to high school with have already graduated, but life took me on a different path.

Working as a private tutor, I've pinched pennies and skipped meals so I can finally start at UCLA this fall with minimal loans. After years of floundering, I'm finally taking steps toward the future I want. With a degree in engineering, my future will be secure. It's at the top of the "degrees that make the most money" list—that's why I chose it.

But now? I can't pay for school when I can't even afford rent.

Elaine is the first to shut her laptop. "I don't think this is going to work."

Sophie reluctantly lowers her phone. "Then what do we do?"

I keep scrolling through rentals without looking up. There has to be something. There *has* to be.

After a beat, Elaine says, "I guess I could go back to living with my parents for a while."

Sophie groans. "David *has* been asking about me moving in with him at some point, but…"

An awkward silence falls, broken only by my increasingly desperate scrolling. But when I realize they're both looking at me, I slam my laptop shut and force a tight-lipped smile.

"Yeah," I say. "You guys should do that. I'll figure something out."

They *should* explore their options. It's not their fault I don't have any.

Because I have no boyfriend. No family. Nobody at all.

"I mean, I don't *want* to live with David," Sophie says quickly. "His roommates suck and I know he'll just expect me to start doing his laundry and shit." Her lower lip trembles. "I want to live with you guys."

"I really don't want to live with my parents, either," Elaine says. "They got a cat a couple months ago, and I'm allergic, so…"

"Guys," I say, hating the fact that I feel like crying. "We're talking last resorts here. What else can we do? We can't afford these places."

"Well…" Sophie's face scrunches. "I guess we'll have to come up with more money."

"Wow," Elaine says. "Why didn't I think of that?"

"I mean, it's not going to be *fun*," she says. "But there are ways."

"Like what?"

"Let's find out."

We all dive back into researching furiously. Ideas get tossed around, each one progressively more outlandish.

"We could donate our eggs," Elaine suggests. "Or sell drugs."

"Or sell feet pics!" Sophie contributes. "Or… more than feet pics…"

"None of these are reliable sources of income," I say, rubbing my temples. "Nobody's going to let us sign a lease with *feet pics* as our main way to pay rent." Not to mention that I don't even want to touch that idea. Not because of prudishness or pride, but because it could ruin my career. Not that I'm going to have a career if I can't figure out how to pay for college…

"Ugh, this is so stupid," Sophie complains. "Why can't we go back to the good old days when artists and writers had rich patrons to pay for everything?" She sinks down on the couch, throwing a dramatic arm over her forehead. "Like, come on, rich people. Do something useful for once."

Elaine rolls her eyes from the other end of the couch, her fingers clicking away on her laptop keyboard.

But I sit up, my thoughts catching on that word: *patron*. "Wait a second."

Elaine's fingers go still. So do Sophie's kicking feet. They both look at me.

"I know that face," Sophie says, expression brightening. "You've thought of something."

"Maybe." I stand up and start to pace the length of the room, nibbling on my thumbnail as I think. "It's a long shot, but…"

My roommates' eyes follow me back and forth, back and forth.

"Spill!" Sophie says.

"Well, I'm just thinking, there *are* modern-day patrons. But not for artists. Or… not exclusively for artists, but there's no reason why they can't be…"

"Ah," Elaine says, her eyes widening.

Sophie's gaze whips back and forth between us, still confused. "Somebody better explain or I'm gonna lose it."

I pause by the window. "Valentines," I say. "Valentines have patrons. And the gig pays well… or so I hear, anyway." I hurry onward, not wanting to be questioned on exactly how much I know about the vampire scene. My roommates would never let me live it down.

The truth is, I've always been enamored by vampires and their glamorous human companions, also known as valentines. It's a practical exchange: valentines donate fresh blood to their fanged patrons, and in return, vampires compensate them generously.

Yet even I can see the romantic side of the lifestyle, too. To live alongside the nocturnal nobility, to attend their lavish, exclusive parties echoing Regency-era decadence…

"Nora, you magnificent bitch," Sophie says. "You're so right. That'd be an assload of money." Her gaze turns dreamy. "Not to mention the perks. The ballgowns, the dancing, the high society life…"

"Getting bitten every day," Elaine adds, wrinkling her nose.

"Hey, some people are into that," Sophie says.

I remember a picture from my magazine—a close-up of a vampire lovingly sinking his teeth into a woman's neck, her face slack with bliss—and flush. "Yeah, I've… I've heard that too." I clear my throat. "I'm sure it's not as glamorous as they make it look. Especially with the social stigma."

No more needs to be said. We're all aware of the downsides to such arrangements. Valentines are alternatively seen as idols and gold diggers, glamorous and debauched. It's often a short-lived arrangement, and I've heard a lot of sad stories about retired valentines struggling to find work and acceptance in society after getting pushed aside. Plus there are the horror stories of vampire-blood addiction and the like.

"I'm sure David won't mind me getting dicked down by the undead as long as I'm getting a valentine salary," Sophie says, derailing my train of thought.

"Sophie!" My face heats further. "I don't think they like being called that. And I-I mean… I'm sure not *all* valentines are hooking up with their patrons, right? That's probably just a stereotype."

Sophie lets out an undignified snort of laughter. "Oh, Nora," she says. "You sweet, innocent baby."

"Debates about the nature of the career aside…" Elaine says. "What are the chances that one of us would be accepted?" Elaine asks, her brow furrowed. "It'd practically be like winning the lottery."

I shrug. Nobody knows what vampires look for in their valentines, but I do know that most people are turned away before even getting a chance to attend one of their famous Valentine's Day balls. "Like I said, it's a long shot. But unless somebody has any better ideas…?" I glance at each of my roommates, who both shake their heads. "It couldn't hurt to try out, if one of you wants to."

Sophie sits up, a grin slowly spreading across her face. "I'm so in."

Elaine, after a moment's consideration, closes her laptop. "Like you said, it can't hurt."

I blow out a breath. "Well, let's figure out how we do this, and I can drive—"

"Oh, hell no," Sophie says with a wicked grin. "This was your idea. You're not getting out of joining us."

I try to fight the blush creeping up the back of my neck. "What? Don't be ridiculous."

Elaine pushes her glasses up her nose, looking at me. "Oh, so it's not ridiculous for us, but it's ridiculous for you?"

"That's not what I mean…" I look away, rubbing the back of my neck. "I'm not that kind of person."

"*What* kind of person?" Sophie asks, placing her hands on her hips and staring at me.

"Oh, so you're asking us to do something you think you're too good for?" Elaine suggests, scowling.

"That's not it!" I pause, flustered, trying to get a hold of my thoughts. That's not what I mean at all. It's not that I'm too good for being a valentine. I mean, it *could* jeopardize my career, but that's not even the point. I don't think I'd make it there in the first place. It's just that both of my roommates are so… unique. Sophie is going to be a famous writer someday; Elaine is just waiting for a break in her acting career. And I *know* both of them are going to make it big someday. They're the kind of people who become valentines. Not people like me, who go to bed at nine p.m., choose an engineering path because it's practical, and carry Tums at all times.

Believing in that kind of hope is dangerous. If I think too hard about all of those pictures I've studied in *Fangs* magazines, try to imagine *myself* in the place of a valentine… me in a beautiful dress, with a beautiful man, his hand grazing my hip…

My face must be bright red by now. My roommates are still staring at me. "Fine," I say. "What the hell. I'll try out too."

Chapter Three

My roommates and I spend all evening calling different valentine agencies around the city. Each time, we meet only rejection. The Valentine's Day Ball, one of the biggest events in the vampire world, is only a week away, and most agencies state that their rosters of hopeful humans are already full. Others snootily inform us that they only take referrals, anyway.

Finally, I reach the last agency on my list, a tiny organization called The Valentine Society.

"There's only one review," I tell my roommates. "But it *is* a five-star one."

Elaine shrugs. "Worth a shot."

I nearly drop my phone when the woman on the line says they're accepting applications. She hardly sounds enthusiastic about it, and this is far from the most prestigious of the businesses we've been looking at, but a tryout is a tryout.

Soon enough the three of us are booked for the next evening. We share our last bottle of rosé to celebrate. Despite my insistence that I don't have a chance of being chosen, I fall asleep with thoughts of ballgowns and fangs.

* * *

The next day, I'm so nervous I can barely eat. But the advice online was adamant about having a hearty meal a few hours before giving blood, so I decide to cook breakfast. But my heart sinks when I open the fridge and realize it's nearly empty aside from half-used condiments and too-old takeout.

The pang of anxiety is familiar. So many times in my childhood, I was left to fend for myself with a fridge just like this. But that means I'm used to pulling together a struggle meal. After a few minutes, I scrounge up some peanut butter and jelly. We're out of bread, but tortillas will work in a pinch.

"Breakfast of champions," I say, passing the surprisingly delicious creations to my roommates as they emerge from their screened-off partitions of the living room.

I spend most of breakfast coaxing my roommates into eating, but I manage a few nibbles before ushering them out the door. They're the ones who have a real shot at this, anyway. I'm just here to make sure they show up on time.

Between the three of us, we only have one car: Elaine's clunky old sedan that hasn't had working air conditioning in years. But I end up driving, as usual, when we're together, because Elaine's road rage has made me break out in stress-induced hives before.

Elaine and Sophie chatter the whole drive over, but we're silent when we lay eyes on our destination. This feels a lot more real with the sight of the narrow, gothic house with its iron gate. We're about to meet a real-life vampire. Something I've daydreamed about for an embarrassingly long time, but I'm not about to show them how nervous and starstruck I am.

"Let's keep in mind they're just people, at the end of the day," I say as calmly as I can manage, as I roll past the gate and park in front of the house.

"Just super rich, super famous people," Sophie says, nodding.

"No different from your average brush with a celebrity at a grocery store, really," Elaine says.

"Except we're the groceries."

"And they're a little bit dead."

"And—"

"Guys," I say, turning off the car. "*Please* be normal."

"This is us being normal," Sophie says.

I sigh, and get out of the car. A moment later they join me. They're uncharacteristically quiet as they stare at the door to the house. I glance at them. While I opted for my usual faded T-shirt and jeans look, they both dressed up for the occasion: Elaine in a sharp blazer and tailored trousers, Sophie in a fluffy, pink monstrosity of a minidress. But despite their earlier enthusiasm, Sophie is wide-eyed, and Elaine is trembling.

"Hey," I say, more softly. "Come here. We've got this." I pull each of them in, and they crowd in for a group hug. "We're doing this for all of us. Remember our promise."

"Right," Elaine says, letting out a shaky breath.

"Fingers crossed that one of us has tasty blood," Sophie whispers.

"And it only takes one." We've already agreed that if one of us is selected, whoever it is will pay for the apartment until the others can come up with the money. We all link our pinkies in a promise and nod solemnly.

I study their faces as I pull away. We may have met online in a moment of mutual desperation, and living together the last few years hasn't always—or ever—been easy, but they're my best friends. Ever since I met them, I knew one of them was going to end up fabulously famous and rich if there's any justice in the world. They just have that kind of star quality. And when it happens, I'll be delighted to just be at their side.

We step inside together, and are greeted by a blond woman who introduces herself as Lissa. I hesitate for a moment when I see her, but after seeing the color in her face and the rise and fall of her chest, I relax. *Human.*

"All three of you, hm?" she asks, eyeing each of us.

I squeeze both of my roommates' hands. "That's right."

"Well, we'll see how that goes," she mutters. Then, before anyone can answer, "This way!"

She leads us down a hallway and into a parlor.

My roommates *ooh* and *aah* under their breath as they look around. I survey everything more skeptically. It's very old-fashioned, the sort of fancy little parlor I'd see in a historical show or something. A round table sits in the center, surrounded by plush chairs. A chandelier hangs above, and old-fashioned bronze sconces on the wall provide lighting, since the curtains are drawn against the dying rays of the sunset.

"Yes, yes, I know," says Lissa, rolling her eyes as she gestures around. "I keep telling him it's all a bit much, but—"

"Lissa, must you? Every time?"

I freeze at a voice behind me. It's pleasant and low with an aristocratic British accent. But there's something about it, no, something about the *presence* at my back, really, that makes my spine stiffen in sudden alarm.

My roommates turn with me. A man stands in the doorway a few feet away. But he isn't a man at all, even though he looks like a perfect gentleman, with his neatly trimmed beard and well-tailored suit. Something about him screams *dangerous*.

Predator.

Vampire.

"My name is Benjamin Acharya," the man says, extending a hand. "Pleasure to meet you."

Somewhere beneath my panic, it registers that it's an odd name for a vampire. Most use their court names—*de Camelia*, for example—rather than a surname.

My friends are frozen on either side of me. After a moment, I shake off the same paralysis and step forward, plastering on a smile as I reach to take his hand.

"The pleasure is—oh, shit."

My attempt at a greeting falls apart as Sophie slumps at my side. I rush to catch her, and only half succeed, bringing us both awkwardly lurching toward the floor. But a moment later, I feel the touch of a cold hand and my body is suddenly weightless.

In the blink of an eye, Benjamin has made his way to us, holding each of us up with an arm.

"Are you quite alright?" he asks, shockingly unfazed.

"I-I'm fine, but she's…" I turn to look at Sophie as Benjamin sets me back on my feet.

"She's fainted," Benjamin says. "Not an abnormal reaction to meeting a vampire for the first time. She'll recover shortly."

"Is there anything we should do?" I ask. I glance at Elaine, who is still standing frozen and wide-eyed.

"Just give her a moment. I'll set her on the chaise here?"

"Sure." I wring my hands, following close behind as Benjamin lifts my friend with startling ease and lays her on the chaise. As I crouch beside her, softly calling her name, she stirs. "Hi, sweetie. You okay?"

Sophie blinks at me, puzzled for a moment before her eyes go wide. "Oh, God," she says, sitting up. I place my hand on her arm, urging her not to move too fast. "I'm so sorry!"

"It happens all the time," Benjamin says from somewhere behind me. The moment he speaks, Sophie's eyes roll back and she swoons again.

I grab her shoulder to steady her and shoot an apologetic smile over my shoulder at the vampire. Truth be told, my heart is still beating erratically as well, but I know it's just a deep-buried instinct acting up. *Stop it*, I scold myself. *He's just a polite man who happens to be undead and fanged.* "Maybe I should take her out to the car."

"That's probably for the best," Benjamin says.

I help Sophie to her feet, put an arm around her shoulders, and guide her outside. Elaine is still standing in the doorway as though paralyzed. "Do you want to come with us?"

"I…" She blinks, takes a deep breath. "No. I can do this."

I nod. "I'll be right back."

I help Sophie down the hallway and out the front door, slow step by slow step, though gradually she becomes better able to support herself.

"I'm sorry," she says, chin wobbling. "I'm really sorry. I didn't know it would be like that."

"Don't worry. He said it's common."

"Still, how *embarrassing*…"

I murmur soothing words and help her to the parked car. I'm easing her into the backseat and encouraging her to drink some water when Elaine comes running, tears in her eyes.

"I'm sorry!" she blurts. "I'm sorry. I can't do it. He was about to bite me and I couldn't—I mean, it was all very sexy and consensual, but I still—"

"Whoa, whoa, whoa." I make sure Sophie is safely in the car before turning and hugging her. "It's okay! It's fine. You tried. We knew this was a long shot, right?"

Elaine buries her face in my shoulder. "But I really wanted it to work," she says.

I shut my eyes, grant myself a brief moment to let the disappointment sink in, and then turn back to practicality. "It's okay," I say again. "We'll figure something else out. Let's get you guys home, and then—"

"Wait." She pulls back, gives me a pleading look. "But you haven't had a chance yet."

I shake my head. "It doesn't matter. It was never gonna be me."

"What do you mean?"

"I mean… I was just here for you guys."

She blinks at me. "But you didn't freak out," she says. "You're the only one who kept your head. You have to try."

I want to argue and get them home so we can start brainstorming new and more practical ideas. But I've never been good at saying *no* to my roommates. It's impossible when Elaine, who is normally so dry and aloof, is giving me this misty, hopeful look. "Fine," I say. "But don't get your hopes up. I'll be back in a few minutes."

Against my better instinct, I trudge back inside alone. I find Benjamin in the parlor, sitting at the table with a cup of tea. His eyebrows rise as I enter the room.

"Ah," he says, setting down his cup. "You're back."

I manage a wan smile. "My friends insisted."

He studies me as I take a seat across from him. There's still a buzz of electricity under my skin from being in the room with him, but it's easier to bear than before. "You don't want to?" he asks.

I shrug. "I was mostly here to make sure they didn't do anything stupid."

"It seems your job is done, in that regard. You're free to go, if you wish."

I hesitate. He's right. My friends are fine, though it's clear none of them have a future in this line of work. There's no reason I *have* to stick around and see if it's possible for me to pass the test myself.

No reason at all, except for that traitorous quiver of hope in my chest. And the fact that if I walk away now, I will forever wonder what could've been.

I'm too embarrassed to voice the sentiment. But after a moment, Benjamin moves over to the couch and gestures to the seat beside him. I slowly cross the room and sit at his side.

This close, I can *feel* the energy he exudes. Every hair on my body prickles, goose bumps shivering over my skin to warn me there's a predator nearby. But Benjamin's eyes are warm as he looks at me, and when he holds out a hand, I lift my wrist for him to grasp.

He gives me an odd look.

"That's the safest place to bite," I say, "right?"

His lips quirk. "You seem to know more about vampires than your reluctance to be here might suggest."

"I—" I flush slightly. "I mean, I've read about this sort of thing. I'm curious about vampires. Who isn't?"

He chuckles, turning my arm in his grasp. His fangs slide out behind his lips, and I can't help but stare. His eyes flick to mine. "May I?"

No turning back now. I nod, feeling ridiculous for the way

my blood is roaring in my ears. I've always thought that vampires were romantic, but I'm certain the reality won't live up to the fantasy of it. It never does, with these sorts of things. There's a reason I prefer fictional men to—

Oh.

His fangs sink into my wrist. There's the slightest prick of pain, and then the world goes hazy. My head feels light, but not in a way like I'm going to faint. More like the feeling after a few drinks, that low, pleasant buzz that makes all of your troubles seem like background noise. My head lolls back as I sigh. It's so… blissful. Like being drunk, but better.

Benjamin pulls away from my wrist, and I am suddenly burdened with self-consciousness. I sit up straight, cheeks flaming, and cross my legs. Then uncross them again, wondering if I'm just bringing attention to the fact that I was turned on by being bitten. What *was* that? Does *everyone* feel that? I side-eye Benjamin to see if he noticed, but he's busy pulling out a dark vial of liquid and dabbing some on a handkerchief.

"Vampire blood," he murmurs.

I flinch back, some of the haze clearing from my mind. "Isn't that a drug?"

"Only when ingested. Like this, it can heal minor injuries without side effects."

He waits for me to offer my wrist again and presses the handkerchief to the puncture marks. They close up in moments.

I study the healing process, fascinated, before looking up to meet Benjamin's eyes. He's watching me—studying me, really, as if waiting for something.

"Well?" he asks.

"Well what?" I shoot back. "Aren't you supposed to tell me

how I taste?"

He huffs a laugh. "First I'm interested in whether or not *you* enjoyed the experience. You seemed reluctant, so…"

My face heats. "Of course I did," I mutter, pushing my glasses up and looking away. "I'm sure everyone does."

"No, they don't," he says. "Your friends had more common reactions. Plenty of people fail, even upon reaching the point of being bitten. But for a few rare people, I have heard, it is quite enjoyable."

I shake my head, unwilling to believe it. This is probably a marketing ploy. "I'm sure it's not that rare." I'm not the sort of person who these things happen to. "So tell me. How'd I taste?"

He looks at me for a long moment, as if trying to read something in my expression. Then he says, finally, "Quite wonderful, actually. Not too sweet, but… rich, smooth. You'd make a strong candidate for a valentine."

I shut my eyes, biting back a curse. *Of course.* This would be so much easier if I could say that I wasn't well-suited for the job for *any* reason. But if I walk away now, it'd be because it's my choice. How could I explain that to my friends? I could lie, of course, but the guilt would eat away at me forever. And aside from that, how could I live with myself if I gave up my future because of fear?

But my future is the problem. Who could take me seriously as an engineer if they see me as some vampire's blood doll? Certain people see valentines as one step above prostitution. I don't agree with it, but I need to be practical.

Plus… could I bring myself to do it? Even if giving blood doesn't concern me, just like Sophie told me, everyone expects valentines to be intimate with their vampire patrons. I'd have to live with one, and if they expected that…

"*That* reaction," Benjamin says, "is what concerns me. You don't seem to want to be here, and that is the most important thing."

I sigh, opening my eyes to look at him again. "It's not that I don't want it," I say. "I… I liked that feeling. A lot. But…" I trail off, and he waits patiently for me to continue. "It's the lifestyle that worries me."

His brows rise. "That's the main appeal for most people."

"Right, but…" I look down at my lap. "Look, I'll be honest. I'm doing this for the money. But it's not the kind of life I want long-term. I was supposed to start school this fall. And I… I'm not…" I shake my head, swallowing past a lump in my throat.

"I understand," Benjamin says. "You're not the first person to come to me with such concerns. Most valentine contracts last a year, and you're under no obligation to continue beyond that. I'll focus on finding you a patron who can be discreet, and out of the public eye as much as possible. Most of us prefer that, despite what the magazines and TV may suggest."

I didn't know that was an option. But my hope dies again as quickly as it flared up. "My public image also… isn't the only thing that concerns me." I drop my gaze. I'm not sure how to put this into words without feeling foolish, but I know I have to say it before I sign anything agreeing to this. It wouldn't be fair to Benjamin or to me. "I'm… not looking for a romantic relationship. And I'm not a casual sort of person when it comes to those things. So… I would prefer to avoid anything, um, intimate. Is that possible?"

I feel stupid even asking. It's like looking for a sugar daddy and asking, *actually, can we just be sugar friends?* But I have to know.

I've had only a couple of romantic relationships in my life, and they were enough for me to decide I don't need that kind of distraction.

Benjamin's brow creases as he considers. "It's not unheard of, but it will make it more difficult to find a patron for you. Feeding is inherently intimate. Most vampires desire the… full experience, shall we say, with their valentine."

My heart sinks, even though I already expected as much. "I see."

"I will do my best to find you the match you're looking for," he says. "That's all I can promise. But you will be paid for the night of the Valentine's Ball, with or without a more long-term arrangement. Are those terms agreeable to you?"

I suppress a sigh. How can I say no to that? Especially with my roommates relying on me? "Okay." I massage my temples. "Can I see the contract?"

Chapter Four

Beside our parked car, Sophie, Elaine, and I share a group hug and a short celebration involving lots of excited squealing. Payment for the Valentine's Day Ball won't solve all of our problems, but the money will give us enough to pay for a first and last month's rent on a new place, so our situation just got a little brighter.

We drive back to our condemned apartment, where that orange notice on the door doesn't scare me quite so badly anymore. Everything important fits in one suitcase, a habit I never broke after a childhood of moving every several months. Then, they drop me back off at Benjamin's, where I'll be staying for the next week to train for the ball.

"I still don't get why you have to *train*," Sophie says, pouting at the little gothic house like it's done this to her personally.

"Vampires are strict about their etiquette," I say. I'd been relieved to hear there was training involved, since I've heard rumors of the strict, old-fashioned expectations at private vampire events. "These balls are basically like traveling back to the Regency era. Lots of rules and dance steps to learn."

"Except they can eat you if you curtsy wrong," Elaine says.

"Benjamin assures me they'll only eat me with consent. I'll

have a blood card with my tasting notes, where they sign up for time slots and everything."

My friends exchange a glance and burst into giggles.

My face flames. "Not like *that*. My God, you two…"

When their laughter finally dies down, silence lingers. As I hesitate, looking from Sophie to Elaine, I find myself fighting back an embarrassing desire to cry.

"You guys will be okay?" I ask.

"Sure," Sophie says. "I'll stay with David."

"And I'll be at my parents' place," Elaine agrees.

"Keep researching new apartments," I say.

"We will." Sophie grins. "Don't have too much fun without us!"

With one last goodbye, I head inside to train for my big night.

* * *

I throw myself into valentine lessons with the same intensity I dedicate to everything else. If I'm going to do this, I plan on doing it well. I show up to our first middle-of-the-night lesson yawning but prepared, with a notebook and pen in hand.

Benjamin smiles when he sees me. "So different than my previous trainee," he says, with a wry shake of his head.

"How many valentines have you arranged matches for?" I ask, remembering that singular rave review.

"Just the one," he says. "The Valentine Society just opened last year, so most applicants go to the larger agencies with vampires who aren't, well… courtless, like I am. And I'm careful with those I select. Most vampires only consider the taste of a human's blood, but to me, it's the enjoyment of being bitten that's most important."

"Is it really so rare?"

He gives me a look. "You saw it for yourself with your friends."

I sink into my chair with my brow furrowed.

Benjamin waits for a moment to see if I have any further questions, and then launches into today's lesson. "We'll begin with an overview of the four vampire courts…"

I dutifully take notes as he talks, sitting in rapt silence. I've always been a good student, and it helps when the subject material is interesting.

"Camelia, of the rose and dagger, is called the court of beauty. Models, actors… many of them are famous, or hoping to be, so it's unlikely to be a good match for your desire for discretion." He moves down the list. "Vulpe may be a possibility. It is the court of artists, represented by the snake and goblet. Some are more public-facing, but others prefer their privacy."

I bite my lip. "I'd… prefer to avoid that court, too."

Benjamin shoots me an amused glance. "Vulpe? Curious. I don't believe I've ever had someone opposed to them."

"Yeah, well." I shrug half-heartedly. "I don't mesh well with artistic types."

His brow furrows.

"I know how it sounds! I just…" The truth is that I made a promise to myself a long time ago: never fall in love with an artist. Not after I spent my entire life feeling like I was second best to my own mother, who always loved her art more than me. I won't put myself in a situation where I'm second best again. But I don't want to touch on my relationship with my mom when I barely know him, so I scramble for an explanation.

"Your reasons are your own. I'll respect your wishes." Benjamin shrugs, and moves on. "The next court is Solomon." He shows me an icon of a moth over a skull's mouth. "They are… certainly private, as you would prefer. They deal with vampire law and the secrets of our species, such as details of the creation of new vampires. But they are considered the most dangerous of the courts."

"I didn't realize being a valentine could be dangerous," I say, my stomach flipping.

"It isn't, generally," he says. "Our treatment of valentines is considered symbolic of our promise to do no harm to humankind, and thus the peace that exists between us. None of us wish to return to the dark days that came before. The court wars, the hunters, living in the shadows…" He shakes his head. "Suffice to say, breaking a valentine contract is one of the most severe crimes in vampire society. And we enforce the law among our own kind, as we swore to humans we would, long ago."

"What if I broke the contract?" I ask.

"You'd be immediately dismissed without payment for the rest of your term and blacklisted by the vampire courts. But short of upholding your duties, there isn't much you could do to violate it. Still… Solomon attracts vampires of a certain character, and a Solomon valentine's duties would likely include attending Solomon *parties*, which are…" His lips twist as he pauses, as though considering how much to say. "Not a good match for your preferences."

"None of this sounds very promising so far," I say, sighing.

"Well, that brings us to the last of the four courts. Celeste, the court of the quill and moon, who dedicate themselves to preserving history over their long lifespans." He taps the icon. "Scholars and historians. If you want a private, quiet life as a valentine, this is your best bet. My last client was placed with a Celeste vampire. However, they *are* the smallest of the courts, and rarely the most enthusiastic partygoers, so I can only hope that there will be someone looking for a valentine at the ball."

I place an elbow on the table, propping my chin up with one hand. It's hard not to let my thoughts run away with that idea. A scholarly vampire… "That sounds like my dream life," I say with a wistful sigh.

Benjamin gives a wry smile. "I will do my best to arrange it for you," he says. "Though I find these situations rarely work out as perfectly as one might hope. You may be surprised by what you end up wanting."

I smile and agree, though privately, I think he's wrong. I know exactly what I want, and I don't intend to bend on the matter.

* * *

Most of Benjamin's lessons are easy, even with my thoughts muddled by sleep deprivation. I've never had a problem memorizing facts or rules, and vampires and etiquette are no different.

But then come the dance lessons.

I memorize the steps of every dance quickly, but Benjamin's

frown is unrelenting.

"You're so stiff," he says. One hand on my lower back tries to coax me into a position my body doesn't seem willing to bend into. "Try to relax. Follow my lead. Feel the music, rather than just performing the steps."

"I'm trying," I huff. "I just don't know *how* to do that." And trying to *force* myself to relax is paradoxical. Sometimes I manage it for a second, but my body tenses as soon as my mind wanders.

I find his instructions aggravatingly vague, impossible to follow. It reminds me of being a child, when my mom attempted to teach me how to paint. Lessons that usually ended with me in frustrated tears. The memory—along with the familiar feeling that this can only end in disappointment for us both—only makes me more awkward.

After cringing my way through another dance, I shut my eyes, letting out a frustrated noise. "I'm hopeless at this."

A moment passes, and a hand pats my shoulder. "Not everyone can be good at everything," Benjamin says. You've got the most important parts of being a valentine down already; the rest of this is just icing on the cake." When I open my eyes, he gives me a wry look. "I promise, dancing is only a minor part of all of this," he says. "You're doing wonderfully, Nora, really."

It's embarrassing how much the praise warms me. I manage a small smile, tucking hair behind my ear, despite my lingering frustration with myself.

I hope he's right. Because after what feels like a ludicrously short period of time, the night of the ball arrives.

* * *

I stare at myself in the mirror.

The dress is white tulle, so delicate it's nearly transparent in the bodice, but with intricate pink flower appliqués providing coverage for my breasts. Below the waist, layers of ethereal fabric and further floral appliqués build into a voluminous, dramatic skirt.

"I look straight out of a fairy tale," I murmur. Though the skirt is full, the sheer bodice shows far more skin than I'm used to. My back is entirely bare, and the tightly laced bodice has coaxed out some cleavage I wasn't aware I had. "Though maybe risqué… Are you sure this isn't too much?"

Lissa gives a distinctly unladylike snort from where she's watching. "Trust me," she says, "you don't have to worry about that. You look perfect." I flush at the praise, especially from her. It's hard to forget how brusque she was when we first met, but she's softened over the last few days I've been here. "Now…" She leans forward, clasping her hands together. "Can I do your makeup too? Please?"

I'm happy to agree, especially since I can't remember the last time I touched a makeup brush. I've never been very good at it. Lissa grumbles as I wrinkle my nose at the tickling sensation. My eyes water every time she comes near them with a pencil. But after a considerable amount of wrangling with my body's aversion to her tools, Lissa spins me around to face the mirror, and I find myself gazing at a new version of myself.

I tilt my head slowly from side to side, admiring her work. I was afraid I'd look ridiculous in heavy makeup, but Lissa used a light touch. I don't look unlike myself, just like a better version, my skin smooth and my face glowing. My cheekbones and lips shimmer, and white liner makes my eyes appear larger than life. My eyelids are brushed with blushing pink to match the rose appliqués on my dress. I look dreamy, ethereal.

"Correction: *now* you look straight out of a fairy tale," Lissa says.

I smile, pushing my glasses up. I insisted on keeping them, despite Lissa trying to get me into contacts. "Thanks, Lissa. This is unreal." But my smile fades the longer I look at myself in the mirror. "You and Benjamin have worked so hard to help me," I say, a lump rising in my throat. "I don't know how to thank you." Or live up to their expectations.

Lissa pats my back in an approximation of a comforting gesture. "Aw, don't get sappy on me now, Nora." She leans in. "Plus, you know, this isn't entirely out of the goodness of our hearts. Benjamin *does* get a finder's fee, and this helps build his business."

I take a deep breath, and the lump recedes. "That does make me feel better."

She grins. "I thought it might." She reaches down to add the last touch to my outfit: a white-and-gold anatomical heart pin, which designates me as an unclaimed valentine. "Ready for the ball, then?"

I don't think I'll ever feel ready. But with Lissa's help, I'm about as close as it's possible to get.

Chapter Five

The Valentine's Day Ball is styled like an indoor garden party. A carpet of rose petals leads down the stairs and into the ballroom, and more flowers twine over the railing and dangle from the chandeliers. I pause to pluck a bloom from the banister as we descend the staircase, bringing it to my nose. It's honey-sweet, and soft as silk between my fingers.

The flowers are all real, and so are the trees that someone has transplanted indoors, their branches dripping with twinkling fairy lights. The ballroom is dim aside from that soft, golden illumination. It doesn't quite reach the edges of the huge room, where whispers of fabric indicate movement I cannot see. Dancers in the center of the ballroom drift in and out of the light, visible and then gone; some disappear into the shadows and don't emerge again.

I'm sure it's intentional that the vampires can see everything in the room, but us humans cannot. It feels both playful and ominous, a sort of fairy-tale menace—*don't stray from the light.*

Most humans get a glimpse of the vampire society through the media, but few ever get a chance to experience it like this. They may exist in the same world as us, but their small population exists almost entirely separately from us. Some might say *above* us. Now it feels like I'm stepping into *their* world, a place that feels ancient and secret, and it is both awe-inspiring and terrifying.

I cling tighter to Benjamin's arm, suppressing a shiver, and turn my attention from the decorations to the partygoers. They teeter on the same edge between beautiful and sinister. Vampires and humans alike are draped in finery, and I quickly forget any concerns that my dress is *too much* when I see a woman wearing a sheer dress with real roses covering only her most private areas, and a man whose chiseled body is shirtless beneath a cape of pink and white carnations.

Everyone and everything here is so gorgeous, so *interesting*. I would love to stand in a corner somewhere and watch the night unfold. But instead, Benjamin leads me into the heart of the crowd. I hold tight to him, fighting the urge to slink back against the wall. My shoulders keep curling inward, like I'm a turtle retreating into its shell; it takes determination to keep my head up and my back straight. I take out my blood card—a paper fan holding my tasting notes, the name of my chaperone, and six slots to sign up for drinking from me—and fan my face with it. But still I can hear my heartbeat in my ears, and the glances of vampires we pass remind me that they can hear it, too. I had time to adjust to being in a vampire's presence during my week with Benjamin, but my adrenaline is still surging as I realize I'm surrounded by potential predators.

"You're safe," Benjamin says in a low voice. He pats my hand, and I realize I'm clutching him so hard, it must hurt. Or at least it would if he were human. "Take a moment, let yourself adapt to it."

"I'm not sure I can," I grit out through a fake smile as another vampire glances our way, giving me a once-over. What the hell am I doing here? What made me think I was in any way cut out for this?

"I promise you can, and you will. Just breathe."

Benjamin leads me in a slow circle around the edges of the party, in and out of the shadowed recesses of the ballroom. By our second pass through, I finally feel like I'm no longer on the verge of passing out. But I'm still far from comfortable. Everywhere I look I see poise and beauty, gold and glamor. I feel more and more like a pigeon in the midst of peacocks. Drab in a way that people would normally overlook, but just makes me stand out more in a place like this.

Yet as time passes and nobody stares at me as though I'm the leper I feel like I am, I gradually relax.

"That's it," Benjamin says, smiling at me. "Do you think you're ready to meet some potential patrons?"

My pulse leaps at the thought, my mouth immediately going dry again, but I force a wobbly smile. This is what I'm here for, after all. I've trained for it, I'm being paid for it. I don't have much hope for finding a long-term patron, but I owe it to Benjamin to try.

And maybe… maybe I owe it to myself, as well.

"Let's do this," I say.

* * *

The first vampire takes my blood card and scans it. I've already memorized the tasting notes Benjamin included: *rich and smooth, with subtle notes of cherry and dark chocolate.*

It makes me sound like a lovely red wine, but the man frowns as he lowers it. "Ah," he says. "I was hoping for something more interesting. The human you brought last year was so *novel.*"

Benjamin's smile is only slightly strained. "You're referring to Miss Burton? I recall you spitting out her blood all over the floor."

"Exactly!" The man grins. "An experience I'll never forget. But this sounds…" He frowns at my card. He still hasn't so much as glanced at me. "Well, forgettable."

I focus on the rose-and-dagger symbol embroidered onto his suit jacket. *A Camelia vampire*, I tell myself. *Not a good match anyway.*

Benjamin plucks the fan out of the other man's hand and returns it to me. "A pity," he says. "I suppose you'll have to find your entertainment elsewhere tonight."

As the vampire stalks off, muttering to himself, Benjamin pats my arm. "Ignore him. You wouldn't have wanted to be bitten by him, anyway. He makes a mess of it."

I nod, but it's hard not to feel his judgment as a blow to my self-esteem. And while the next few vampires we approach aren't such assholes about it, they express similar sentiments. *And here I thought you were a purveyor of more interesting flavors,* one says, while another questions, *Nothing more exotic this time?*

Benjamin's frustration grows with each conversation that goes nowhere, and I can't help but feel responsible for it.

"I'm sorry," I say, though I'm not sure for what.

"Don't be," he says. "The same arseholes who rejected Amelia for having an unusual flavor are now rejecting you for having a pleasant one. It has nothing to do with you, and everything to do with my courtless status and their power plays."

I'm not sure I believe him, nor am I surprised by the way things are going. I've spent my entire life being unremarkable, so it's no shock to me now.

* * *

After several rejections in a row, I ask for a moment away from the ballroom. It's raining outside, a quiet patter against the distant rooftop, so Benjamin takes me deeper into the mansion. We wander through quiet hallways, occupied by smaller groups or vampire-valentine duos seeking a private moment. We pass by a set of double doors that I suspect is a library, but when I reach for the handle, Benjamin shakes his head.

"Occupied," he says, and urges me onward.

Gentle piano music drifts out of another room, and we pause in the doorway to listen before continuing on. Next is a gallery of sorts, and I pause, my eyes drawn to the walls and the paintings that line them. After a moment, I let go of Benjamin's arm and step inside to study them. He hangs back to give me space, though I can feel his eyes on me.

Despite my better judgment, I always find myself drawn to art. There is a comforting type of familiarity in it. My mother could never teach me talent and passion, but she did succeed at giving me an eye for it.

I walk slowly through the room. My eyes pass over most of the paintings—lovely, but missing personality—before settling on a Baroque-influenced depiction of a Paris café. An everyday scene captured in deep colors and dramatic lighting, drawing the eye to details one would normally overlook: a still-smoking pipe left on a table, a flower on the sidewalk that has been crushed beneath someone's heel.

It's… interesting. I find myself staring at it for longer than I intended. I walk slowly down the wall, following a line of framed paintings that must have come from the same artist's hand. There's a lighthouse overlooking a stormy sea, a beautiful cathedral drawn in fuzzy detail with a bedraggled stray cat in the foreground, a candle dripping wax on a windowsill overlooking a cliff, a glass of red wine toppled over and spilling over the edge of a table.

My mom always told me that art is successful if it makes you feel something, but I've found that most things she calls *fine art* don't do anything for me. This, though, stirs something in my chest. It feels more honest than most art. Ugly and beautiful at the same time, highlighting the details that most people wouldn't notice.

I stop at the last, where a small cluster of other valentines have gathered. I gaze up at it alongside them. This one depicts a tree on a sunny hillside, all soft edges and bright colors.

"Isn't it just beautiful?" one of the other women asks, staring up at the painting.

Another sighs. "Gorgeous. A shame it was his last."

"His last?" I'm too curious; I have to butt in to their conversation. "Did he pass away?"

A man huffs as if it's a stupid question. "Of course not. This is the work of Lord Claude de Vulpe."

He says it like the name should mean something to me. It does give me a glimmer of familiarity, though I can't put my finger on it. It does, however, tell me that the artist is a vampire.

"Then why has he stopped painting?"

"I heard he went mad," someone whispers behind her fanned-out blood card.

"I heard he has some grudge against the Vulpe Court," another person contributes.

"Nobody knows," the man says with a shrug. "But he hasn't painted since he was turned into a vampire."

"Regardless," the woman says, still gazing up at the painting with adoration that almost seems fake, like she's posing for some reason. "I think it's his best work."

I snort a laugh, unable to help myself. "Really?" They all turn to look at me, wearing a unified expression of *who the hell are you to comment?* My face heats, but I'm too deep to back out now. "I mean… it's pretty, sure. But it's so… I don't know. Empty, compared to the rest. All of the others had something to say. And this one is just…" I gesture vaguely with one hand, and then stop, realizing that the valentines are still staring—but no longer at me.

Instead they're all looking somewhere behind me. I turn, and startle as I realize someone is standing just a few feet away, where I'm sure there was no one a few seconds ago.

Only a vampire could move so quickly and quietly.

This man has a face that looks like it belongs in marble, all hard angles and hollow cheeks, lush lips, and long eyelashes. Devastatingly pretty, with sad eyes of the palest blue. He's very tall, even with the lazy slouch of his shoulders. A disarray of brown curls lay over his ears and forehead. His fine white shirt is wrinkled and half-untucked from his tailored trousers, his sleeves pushed haphazardly up his forearms.

I have an urge to push back his hair and fix his shirt, but I'm not sure if it's because the lack of care annoys me or because I want an excuse to touch him.

Either way, it's an inappropriate thought, especially because he is currently looking at me as though I just walked over and yanked out one of his perfect, messy curls.

"You don't like it?" he asks. There's the slightest hint of a French accent in his voice, which would be sultry if he didn't sound so wounded.

I follow his assessing gaze to the painting behind me. But before I can answer, the valentines on either side of me immediately dip into bows and curtsies, one of them letting out a choked, panicky sound.

"It's an honor," says one.

"Such a surprise to see you," another says, "Lord Claude."

Chapter Six

My eyes dart to the painting we were discussing, and I dip into a belated curtsy, dropping my eyes away from that damning signature: *Claude de Vulpe.*

"It's the last thing I ever painted," the vampire says, pulling my eyes back to him. He wears no indication of his court, which is an oddity, but it's not surprising to learn he's a Vulpe vampire. An artist through and through, from his sad eyes to his slender fingers to his obvious sensitivity. He's staring at me with his perfect face creased. "Perhaps the last thing I will ever paint. Most people like it the best. But you do not?"

"I… I meant no disrespect," I stammer, not sure what else to say. It's not like I can lie now when he so obviously overheard me speaking about it. I never would have said anything if I had an inkling the artist was *here*, especially when I'm well-acquainted with how sensitive those types can be about their work, but now I feel backed into a corner.

"What don't you like about it?" he asks, folding his arms over his chest and continuing to stare at me.

I slowly rise again, my eyes still on the floor. "I didn't mean… That is… it's very pretty, I just have no eye for these sorts of things."

When I glance up at the vampire, he waves a hand as if physically brushing away my excuses. Rings glitter on his long, pale fingers.

"I don't care about that. I care about why you don't like it."

"I…" I stare at him, my heart thumping in my ears, trying to think of something to say. But there is nothing that comes to mind that isn't horribly rude. I bob in another, more awkward curtsy. "I prefer not to say. Thank you. Goodnight!"

I rush away as fast as I can in these heels, my face aflame with embarrassment.

Benjamin is thankfully nearby, talking quietly with another vampire while remaining within my sightline. He startles as I slip my arm into his and press close to his side.

"Nora," he says, surprised. "Are you—"

"Is he following me?" I hiss, clinging tighter to his arm.

He glances behind me, brow furrowed, and then straightens up in abrupt shock. "Lord de Vulpe," he says, with a small bow.

I slowly turn, unable to keep the grimace off my face as I see that the painter I insulted has indeed followed me here.

"Good evening," he says. "You are her chaperone, then?"

"Indeed. Lord Benjamin Acharya."

Claude inclines his head. "I would like to request a slot on her blood card, if I may."

"You may not," I blurt.

Both vampires blink at me. Benjamin looks appalled by my behavior, Claude rather wounded.

"A moment, please," Benjamin says before Claude can answer, and leads me into the nearby corner, glancing over his shoulder to ensure that Claude isn't following us. "What is this about?" he asks me in a low voice.

I fan myself; my face is still hot from our encounter in the gallery, and the last thing I want to do is recount it to Benjamin. "I can't explain it. Just… anyone but him. Please."

"Do you believe him to be dangerous?" he asks, studying my face.

I shake my head. "No, it's not that."

"Has he given some offense?"

"Well… no." I blow out a frustrated breath. "I think I may have offended *him*."

Benjamin's eyebrows rise. "So you intend to rectify this by… further insulting him?"

"I…" I open my mouth, shut it, shake my head in frustration. "He's a *painter*. I made my feelings quite clear, didn't I?"

"It's just a taste of your blood, you're making no commitment," Benjamin says. "It may help attract other suitors, if they see Lord Claude take an interest in you. He usually spends these parties…" He glances over my shoulder, and inclines his chin. "Well, like that."

I turn to see Claude standing by the window and staring out at the grounds, his mouth downturned and his brow furrowed in an expression of picture-perfect broodiness.

"This is exactly what I mean," I hiss, turning back to Benjamin. "What's his *deal*?"

"Well…" Benjamin leans in, lowering his voice. "They used to call him a prodigy. He was an incredibly gifted painter in life, and so the Vulpe Court was eager to offer him the bite and welcome him into their ranks. But they say he hasn't picked up a paintbrush since, much to the displeasure of his court." He shrugs. "That's all I know. Rumors, mostly."

I bite my lip, cursing myself for my blunder once more. Of course I would manage to insult not only a sensitive artist, but a famously *tortured* artist.

"That doesn't mean he has to be so melodramatic about it," I grumble, trying to fight back the wave of guilt as I think back to that sorrowful look in his eyes.

One corner of Benjamin's lips rises before he tamps it back down.

"This isn't funny!"

"Yes, well…" He shrugs, glancing again at Claude and then back to me. "It's your choice, Nora, but I truly can't see any harm in giving him your time. By all accounts, he's a perfect gentleman, not someone you need to be worried about."

A *no* is ready on my lips, but I hesitate. Curiosity drives me to glance over my shoulder at Claude again, studying the sharp angle of his jaw from the side, the perfect tousle of his curls.

That's the harm, I realize. That's why I'm worried: because even a glance at him has my stomach fluttering with girlish nerves. Even when he's being theatrically sulky like he is now, I can't deny my attraction to him. If only he weren't so… so…

He glances over, catches my gaze, and straightens from his melancholy slouch, a glimmer of hope in his eyes.

I turn back to Benjamin and sigh. "I guess I do owe him after insulting his painting."

"Good lord, Nora," he mutters with a shake of his head. Then he leads me back over to the vampire now leaning against the wall with his arms folded over his chest. Is he *posing*? I believe he might be.

I force a thin-lipped smile and hold out my blood card in invitation. Claude holds my gaze as he reaches out to take it from me, one cold finger nudging against mine as he slides the fan out of my grip. I watch him write his name in my next slot, and drop my gaze as soon as he looks up at me.

"Thank you for reconsidering," he says, holding out my blood card. He forces me to reach out to take it, and our eyes meet again, sending a bolt of heat through my body. He smiles like he knows exactly what effect he's having on me. "I'll see you in…" He checks his watch. "An hour and a half."

* * *

As time meanders by, I begin to think that I was overreacting. There is no shortage of beautiful people at this party. Surely I'm exaggerating the effect that Claude had on me because the idea frightened me. What I felt was nerves and embarrassment after insulting him, not *butterflies* like I'm some hapless schoolgirl with her first crush.

I've nearly managed to convince myself it's true by the time Benjamin is leading me to our meeting place with Lord Claude. Then my eyes find him across the room, where he lounges in that damnably casual-but-poised way of his, and my heart starts to beat double time. By the time I sink onto the couch beside him, the goddamn butterflies are back in full force.

Stupid, stupid, stupid, I chastise myself, taking my time smoothing out my skirts to avoid looking at him. I knew this was a mistake. I should've insisted on staying away from him. Something about him makes my brain go all fuzzy, and I can't afford that right now.

When cold fingers graze my wrist, I freeze. My eyes dart to where Claude's pale hand holds mine in a feather-soft grip, his thumb pressed to my pulse point. I swallow before lifting my gaze to meet his.

"Your heart is beating very fast," he says, thumb rubbing slow circles over my wrist. "Am I making you nervous?"

"No," I say, while my pulse betrays me. I breathe in deeply through my nose, let it out from my mouth, and snatch my wrist back from him. He doesn't try to hold on, but even when I'm free of him, I still feel the imprint of his cold fingertips where they so delicately gripped me. "I'm just not used to being around vampires."

"I see." He studies me. "We don't have to do this. I just wanted a chance to talk to—"

"I'd rather you bite me," I say.

His lips twist. "Is my company so terrible?"

I sniff and look away, refusing to dignify that with a response.

"So cruel to me," he says. "What have I done to deserve this treatment?"

I glance sideways at him without turning my head. "The better question is, why do you seem like you're enjoying it?"

"Most people try to flatter me, or treat me like I'm made of glass. Your blatant hatred is rather refreshing."

I purse my lips and hold out my wrist. "Can we just get this over with?"

He regards me for a moment. "Alright," he agrees, more easily than I expected. "But you're going to have to move closer, I'm afraid."

I scoot an inch closer on the couch.

"Closer than that," he says.

I scoot again, begrudgingly. My knee brushes against his.

And suddenly I'm weightless, moving, and then blinking *up* at him as he leans over me. It takes my brain a moment to right itself.

I'm leaning across his lap. One of his arms supports my upper back; the other holds my wrist. Like before, his grip is soft, belying the strength he must have for him to effortlessly maneuver me like he just did.

"This is more comfortable, no?" he asks, a stray curl falling over his forehead as he looks down at me.

I am breathless. Out of sorts. Part of me wants to be furious with him, but I can't fight the slow unfurling of warmth in my stomach, the heat creeping into my face.

This is just a comfortable position for him to bite me, I tell myself. That's why I'm nodding. Never mind the fact I don't trust myself enough to speak.

Claude watches me through heavily lidded eyes as he lifts my wrist to his mouth. My skin prickles with awareness of his teeth in close proximity, and the heat in my belly rises to a dangerous simmer.

"Are you ready?" he asks.

"Yes," I whisper.

He kisses my wrist.

That's what it feels like. The soft press of lips, a hint of tongue against my skin. There's only the slightest prick of fangs, so gentle it seems impossible until I feel the deep *pull* of him drinking from me.

And then I'm melting into his lap, sinking into the couch. Only his grip on me keeps me up, his arm holding me tighter against his chest. My eyelids flutter and my lips part. I'm hyperaware of every inch of my own skin. Every breath sends new, fizzing pleasure through my veins, slowly condensing into a throb in my lower belly.

"Oh."

I think it's me who makes that soft exhale of a noise, but

no, it's Claude, pulling back from my wrist with a strange expression. His pupils have blown wide, nearly covering the blue of his eyes, and his gaze is locked on my wrist, where a trickle of blood is still leaking from the puncture wounds he left.

He leans forward and licks it, and I shiver at the sensation of his tongue against my skin.

"Claude," I say. He doesn't respond to his name. His fangs are still out, his mouth open, a bare half inch away from biting me again. "Claude," I say again, louder.

Footsteps. Claude blinks, finally focusing on my face, and then someone behind me.

"Is everything alright here?" Benjamin asks.

Claude shakes his head—whether in response or to clear it, I'm not sure—and guides me into an upright position. My body still feels weak and languorous after that bite, but I force myself to stand on wobbling legs. I'm suddenly all too aware of what just happened, what I just *felt*, and the fact that we were very much in public. It's a thousand times worse than being caught with a copy of *Fangs*, which until recently was one of my biggest fears. I'm sure my face is stained bright red, broadcasting my filthy thoughts to everyone in the room.

Benjamin slides an arm around my waist, providing subtle support. I lean into him, grateful.

"Get a hold of yourself," he whispers.

I shoot him a baffled, offended look, but he isn't looking at me. He's looking at Claude, who is still staring at me, a dazed look in his dilated eyes.

At Benjamin's chastisement he finally looks away, dropping his gaze to the floor. He lifts a thumb to rub over his lower lip and says nothing.

Benjamin urges me back one step, and then another, before he turns us around and leads us away. He takes us to a quiet corner of the ball and pricks his thumb on his fang before pressing it to the puncture marks on my wrist.

I look up at him, trying to shake off my sluggishness and read the troubled expression on his face. "Is everything okay?" I ask.

"I believe so." He studies my wrist until the wounds heal, and then drops it and looks me in the eyes. "Are you well?"

"I'm fine," I say. Better than fine, really. That bite left me with a pleasant, tingling sort of wooziness, as though I've had a few glasses of wine. It felt good when Benjamin bit me, but that was something else entirely. "Did something happen?"

"No, but it nearly did." Benjamin glances at the crowd around us. "That expression on his face… I know the look of a man on the verge of losing control to his bloodlust, and he was very, very close."

Bloodlust? I think back to that moment, the way he held me and looked at me, and can't make sense of the word. "Are you sure? He was so gentle with me."

"I'm sure," he says. "And that makes it even more dangerous. Vampires like that…" He shakes his head. "He could have drained you past the point of safety before you realized something was wrong."

"Well…" I wring my hands, uncertain what to say. I have the strangest urge to defend Claude, even though just minutes ago I was uttering the words *anyone but him.* "He didn't hurt me. And if he had really been a threat, I'm sure you would have stopped him."

Benjamin chokes out a sound that might be a cough, or a startled laugh. "Your faith in me is admirable, but misplaced,

I'm afraid."

My eyebrows shoot up. "What? Surely you're stronger than him. He's so…" I shrug, unable to even find the words for it. His perfect curls, his blue eyes, his long, pale fingers that gripped me so gently. Even if Benjamin hadn't told me he was an artist, I would've known it at a glance. That's how he seems. Sensitive, almost vulnerable.

"He's nearly one hundred and fifty years old," Benjamin says, shocking me anew. "Which is quite a bit older than I am. Trust me on this, Nora. Even without the backing of his court, and my lack thereof, I would have trouble handling him." Benjamin's expression is grim, but as he turns to me, it softens. "In any case, I'm glad you're safe. No harm done. Shall we?"

I take his arm and let him lead me back to the party, my skin still tingling from the ghost of Claude's mouth.

Chapter Seven

It seems impossible to return to the ball as though everything is normal after what I just experienced. I let Benjamin lead me around, smile and nod when it's required of me, but my mind keeps wandering. Every time I see a vampire entwined with another human on a chaise somewhere, my knees go weak with the memory of Claude holding me on that couch. My eyes keep searching for a sign of dark curls and blue eyes in the crowd, but I don't see Claude anywhere.

Until I turn around and he's right in front of me.

Benjamin stiffens at my side, pulling me closer. "Lord Claude," he says, making it sound like both a warning and a question.

I study Claude in silence, trying to see the apparent danger that Benjamin sees. I still can't; he seems too pretty to be threatening, though maybe his apparent insouciance is a deliberate mask.

"I would like to apologize," Claude says, and inclines himself in a low bow. Benjamin looks startled, and several nearby heads turn in our direction; clearly, someone like Claude bowing to someone like Benjamin isn't commonplace.

"I accept your apology," Benjamin says, though there's still tension in his voice.

Claude straightens. "I'd also like to request another slot on Nora's blood card."

I'm glad he's looking at Benjamin instead of me, because I'm pretty sure my face shows about five different emotions in the span of two seconds.

Benjamin is silent for a moment. Maybe he's waiting for me to weigh in, but I'm flabbergasted.

"I don't believe that's the best idea," he says, after a moment.

"I know what you saw back there, but I assure you, I remained quite in control," Claude says.

"You looked like you wanted to devour her whole," Benjamin says.

"But I did not," Claude says, not denying it. When Benjamin remains implacable, he turns to me. "Please, Nora," he says.

My mouth goes dry as I stare into those long-lashed eyes, so blue I could drown in them. My heart skips a beat as I realize I want to say yes. I want to feel that sharp-edged kiss on my wrist again—or on the curve of my neck. I can picture myself swooning against him as he drinks my lifeblood, his strong arms cradling me…

And that terrifies me.

"No," I say. "I trust my patron's guidance."

Claude stares at me. But he doesn't try to press me like he did Benjamin. Instead he nods stiffly, turns, and walks to the nearest window, staring out at the grounds with an expression like a storm cloud. Sulking again, but at least he's doing it away from me.

I let out a small, shaky breath.

Benjamin touches the small of my back. "Something

wrong?"

"No. Nothing. I just…" *Almost lost sight of what I'm here for. This isn't some fairy tale, and I meant what I said to Benjamin: not an artist.* I don't need that kind of flighty dramaticism right now. I need someone steady and reliable, who will be on the same page as I am about this being a practical exchange of services. "I'd like to meet some other potential patrons, please."

Anyone but him, I remind myself, but it takes every ounce of willpower in my body to resist looking over my shoulder at him as I walk away.

* * *

At the very least, Claude's attention seems to have broken down whatever barrier made me unapproachable. Soon enough, a pretty, dark-skinned woman with a Solomon moth earring comes asking after my blood card. But after a few minutes of conversation about my background and my tasting notes, I notice she keeps glancing off to the side, her brow creased. I follow her gaze to see Claude standing nearby, leaning against the wall, watching us without making any attempt to disguise either his interest or his dour expression.

The woman excuses herself shortly thereafter, and I suppress a sigh. Benjamin leads me to the other side of the ballroom to talk to a pair of Celeste vampires. They seem more interested in hearing about my future studies than my blood, yet again, I notice their attention drifting after a few minutes. I turn around and see Claude, once more hovering nearby, now sitting on a chaise with one hand propping his chin up and his blue eyes locked on me.

The Celeste vampires soon find an excuse to leave us. Without requesting a slot on my blood card, of course. It's still entirely empty except for Claude's name claiming the first line, and we have mere minutes until I'm supposed to be giving blood for the second time tonight. The night is still young, but I'm hyperaware that I have a limited amount of time to find a potential patron, which will be especially hard given my particular needs.

I grit my teeth, looking up at Benjamin. "How do I get rid of him?"

Benjamin grimaces and presses his fingers to the bridge of his nose. "I hate to leave you, but perhaps if I try approaching some potential patrons without you to make arrangements…"

"Yes," I say immediately. "Please do. I insist."

"You're certain you'll be fine?"

"Yes. I'll stay right here." Surely he won't dare to do anything in full view of the ballroom.

Benjamin looks torn, but after a moment, he nods and steps into the crowd.

Leaving me with Claude. There *is* an entire ballroom of people nearby, and the chaise he's chosen is a few yards away, but somehow it still feels as though the two of us are alone.

I know I should ignore him. But I can't help myself.

"Claude," I hiss.

He stares up at the ceiling.

"Lord Claude de Vulpe," I say, louder.

He blinks slowly and lazily, like a cat, one leg swinging idly along the side of the chaise.

"Stop pretending you can't hear me!"

He still doesn't look over, but the corners of his lips curl subtly upward.

Burning with indignation, I consider tossing my blood card at him, but realize Benjamin took it with him to convince other patrons of my merits. Instead, I dig into my purse and grab the first thing I can find—a handkerchief. I ball it up and lob it at Claude.

His hand darts out, impossibly fast, and catches it midair. He glances sideways at me, one eyebrow raised.

Catching myself gaping, I clear my throat and regain my dignity. "You obviously craved my attention. Now you have it. What do you want?"

"Dahlias," he says.

I blink. "...What?"

"On your dress." He gestures to the flower appliqués. "They symbolize eternal love, in the Victorian language of flowers."

I blink again. "Okay?"

"That is to say..." He sits up, fist tightening around my handkerchief. "You know what I want."

I fold my arms over my chest. My heart is hammering, and I hate that it's not entirely annoyance that's bringing a flush to my cheeks. "I already told you no."

"And I respected your no," he says. "But did you think that was going to make me sit back and watch someone else have you?"

The heat in my face deepens. "Don't say it like that."

His brow furrows. "Like what?"

"*Have me*," I repeat. "You make it sound intimate."

He tilts his head, studying me. "It is."

"You drink blood every night. It can't possibly be an *intimate* experience every time."

"Mm, no. It isn't always." His eyes seem to pierce right through me. Those breathtaking ocean depths. "But what happened between us was."

"It-it wasn't—" I stutter and then look away. If I force the words out, it will only make it more obvious that they're a lie. "Look, I'll be honest, that's the problem. I'm not interested in intimacy."

Claude shoots me a skeptical look. "You do realize the nature of a valentine is—"

"Transactional," I finish for him. My face is so hot it's probably steaming. "My blood tastes good, or so I've heard. And I need the money. That's all this is for me. A job."

I can't risk it being anything more, I want to explain, but it's too embarrassing to say aloud when he's looking at me so intently.

Claude drops his gaze to the floor. Then he lifts his eyes to me again and stands. He crosses the space between us in three long, determined strides.

I startle at the speed of it, but I don't step away. Maybe the smart thing would be to yell for Benjamin, but no matter what he's said, I can't bring myself to see Claude as a threat. And his eyes don't have that dazed look from before when he drank from me. They're clear and focused, and very blue as he looks down at me.

"I can make that work," he says.

It takes me a second to remember what we're talking about. Right—a job. A transaction.

I shake my head. "I don't believe you."

"I'm serious." He leans closer. Then he pauses, registering the way I automatically lean back from him. It's not that I'm afraid, it's just hard to think with his face so close to me. But maybe he misreads my expression, because after a moment he pulls back.

Then he drops to one knee in front of me.

My face heats. "What are you doing?" I hiss.

"Showing you how serious I am," he says.

"People are staring!" And whispering. Laughing.

Yet Claude only shrugs, his eyes never leaving mine. "I don't care. I need to explain—"

"*Claude,*" a voice says.

He seemed so immune to the earlier whispers and stares, but Claude snaps to sudden attention—his head up, his spine straight. He rises to his feet and turns slowly toward the source.

Benjamin is approaching us with an unfamiliar vampire at his side. It's the stranger that Claude's attention is instantly focused on—a tall man with tousled brown waves falling to his broad shoulders. He wears a classic black suit with only a single adornment: a golden snake pinned to his lapel. His face is smooth, expressionless, but when his green eyes flick to mine, it feels as though I've been plunged into ice water.

I only breathe when they shift away from me. My throat still feels tight, my heart thumping rapidly. I look at Benjamin, who I realize is standing behind the man instead of directly at his side, with his gaze lowered to the floor. And then to Claude, who still hasn't moved since this vampire said his name.

"Sire," Claude murmurs, lowering his head.

"You're making a spectacle of yourself," the man says. He flicks his wrist. "Go."

Claude leaves without a glance back at me, his head still lowered.

My stomach swoops as the man's attention returns to me. It isn't the same fluttering feeling that Claude gave me, but an unpleasant, deep twist. His gaze pins me as he moves closer, and I weave my fingers together behind my back to prevent them from trembling.

Benjamin stands beside him, hands clasped behind his back. "Nora. I'd like to introduce you to Lord Ambrose de Vulpe. He sought me out to inquire about your blood."

I steal a sideways glance at Benjamin. His posture is stiff. *He sought me out*, he specified. He isn't giving me an option like he did with Claude, even though he knows of my aversion to the Vulpe court.

The warning is clear: this man is dangerous.

Chapter Eight

I force a tight smile, staring at Ambrose's cheek to give the appearance of politeness without having to look into those eerie eyes. "A pleasure to make your acquaintance, Lord Ambrose."

"The pleasure is mine," he says. He takes my hand and lifts it to his mouth. The kiss he grazes against my knuckle is gentle, but his grip is hard enough to hurt. "I heard my wayward fledgling was causing trouble for you."

Right. Claude called him *sire.* Benjamin told me that Claude is older and stronger than he appears, and this is the man who created him. If Claude is one hundred and fifty, then… the mere idea of how old Ambrose must be makes me feel lightheaded. "Oh, he wasn't causing trouble," I say, my voice trembling. "We were just joking around."

"Curious." Ambrose lowers my hand from his lips but doesn't release it. "Claude is not often prone to humor."

I'm not sure how to respond, so I say nothing.

"Nor does he often take such an interest in humans," Ambrose continues after a moment. He's still holding my hand too tightly; I swear I can feel my bones grind together. "He used to dabble in romantic follies, but it has been a long while.

I confess I am curious about why you caught his eye. I had to have a look for myself." He smiles, a glint of fang. "Or should I say, a taste?"

There's only one answer I can possibly give. I hold out my free hand to Benjamin, and he delivers my blood card. I present it to Ambrose, smiling silently because I'm afraid that a quake in my voice will betray me.

After a cursory glance at my tasting notes, he signs his name under my next slot. He hands the fan to Benjamin rather than returning it to me, and then grabs my hand without waiting for me to offer. His fingers are shockingly cold and strong as they encircle my wrist. He pulls me to a seat on a nearby couch.

"May I?" he asks, as if he isn't already holding me in a viselike grip. His expression is smooth, his posture casual; it doesn't seem like he's intending to hurt me, but rather that he's oblivious to the fact he might be. Such strength paired with such indifference strikes instinctive terror deep within me.

But I swallow it down, even as my heart thuds in my ears. I resist the urge to look at Benjamin or otherwise falter. Ambrose has already signed my card; asking is just a courtesy, and I don't want to cause a scene or a scandal by backing out for no reason. It's just a bite, and my past ones have been quite pleasant. Surely this can't be too bad, even though something about this vampire sets my teeth on edge.

"Of course," I say through a fake smile.

His fangs sink into me not a half second later, and I bite my lip to suppress a yelp. It *hurts* in a way other bites haven't, and there's an uncomfortable pulling sensation that makes me feel dizzy. It doesn't last long, but as he pulls away, it leaves me lightheaded.

"Mm." Ambrose licks his lips, looking thoughtful, and shrugs. "Not as sweet as I prefer." He directs the words at Benjamin instead of me. "I must admit I don't see what the fuss is about."

Benjamin smiles stiffly. "We all have our tastes."

Ambrose walks away without another word, leaving me bleeding on the chaise. Teeth gritted, I press my hand to the wound until Benjamin sits beside me and heals it with a touch of his blood. But even as the puncture marks on my wrist seal, bruises darken around them where Ambrose's fingers gripped me.

"Are you alright?" Benjamin asks.

I nod. "It was… unpleasant, but I'm fine." I brush hair out of my face and let out a breath, then look up at Benjamin. "What in the world just happened?"

He's watching the crowd where Ambrose disappeared, his brows pulled together in a troubled expression. "I'm not certain," he says. "But I'm quite sure we don't want to end up involved in whatever it is." He looks back at me. "At least it seems to have gotten rid of your unwanted suitor."

I think about Claude's sad gaze and gentle touch, at odds with his sire's punishing grip and eerie stare. But Benjamin is right. Claude wasn't what I wanted in a patron, and whatever dynamic created such tension between him and his sire, it's better for me to stay away from it.

* * *

The hours blur together as the evening goes on. I fill up a plate at the buffet table, bypassing the champagne fountain and mountains of baked goods to find more vitamin-rich options like meat, spinach, and fruit. I end up giving most of it away to other valentines when I find them delicately snacking on chocolate-covered strawberries and macarons.

"Where are their chaperones?" I huff when Benjamin gently steers me away. "That man looked like he was about to pass out, and he was eating pure sugar!"

He leads me to a couch and places a fresh plate into my hands, loaded with the same options I chose for myself. "A lot of agencies consider their work done when they arrive at the ball," he says. "They don't chaperone like I do."

I frown as I bite into a mini beef wellington, too distracted to appreciate the decadent bite of golden pastry and tender meat. "Well, they should."

He smiles. "I agree. It's one reason why I opened my agency. To make things safer for hopeful valentines." He nudges my plate. "Eat up. The night is young."

A number of vampires approach Benjamin and me to inquire about my blood card. I spend some time with a soft-spoken woman with Celeste's moon symbol hanging around her neck, and a charming young man with a Camelia rose pinned to his lapel. Yet even as I force a smile and say everything I'm supposed to say, my mind is far away, and my gaze keeps wandering to the crowd around us.

But Claude is gone. He's no longer blocking my chances at meeting a more suitable patron, and I have no problem filling up the remaining slots on my blood card. It's exactly what I wanted.

But no other vampire's bite feels the way his did. None

send that delicious shiver up my spine. I'm grateful each time Benjamin steps in to announce they took enough blood.

"It's for the best," I murmur to myself, sitting with my eyes closed as Benjamin heals my wrist for the last time. I'm a little lightheaded after this last bloodletting, but I haven't fainted, which is more than I can say for a number of other humans who had to be carried out of the ballroom.

"What is?"

I was talking to myself, but I didn't account for vampires and their heightened senses. "Oh, um. That I didn't find a patron, I mean."

Benjamin huffs a laugh. "What makes you think you didn't?"

I open my eyes and blink at him, perplexed. "Nobody asked."

"That's normal. You'll receive official offers tomorrow evening, after the vampires get approval from their courts."

"Oh." My brow furrows. "I didn't realize courts were involved in the process."

"A valentine contract binds them to protect you, in your patron's name, so yes."

There's still hope… but I'm afraid to let myself feel it. "None of them seemed to particularly like me, though." Except for Claude. That goes unspoken.

"I don't think you were paying attention," Benjamin says, his tone equal parts amused and chastising. "It seemed like your mind was on something else. Or… someone else?" He arches a brow.

A flush heats my face. "I don't know what you mean." I take off my glasses and busy myself cleaning them. "Well, it's over now, right? At least I didn't have to embarrass myself on the dance floor."

"Oh, I'm not letting you off that easy." Benjamin stands.

When I put my glasses back on, he sharpens into focus, one hand extended toward me. "You can't leave your first ball without at least one dance."

I hesitate. "You *know* what my dancing looks like…"

"Trust me, I've seen worse. Will you do me the honor?"

My hand hovers over his before I place it in his grasp. Despite my reservations, I can't help but smile as he lifts me to my feet and pulls me to the dance floor. I don't do any better than I did in training, but Benjamin leads me effortlessly in a way that makes me feel elegant nonetheless. Soon, the way he spins and dips me has me laughing and breathless, grateful for his steady, friendly presence among all of the tumult tonight.

Still, as the music dies away, I find myself searching the crowd for a pair of sad blue eyes.

Chapter Nine

I wake the evening after the ball, groggy and confused by my still-new sleep schedule, with my feet aching from the long night. As I shuffle out to the parlor in slippers, I curse the existence of high heels.

"Good evening," Benjamin says as I drag myself in. He's sitting on the chaise with Lissa, their knees touching, and they look suspiciously cozy and disgustingly awake.

I grunt, pouring myself a cup of coffee, and collapse into a chair. I'm aware I look like a disaster in my sweatpants and messy bun, but I don't care.

"Looks like you had fun last night," Lissa teases.

I glower at her over the rim of my mug. I'm tempted to tease her back about her closeness with Benjamin, but I'm not awake enough to find the words.

"I'm delighted to report that you've received two offers of patronage," Benjamin says. "Pending some final negotiations."

That wakes me up. I set down my mug as my heart starts to thump faster. "Two?"

"Indeed." He smiles warmly, sliding over two envelopes.

I carefully open one. My eyes skim over the details: *offer of patronage… one year… a* generous *salary…* before skipping to the name at the bottom.

My eyebrows knot together. "Lord Joseph de Camelia…"

"The gentleman who took the last slot on your blood card," Benjamin reminds me.

"Right, of course." I try to conjure up the memory of his face, or something we talked about, but nothing stands out. My mind was elsewhere.

"He has three valentines currently, but assures me you would have an honored place among them. I haven't spoken to him about the precise details of what you're looking for. He may be more open to the idea of a non-intimate relationship if you're not the only valentine in the household."

"Right. That's good." Yet I can't seem to drum up much enthusiasm about it.

Benjamin studies me across the table like he can see everything I'm not admitting and then nudges the second offer across the table.

This time, I look straight at the signature at the bottom, and my stomach twists oddly.

"Lady Katherine de Celeste."

"Ah, yes. I did have the chance to broach the topic of intimacy—or lack thereof—with her. She seemed disappointed, but it's a good sign that she was still willing to make an offer. Perhaps she's reconsidered, or…"

My mind drifts as Benjamin continues talking. I remember Katherine from the end of the night. She was kind, a bit flirty in a coy and soft-spoken way, certainly attractive. She's from Celeste, which Benjamin suggested would be the best court for me to sign with. From what he says, we could be a great match.

So there's no reason I should be disappointed that the

second—final—offer was from her and not someone else. No reason that I should have been hoping to see one particular name written at the bottom of one of the offers.

I realize Benjamin has stopped speaking, and glance up at him. He's giving me a knowing look that makes heat rise to my face.

"I was expecting Lord Claude to offer as well," he says. "I couldn't say why he didn't. His interest was obvious."

"I mean, it's good that he didn't," I say quickly. Perhaps too quickly. "We wouldn't have been a good match. Obviously. I'm just… surprised, is all."

Benjamin studies me for a moment. "There are a dozen reasons why he may have declined to offer, and few of them have anything to do with you," he says. "I wouldn't worry about it. As you say, it's for the best."

I bite my lip and nod, trying to force down the confusing emotions threatening to rise up. "So… how should we proceed with these two?"

"If you don't have a strong preference for either one, I'll contact them each and negotiate. Make sure that they are on the same page as you when it comes to matters of intimacy."

"Right," I say. Another sip of coffee, and my brain is finally starting to wake up. I need to push aside these annoying thoughts about Claude and focus, because this is really happening. I have offers of patronage. I could be a valentine, not just for a night.

It doesn't feel real yet. If this is actually happening, I should let my roommates know… and withdraw my attendance at college in the fall, since I won't be able to attend. The thought puts a pit in my stomach. I'm putting off the future I want once again.

But it's only for a year. One year, and I'll have enough money for school and rent and whatever the hell else I want. I'm securing my future by doing this, even though it doesn't feel like it right now.

"Everything okay?" Benjamin asks, noting my silence.

"Um, yes. Just tired." I rub the bridge of my nose. "But, yes, that sounds good. See what you can find out, and I'll think about it."

While Benjamin heads out to make phone calls to the two offering vampires, I return to my bedroom and curl up under the covers to rest. No matter how hard I try to logic myself out of it, I can't fight the weird disappointment souring my stomach. There is no reason I should feel like this. I should be honored that I received an offer, let alone two, and excited that I might be able to find a match when we both thought it was such a long shot. I'll spend one year being pampered and well-paid, and then I can have everything I've always wanted. It's not a bad deal.

But try as I might, I can't stop thinking of Claude's blue eyes. The way it felt when he bit me. I can't help but imagine what it might be like if I were a different person, with a different life, and was ready to free-fall into the unknown with him.

Rain drums against the window as if reflecting my mood. After a couple of hours of tossing, turning, and scrolling mindlessly on my phone, I jump at the sound of a knock on the door. I expect Benjamin with news of the offers I received, but instead I open it to find Lissa on the other side, wearing a Cheshire grin.

"What?" I ask, eyeing her. "Why do you look like you're up to no good?"

She cups a hand around her mouth and whispers, "I don't

think I'm supposed to be telling you, but you have a visitor."

My heart leaps. I shove it back down. "What kind of visitor?" Probably one of the two offering vampires here to negotiate in person.

"The kind of visitor who wanders in from the rain with a sopping-wet coat and big blue eyes, asking about you."

Chapter Ten

I consider getting dressed and ready but quickly discard the thought. The last thing I want is to look like I was waiting for Claude to arrive… even though a part of me was, if only to get an explanation about why he didn't offer. So I walk down to the parlor in my pajamas and a messy bun, shooing away Lissa as she tries to follow to eavesdrop.

My heart is pounding as I enter the room. Lissa's description was more than enough for me to know who to expect, but still, it's a shock to see the reality of it.

Lord Claude sits at the table, his hands clasped on his lap. Wet curls are plastered to his forehead, and his once-white shirt is now almost entirely see-through as it clings to his pale skin. Every hard line of his lean body is laid out in a way that makes me have to look away before I start blushing. Did he walk through the rain to get here? Surely not. But I can picture him standing in it, staring at the door to Benjamin's house, rain soaking him to the bone before he lifted one slender hand to knock.

When his pale eyes rise to find mine, I realize that I'm smiling. I tamp it down and drop into a perfectly polite curtsy, despite the fact I'm in sweatpants and slippers. "Lord Claude."

"Nora," he murmurs, and pushes wet hair out of his face, running his fingers through it as if suddenly realizing what a mess he is. It makes me want to laugh, thinking that *he's* self-conscious when I'm here in my bare face and pajamas. Yet the way his eyes rake over me feels no less intense than it did when I was in a ballgown.

Benjamin looks between us, his expression world-weary and deeply unamused. "I don't recall sending for you, Nora."

I blink at him innocently. "I was just coming to ask if there was any update. What's this about?"

Benjamin shakes his head. It's obvious from his expression that he doesn't believe me. "I'm not sure. Lord Claude was just about to explain why he showed up on my doorstep unannounced." He waves a hand. "You might as well sit, I suppose."

I cross the room slowly, feeling as though my knees may give out at any moment. My thoughts are a mess as I take a seat beside Benjamin, not daring to sit too close to Claude. "Well, let's hear it, then."

"Yes. Well." Claude glances down at his hands, idly spinning one of the several rings he's wearing. "I shall be up front. I'm here to make an offer of patronage."

My heart skips a beat. I try not to let my face betray any of the emotions coursing through me. There's no reason I should be excited about this, I tell myself. I was very clear with him, with Benjamin, with everyone about *not* wanting a vampire from the Vulpe Court. And also about *not* wanting to sign with Claude, specifically. Yet...

"You're aware there are proper channels for delivering such offers, which do not involve showing up at my house in the middle of the night," Benjamin says.

"Well, yes, but—"

"And that a written contract is required to formally make an offer," he continues, as if Claude hadn't spoken. "Do you have one prepared?"

Claude hesitates. "That's… No, but—"

"Because someone coming to me in such a way, unannounced and unprepared, might tempt me to think that said person was acting upon a whim rather than careful consideration for what an agreement might mean," Benjamin says. "Or, worse, that said person has something to hide."

Benjamin is, as ever, almost aggressively polite. His tone is measured and calm. Yet it's impossible to miss the bite in his words.

Claude looks just as taken aback as I feel. After a moment of sputtering, he holds up his hands as if in surrender.

"I merely wanted a chance to explain in person."

"So Lord Ambrose is aware you are making an offer?"

Claude opens his mouth, shuts it, meets Benjamin's weighted gaze. "That… is beside the point."

"I'm not certain I believe that, Lord Claude. You may think that being courtless makes me oblivious to the inner workings of court politics, but I am not a fool, and I refuse to allow a valentine under my protection to be dragged unwillingly into a dangerous conflict. So I must ask that you—"

Claude slaps one of his hands down on the table hard enough that it shakes. I jump in my seat. Benjamin goes still halfway through the act of lifting his teacup to his mouth.

Claude shuts his eyes for a moment, jaw working, and then opens them and levels his gaze on Benjamin. For a moment, the two vampires stare at each other down the length of the table. Then Claude says, softly, "Please allow me a chance to explain myself."

Benjamin sets down his teacup without taking a sip. "Very well. Explain, Lord Claude."

Claude retracts his hand into his lap again, takes a moment to compose himself before speaking. "I believe that I gave the wrong impression at the Valentine's Day Ball," he says. "Miss Nora expressed that she has no interest in an intimate relationship." He glances at me, so briefly I barely have time to register it before he's looking at Benjamin again. "And it just so happens that our interests are aligned in that matter."

I blink, studying his face for signs that he's not being truthful, but his expression is frustratingly opaque.

"You seemed drawn to Nora at the ball," Benjamin says.

"I was," Claude says. "But it is not a romantic interest. What calls to me is her blood."

I'm glad that he's looking at Benjamin when he says it, because I'm sure that hurt is written all over my face. I stare down at my lap as I try to subdue it. There's no reason for me to be offended by that. As he said, this is exactly what I want too. Isn't it?

"I am interested in her as a valentine for one reason, and one reason only," Claude says, digging the knife deeper into my chest with each word. "The taste of her blood makes me want to paint again. If I came off as desperate, it was only for that feeling. As I'm sure you've heard, I've been chasing it for a very long time now."

There's an odd sinking feeling in my gut. I dislike the idea of being any artist's muse. Artists are so flighty; it's always seemed a precarious position at best…

"Forgive me, I'm not sure I believe that," Benjamin says.

Claude's smile is so thin it almost looks pained, but he

doesn't appear surprised. "We'll add it to our contract."

Benjamin's eyebrows leap nearly to his hairline. I've never seen him so taken aback. "What? You can't honestly mean that."

"I do," Claude says. "We'll have a clause stating that any intimate contact between us will violate the contract."

I look between them, feeling like I'm missing something. "I mean, that sounds perfect to me…"

Benjamin leans back in his chair, his brow furrowed. "It would be… unusual. To say the least."

"I don't care about doing things the usual way," Claude says. He folds his arms over his chest and looks at me. "I must still be allowed to bite you, of course. That will be excluded from acts of intimacy."

"Fine with me," I say after a beat.

"What about your sire?" Benjamin asks. "There was tension between the two of you at the ball."

"He feared that Nora would be a distraction from my purpose, but I have reassured him that it is quite the opposite," Claude says without batting an eye at the question. "If anyone is more disappointed in my lack of inspiration than I am, it would be Ambrose. He had such high hopes for me."

"So you *have* spoken to him on the matter," Benjamin says. "I thought you didn't require your sire's permission?"

"I don't," Claude says, "but I do respect his opinion, and I am pleased to have his blessing in the matter."

"And the Vulpe Court?"

Claude's hands still briefly, and then he resumes spinning his ring. "I am confident they will follow my sire's lead."

After a moment's thought, Benjamin excuses us to consider the offer. We step into the hallway, leaving Claude alone in the parlor, staring down at his untouched cup of tea.

"Well, what do you think?" Benjamin asks.

I hesitate. What *do* I think? My thoughts are such a muddle, I can barely decipher them. As little as I want to admit it, part of me is drawn to Claude, but I'm not sure I can *trust* that part. I shut my eyes, try to tune out the confusing tangle of my emotions and focus on the practicalities. It's easier to work things through without Claude's damnably distracting face in front of me, but still far from *easy*.

"On paper, his offer sounds like exactly what I've been looking for," I say. "But…"

"He's exactly the kind of person you've been saying you *don't* want this entire time," Benjamin finishes for me.

"Yet he offered to include an intimacy clause in the contract," I say, nibbling my thumbnail. Benjamin's face shifts at that, and I home in on him. "Would the others be willing to do the same?"

He clears his throat. "I… highly doubt it. It really would be unusual, Nora. I find it strange that he suggested it. I'm hesitant to even broach the subject with other vampires, because it would be offensive. And their courts would never approve. Valentine contracts are a serious matter."

"But Claude is willing to do it," I say. "So… he's being honest about his intentions? He just wants me as a source of blood, and muse, which is…" I shrug, hoping my attempt at nonchalance looks convincing. "I can do that."

"There's also the situation with his sire to consider," Benjamin says. "I know he told us it won't be an issue, but I misliked what I gleaned of their relationship at the ball. I'm afraid of you being pulled into the middle of whatever is happening between them."

I heave a sigh. "Is it possible to have some time to think about it?"

"Of course," Benjamin says. "That will give me time to ask around, as well. I'll see what I can find out about Claude's reputation, and that of his sire, along with confirming about intimacy with the other vampires who offered."

We return to the room to break the news, and I say my goodbyes to Claude. If he's disappointed in not receiving an immediate answer, he doesn't show it. He just bends to brush a kiss over the back of my knuckles, bids me farewell, and leaves me with my head spinning.

* * *

The next night, when Benjamin and I sit down to discuss it all, he breaks the news: both of the other offers have been withdrawn, with the patrons citing a refusal to sign any sort of intimacy clause like Claude did.

"I'm not surprised," he says. "I'm rather astounded that Lord Claude *did* agree, in fact."

"And what did you find out about Lord Ambrose?" I ask.

Benjamin shrugs. "The Vulpe Court sings his praises," he says. "They admitted there is tension between Ambrose and Claude, said to be due to Claude's unwillingness to paint since he was turned. Everyone seems to hope you're the solution to that, so they'll support the unusual nature of your contract."

I sigh, rubbing the bridge of my nose. "I don't *love* the idea of being his supposed muse, but..." I shrug. "On paper, it's everything I want."

76

I can't help but be reminded of my words at the ball: *anyone but him.* Yet now, here I am, signing my name on Lord Claude de Vulpe's contract.

Chapter Eleven

My first glimpse of Claude's home—*my* home, for the next year—takes my breath away. I was half expecting someone as dramatic as Claude to live in some kind of abandoned, moody old mansion. Instead the house is boxy and modern, all smooth gray walls and big, bold windows, and perched on a cliff overlooking the sea. I get the shivers just imagining the view.

When I get out of the car, I take a deep breath of salty air and smile. The wind tugs at my hair and clothing, carrying the sound of waves and the smell of the ocean. The Bay Area is just about an hour from LA by plane, and it feels like a different world. Especially since Claude's abode is hours away from the nearest city, far from the smog and the crowds.

I walk to the edge of the driveway and gaze over the side of the cliff. Beneath the night sky, the waves are so dark, they're nearly black.

When I turn back to the house, I see Claude waiting on the porch, watching me. He wears a white shirt with billowing sleeves and a deep V-neck, revealing a generous sliver of his pale chest.

My mouth goes suddenly dry as the reality of the situation

crashes into me. This is how it's going to be for the next year: me, this frustratingly attractive vampire, and a contract that forbids intimacy between us. How did I ever think this would be anything except *outrageously* awkward?

I curtsy and duck my face to hide my sudden trepidation. "Lord Claude."

He studies me. "There's no need for that formality. Welcome to your new home."

For the next year, I add silently. I step forward and take his proffered arm, letting him lead me inside. He gives me a tour of the premises, which are clean and white and angular, much like the exterior. The walls are oddly bare, and the windows that looked pretty for the outside give me a strange feeling now that I'm here, like I'm a creature under observation. Claude shows me the living room with its raised ceiling and square sofas, the dining room with its glass table and high-backed chairs, and my own bedroom, with a four-poster bed and crisp white sheets, and a bookshelf organized carefully by color and size.

"I hope everything is to your liking," he says.

"It's nice," I say.

He glances at me sideways. "Ah," he says. "You hate it."

"What? No!" My face flames scarlet.

"You hate it almost as much as you hated my painting."

"I never said—"

"You're not a very good liar, you know. Better to just tell the truth."

I sigh, and relent. "I guess I'm just surprised. This doesn't seem like a place where you would live."

"Not all vampires live in mysterious gothic mansions, you know," he says. "Some of us have adapted to the modern world."

"I know that! It's just so…" I fumble, unsure how to put it into words. It's more like a staged home than a lived-in one. The sort of place you feel like you'll dirty just by existing. Cold, impersonal, unwelcoming. "…Clean."

He stares at me. I stare back, feeling dumber by the moment.

"Well," he says eventually. "I'll give you some time to settle in. Dinner will be at three, if it would please you to join me."

He leaves me there before I have a chance to respond. I sigh, setting down my purse and flopping onto the too-big bed.

Just a year, I tell myself as I stare up at the glaringly white ceiling. But right now, it feels like an impossibly long stretch of time.

** * **

I doze on and off—I'm still adjusting to a vampire's nocturnal schedule after a lifetime of being an early riser. But despite feeling like I'd rather hole myself up in my room until I can forget the embarrassment of our earlier conversation, I head out to join Claude in the dining room at three a.m., like he asked.

I pause in the doorway, struck by the sight of him sitting at the end of the long glass table. With a cluster of lit candles and the beautiful view of the sea through the window, it should be romantic, but there's something sad about him sitting there at this big table alone.

"Is it just the two of us?" I ask, still standing in the doorway.

Claude glances up at me and frowns. "Who else would be

here?"

I step into the room, shrugging. "I don't know. I thought maybe you'd have staff, or…?"

"No," he says. "It's just me. Sorry to disappoint."

I shake my head, tucking hair behind my ear as I take my place at the opposite end of the table, where my plate has been set. There's a Mediterranean salad, crisp greens with bursts of ripe red tomato and crumbly feta, along with a rather generous pour of red wine. "Then who made the food?"

He blinks, as if surprised by the question. "I did."

"You can *cook*?"

He blinks. "Well, it's a salad tonight, so there wasn't much cooking involved, but… yes."

"You know what I mean," I say. "You can't taste food, so how can you prepare it?"

He quirks a brow. "Still perfectly capable of following a recipe, I assure you."

I flush, feeling foolish. "I… guess I didn't think of that."

He stares at me, one corner of his mouth curling. "You're surprised at my ability to perform basic tasks and maintain a clean house," he says. "These assumptions are interesting."

I stab a forkful of salad to save myself from speaking further, since I seem to only be able to blurt out the wrong things. It's good—fresh and vibrant, with a pleasant sharpness from the vinaigrette. Claude is watching me across the table, so I smile after I swallow my first mouthful. "It's good. Thank you."

His eyebrows rise. "A compliment? How novel."

I roll my eyes and take another bite. "I wasn't aware compliments were part of my job description." After a third bite—and the peculiar sensation of being watched as I eat—I frown at him. "You aren't eating."

He wets his lips, and a hint of fang catches the light. "I'll eat after you do."

"Oh," I say. "Right." I take a gulp of wine to hide my flush. I can't help but remember the way he cradled me as he bit me at the ball, and the heat rushing to every part of my body. But surely I'll get used to the sensation if I'm doing it every night. I have to. Right?

The room is quiet as I eat. The whole *house* is quiet, almost stiflingly so. I didn't imagine that it would be just the two of us in this big house. And before I came, it was just him. Maybe it should sound pleasant, after my lifetime of cramped spaces and nosy roommates, but instead it sounds… lonely.

I'm not the dramatic artsy type like he is, though. He probably loves brooding in solitude on the porch, looking out at the ocean. He probably prefers it this way. I wonder if I'll start to get on his nerves, after a while.

When I finish eating, I dab at my lips with my napkin, set it aside, and then sit there, unsure what to do with myself. Claude is still watching me across the table, his expression impossible to read.

After a moment, he gestures with two fingers and says, "Come here."

I raise my eyebrows pointedly.

His lips twitch faintly upward. "Please."

Good enough, I suppose. I push up from my chair and slowly cross the length of the table. The room feels somehow quieter than before, each click of my heels on the tile echoing faintly. Claude's eyes never leave me. When I reach his chair, he pushes back from the table and holds out his hand.

My face warms. Does he expect me to sit on his lap again? It feels different when it's just the two of us alone in this house.

But we do have a contract. And I *did* nearly swoon when he bit me at the ball. I suppose it would be awkward to do it standing, so maybe this *is* the best option.

Claude is still looking up at me, smiling and expectant. After a moment, I place my hand in his and sit sideways across his knees. It's surprisingly comfortable, especially with his arm supporting my lower back.

But it brings us close together. Very close. If I turned my face to the side, our lips would be centimeters apart. So I don't. I pointedly keep my gaze turned away as he lifts my wrist to his mouth.

Again, his bite is as gentle as a kiss. And again, it sends heat rushing through every part of my body. My eyelids flutter shut; I feel the rush of blood beneath my skin, the pulse of my heart, each beat making the heat inside of me deeper, brighter, hotter. My breath quickens, and then slows as I melt into Claude's arms. I thought my memory of the ball had exaggerated the power of his bite, but it feels so good. *Too* good. An intoxicating rush that leaves me aching.

I open my eyes as he pulls away. He bites his own lip and kisses the puncture marks on my wrist, sealing them with his blood. "Thank you," he murmurs, looking at me with half-lidded eyes.

It would be so easy to lean in and kiss him. I imagine his lips parting for mine, the faintest brush of fangs, his cool fingers against my heated skin…

Then I shake it off and force myself to stand, using the edge of the table to steady myself until my legs feel strong enough to hold me.

"What now?" I ask, trying to sound brusque. As impossible as it seems, this is going to be every night for the next year. I have to find a way to distance myself.

Claude leans back in his chair and shrugs. He looks exactly as casual as I am trying— and failing—to pretend to be. "You look exhausted, so take the rest of the night to get yourself settled." His head lolls back against the cushioned chair, sated and lazy. "Meet me here tomorrow evening."

"And then what?"

His blue eyes are bright as they meet mine. "And then I'll paint."

Chapter Twelve

My room feels too large, too decadent, too quiet. More like a hotel room than a bedroom. Unpacking my suitcase and filling the room with my small collection of belongings—books, mostly—doesn't help much. I don't have nearly enough stuff to fill all the space. I haven't even filled a third of the walk-in closet, even with the extra dresses that Benjamin and Lissa sent with me.

I thought it would be a relief to have this much time and space to myself. It's like nothing I've ever experienced. As a kid, my mom moved us from cramped apartment to cramped apartment, and later we lived out of her van. Ever since I broke free from her, I've lived with roommates like Elaine and Sophie, sharing too-small spaces to save money. I've never had an entire room to myself before.

But the house is so silent, it feels almost oppressive. It's strange to think that before I was here, it was just Claude by himself in this big, remote place. There is something about it that doesn't fit him. Yet then again, I hardly know him; he's already called me out for making all manner of assumptions about him, so I should probably stop doing it.

I should probably stop thinking about him so much in the

first place. I'm here because I'm getting paid, and it's not my job to figure out the enigma that is Lord Claude de Vulpe.

I dig my phone out of my purse and send Benjamin a text to let him know all is well. I was surprised to hear that a vampire had a cell phone, to which he sheepishly admitted that most vampires despise them, but Lissa insisted upon him learning to use one.

His response comes almost immediately: *Happy to hear. Don't hesitate to contact me if you need anything. - Benjamin*

Grinning at the way he signs his texts like an old man, I open up my group chat with Elaine and Sophie.

I made it to Claude's place, I type. *It's gorgeous. I'll have to see if I can invite you guys for a visit soon.*

I stare at the screen for a while, waiting for a response, but none comes. It gives me a pang of anxiety. They seemed happy for me when I told them I found a patron, but they both waved away my attempts to talk about paying for an apartment for them while I'm away. Sophie's staying with David, and Elaine with her parents, like they originally planned. I was always the only one without any options.

I'm relieved they'll be fine without me, of course, but it also leaves me feeling unsettled. Living together was the beginning of our friendship; what if moving out is the end of it? What if they don't want me now that they don't need me?

After nearly a half hour of agonizing, I finally realize they're probably not responding because it's the middle of the goddamn night. It's late even for my nocturnal schedule right now.

I should be exhausted, but still, I stare up at the ceiling for a long time before I manage to fall asleep.

***

I'm not sure my mind will ever get used to waking at sunset, but at least my body is starting to adjust to the nocturnal cycle. Claude didn't specify a time to meet him, so I allow myself the luxury of a slow morning—or evening, that is. I take a long, warm shower, drag a comb through my hair, and stare at my closet before selecting a simple white sundress. Am I supposed to dress fancier? Do my hair and makeup? I don't know what's expected of me. But the lack of caffeine is starting to make my head hurt, so I head into the house as is, resolving to find some coffee before I do anything more.

Memory takes me back to the kitchen Claude showed me last night during his tour. It's modern and spacious, with pale granite countertops and white cabinets. So strange to imagine Claude in here preparing a meal for me last night; stranger still to imagine that it must've sat here unused for years, since only Claude was living here, with no need for meals beyond blood.

The thought gives me a pang of worry. Does he keep the kitchen stocked? He must've bought some things, to be able to make my dinner last night, but would he have thought to stock up on necessities? What about coffee? If he doesn't drink it himself, it must've been years since he had to think about things like that...

My gut is in knots as I head to the fridge, already bracing myself for the familiar sight of empty shelves.

I pull open the fridge and stop short, staring. Utterly dumbfounded.

The fridge is... *well stocked* would be an understatement.

Full feels like an understatement. It is practically overflowing. There are a half-dozen varieties of milk and cream, neat piles of fruit, bottles of juice and sparkling water, an absurd amount of different types of cheese. Ripe red tomatoes and fresh green lettuce, a variety of bell peppers. Bundles of herbs and stacks of perfectly marbled steaks, a rack of lamb, an entire rotisserie chicken. All of it neatly arranged and fresh.

At the bottom is a small drawer containing vials of red liquid, neatly labeled with a date. That's all that *he* needs to sustain himself, so the rest… must be for me.

I can't stop staring.

"Good evening."

I startle at the voice and whirl around to see Claude leaning against the island counter in the middle of the kitchen, smiling at me.

I point at the fridge.

He looks at it, and then back at me, head tilting to one side. "Did I forget something?"

"No! Claude, this is…" I throw up my hands. "How much do you think I eat?"

He blinks. "I have no idea. And I wasn't sure what you'd like, so I got everything I could think of."

"This is way too much! I can't possibly eat it all before it goes bad."

He shrugs. "I'll toss whatever you don't use."

"No! That's so…" I fumble for words. "*Wasteful.*"

"If it's for you, it's not wasted." Still smiling, he crosses the kitchen to the espresso machine, which I failed to notice before. It's so shiny, it must be new. "How do you take your coffee?"

I sigh, massaging my temples. "I can make it myself."

"Again you think me incapable?" He's already taking a mug from the cabinet.

"No! I just…" I cross the kitchen and try to grab the mug from his hands. He holds it above his head, out of my reach, and looks down at me quizzically. "Claude," I sigh, stepping back and folding my arms over my chest. "This isn't necessary. I can take care of myself."

"I'm sure you can," he says, and sets the mug below the way-too-fancy machine, his long fingers darting over buttons too quickly for me to follow.

I lean back against the counter, feeling aggravated for reasons I can't put into words.

"You don't need to do all this," I mumble, feeling like a petulant child but unable to shake the discomfort.

"I know," he says. And then, again, "How do you take your coffee?"

So I end up sitting at the dining table, hands wrapped around a mug of coffee that is sweet with just a touch of cream, exactly how I like it. When I asked for yogurt for breakfast, thinking that was a simple option, Claude made me a parfait, layered with granola and fresh berries.

I take a bite and sigh. It's perfect. All of this is so perfect that it sets my teeth on edge. Nobody's ever taken care of me like this, and it gives me an uncomfortable itch beneath my skin. It's like I'm being a burden, even though I know I didn't ask for any of this. Which makes me feel horrendously ungrateful, and undeserving, and uncomfortable. Along with making me fear that he will expect more from me than I can possibly give.

Claude is watching me from across the table, just like he did at dinner, so I force a smile even though my throat is tight.

"Thank you," I say. My lack of enthusiasm feels like another failure on my part. I try to shrug it off and eat as much as I can manage—which is about half of what he prepared me. "So you're painting today? Do you want me to…?"

"Yes," he says, even though I'm not quite sure what I was asking. "May I drink from you? For… inspiration?"

"Of course," I say, my heart already pounding in anticipation. I set my napkin aside and walk to him, as I did last night. Again, I sit in his lap and surrender myself to the sweet sharpness of his bite.

Could I ever get used to this sensation? It seems impossible that every time should ravage my senses the same way, and yet… here I am, biting back a whimper as Claude drinks from my wrist.

My only solace is that I'm not the only one affected. As he sets me on my feet, there's a fresh, flushed look about him, my blood lending color to his lips and cheeks. And his eyes are bright, pupils so large, he looks almost drugged.

"Yes," he murmurs to himself. He stands, takes me by the hand, and brings me toward the back of the house. "Here, come, come. To my studio."

I let him lead me, curiosity overtaking me as he opens a room that his earlier tour did not include. My breath catches as I step inside. It is a smaller room but might just be the most beautiful one in the house. Moonlight makes the white walls and tile glow. An easel is set up in the center of the room, along with a small wooden table topped with paints and supplies. The workstation faces the far wall, which is made entirely of glass, curtains pulled back to present a gorgeous view of the sea. As I step toward it and look down, I can see the rocky plunge of the cliffs below, the crash of frothing waves against them. I press my fingertips to the glass, staring downward until my knees tremble and my stomach swoops, imagining the drop.

If anything could inspire a man to paint, surely it must be this: the ferocious dark beauty of the sea, just a pane of glass away. Smiling, I look back over my shoulder at Claude. "It's beautiful."

"Indeed," he agrees, looking at me instead of the view. His brow is furrowed as though he's trying to figure something out. "Mmm… sit here for me, please." He gestures to an alcove seat at a corner of the room, just below the glass wall. I'm happy to oblige, thinking he wants me out of the way. The white cushions are plush, and the seat has the perfect view out the window. I pull my knees to my chest and gaze out, taken again by the moonlit cliffs outside, the dark sea beyond. It's quite cozy here, probably a wonderful place to read during the daytime. Maybe even the moonlight would be enough, on a night like this.

"Oh, just like that," Claude murmurs. "That look on your face… Lovely."

My attention snaps back to him. He's standing in front of his canvas, mixing paints, but when he catches me looking, he glances up and frowns.

"You're going to have to sit still," he admonishes.

"Wait a minute," I say. "Are you painting *me*?"

He blinks. "Well, yes. What did you think I was painting?"

Heat creeps into my face. "I… well… I don't know! Your other paintings were all of places and things. Scenes, not people." The cafe, the cathedral, the lighthouse. I'm surprised how vividly I can recall the paintings I saw at the ball, and I'm certain not one of them included a person.

"True," he says, dipping his brush into the paint. "But as you may recall, it's been a very long time. Seems as good a time as any to reinvent myself, no?"

"I…" I squirm in my seat, one foot tapping on the cushions, suddenly itching to be anywhere but here beneath his penetrating gaze. "I didn't even do my makeup."

"So? You are beautiful without it."

He says it so casually. My face is so hot, it must be glowing red. "Surely there are better things to paint."

He gives me an assessing look, and then shrugs. "I find myself hard-pressed to think of any."

"But I'm just…" I gesture at myself, fumbling to think of any appropriate words. Unremarkable? Ordinary? Plain? *Human?*

"Just the woman who reawakened my muse?" he suggests.

"I mean, sure. Maybe there's something different about my *blood*. But I figured you would drink it and paint something beautiful."

"That is precisely what I intend to do," he says, his eyes never leaving me.

I turn away from him, staring determinedly out the window to prevent him from seeing me blush. I'm scrambling for an argument, but I can't seem to find one that makes sense, other than a petulant *This isn't what I wanted.*

"That's a good pose as well," Claude murmurs.

"I'm not posing," I snap at him. "I'm just sitting."

"You're a natural, then."

"Stop it!" I turn back to him. He meets my glower with an innocent blink.

"Stop what?"

"Teasing me." Despite my best efforts to maintain my composure, the heat in my face tells me I've failed. I wind my fingers together in my lap.

"Nora," he says after a moment. "I'm not teasing."

I continue staring down into my lap, unable to meet his gaze. He sounds sincere, but everything within me rebels against what he's saying. It's so much easier for me to accept that he's full of shit. That this is some sort of game. Maybe his revenge on me for insisting we maintain a professional relationship— he'll tease me relentlessly, make me blush and stutter like a fool, just so he can laugh at me.

A beat passes.

"May I paint you now?" he asks. "I'd like to chase this feeling while I still have it."

I swallow. What choice do I have? This is my job. I signed a contract. "Fine," I say.

Chapter Thirteen

Time ticks by. Seconds, then minutes, then at least an hour. The silence is broken only by Claude's occasional muttering and movements. I refuse to look up and see what he's doing, though occasionally I can see him pacing out of the corner of my eye, studying me from different angles.

I hate every second of it. The more he looks at me, the more certain I become that he's finding new flaws. I'm trying my best not to move, like he asked, but the urge to fidget is almost impossible to resist. Every time I push my glasses up, Claude grumbles under his breath. I keep catching myself slouching, or shifting, or fighting the urge to fix my hair or clothing. I'm trying to zone out and lose myself in thought, but I feel agonizingly trapped in my own body, aware of every inch of myself in a way that makes me itch.

The way I'm sitting feels stiff and unnatural. Does it look weird? Is my hair in place? Why didn't I check *before* he started this process? Now I'm locked into this pose, and my every flaw will be immortalized in a painting. Not just any painting, but Claude de Vulpe's *first* painting since being turned into a vampire. It's undoubtedly going to explode into public awareness, and then everyone will be looking at me, *scrutinizing* me...

I suffer in silence for as long as I can handle. Then I clear my throat and glance over at Claude. He's standing in front of his easel, paintbrush raised, a frown etched onto his perfect features.

"I could use a break," I say, and finally scratch the itch on my lip that's been driving me half mad.

"What?" Claude startles, eyes shifting to me and then back to his canvas. "Oh. Already?"

"...It's been at least an hour."

"It can't possibly have been..." He looks down at his watch and pauses, lips pressing into a thin line. "Ah. So it has." He runs a hand through his hair, frowning. "Very well. A break."

I stand and stretch, groaning with relief. My back releases a satisfying crack. As comfortable as the window seat is, any one position starts to feel terrible after enough time has passed. "Did you get what you wanted?" I ask.

"Hm? Oh. Well..." Claude frowns at his canvas. "You were perfect."

I frown. "That wasn't an answer."

"It's a slow process," he says, defensiveness creeping into his tone. "Especially when one is as rusty as I."

"Well, let me see..." I step toward him, and he yanks the easel back so hard, I'm surprised it doesn't break in his hands.

"Not yet."

I stop, fold my arms over my chest. "Why not?"

"It's not finished," he says. Still defensive. "I'm particular about people seeing my works in progress."

I study him, skeptical. He stares back, poker-faced, one hand still gripping the corner of the canvas as though he intends to rip it in two before letting me see it. Come to think of it, that does seem like the sort of dramatic thing he would do.

I sigh, relenting. "Fine. But I do have to see it at some point, you know."

"Of course," he says. "When it's done."

* * *

I expect to resume the process after a short break, but Claude disappears on me. I spend most of the night in my room, scrolling on my laptop and anticipating a knock at the door.

Sitting. Waiting. Doing nothing. I'm not used to spending my time like this, and it grates on me. I feel so lazy and useless. But there's nothing to be done. Eventually, the smell of food cooking draws me out to the kitchen. Claude stands at the stove over what looks like a pot of stew.

"Beef bourguignon," he says proudly, his lilting accent coming out full force, without turning to look at me. Apparently my bare feet on the tile are enough for him to identify my presence. "Lots of iron. Good for you after giving blood. I looked it up."

I hesitantly approach, taking a deep breath of the meat and red wine. Rich, savory, decadent. "Smells good. Can I help?"

"No, no. I forbid it. Go, sit, it will be done soon."

He brushes off my further attempts, and I sigh and relent, heading into the dining room. I'm still dressed in the outfit I wore earlier, since I wasn't sure if he'd be painting me again, and I feel entirely undeserving of this princess treatment.

Nobody's ever cooked for me like this. As a child, I learned to cook myself, because my mom would sometimes get so engrossed in her paintings that she'd forget to feed herself, let alone me. It was the same with my roommates; I was always the one cooking up big meals to make sure everyone had something to eat.

After a while, it became part of my identity. I'm the one who takes care of people. Now that the opposite is true, I feel restless and uncomfortable.

But surely this can't last forever. Claude likely just wants to make a good impression on me for our first few days together.

I keep telling myself that, even though all the way through dinner, Claude watches me eat like there's nothing else he'd rather do.

* * *

The next evening starts much the same. Claude brings me coffee and breakfast. He drinks from me again; I try and fail not to be affected by it, again. Then we take our places in his studio: me in the window seat, him at his easel.

He frowns, rubbing the back of his neck while staring at me. "That's not how you were sitting yesterday."

"Isn't it?" I look down at myself, eyebrows pulling together as I try to recall.

"No," he says. "Your hand was resting on your thigh."

"Like this?"

"Lower."

"Here…?"

"No," he says, a frustrated edge to his voice. "And your face was more turned toward the window."

"Okay…" I try turning, but I can see him shaking his head out of the corner of my eye.

"Your hair is wrong, too. There was a strand falling over your eye yesterday…"

I sigh. "What do you expect me to do? I can't control every little thing."

One second he's next to his easel. The next he's at my side. I jump and stare up at him as one of his cool hands takes my wrist and carefully moves it.

"There," he murmurs. "That's where it was. And your face…" His fingers gently grasp my chin, tilting it just so. "Yes. That's it."

His fingers feel cold against my suddenly hot skin. He's very near, his eyes intense as they study me. I want to break the tension somehow, maybe make a joke or complain about his micromanagement, but instead I find myself tongue-tied as he maneuvers me into place.

"One last thing," he murmurs, and coaxes one strand of hair out, draping it over my forehead. "And… perfect."

He steps back, and I can breathe again. As he returns to his position at the easel, I curse myself for the foolish reaction. Claude is being perfectly professional, and here I am getting worked up about him touching me.

But the excitement of it quickly drains, leaving me itchy and restless again. Claude complains every time that I move, so I try to hold my position. There's nothing to do but stare out the window, and while the view is lovely, I'm already starting to get sick of it.

When I shift to scratch an itch on my nose, Claude makes a soft, perturbed noise, and I glower at him. "I'm not an inanimate object, you know," I snap. "You could always go back to painting landscapes if you're so averse to me moving about."

Claude sighs, twirling a paintbrush in his fingers. "It's just that I want it to be perfect."

Then you should paint something else. I bite back the comment, and the desire to fidget more out of spite. It'll only draw this process out more. "How long do I need to do this?" I ask.

Claude frowns at his canvas. "I'm not sure."

I sigh. "Wonderful," I mutter, and return to staring out at the sea. My portrait is probably going to end up with a permanent scowl, but I guess that would be a faithful representation.

I shouldn't complain. I'm getting paid for this. Paid *very well*, to sit here doing nothing. I'm sure a lot of people would be happy for this job, and this house, and Claude's insistence on taking care of me. There must be some defect in me to be annoyed with it, even for a second.

But for me, the future I've always strived for is being entirely self-sufficient and stable. This undermines all of my ideas of what I want for myself… and I'm terrified of getting used to being taken care of when I know it's a temporary situation.

I force myself to sit as quiet and motionless as possible. I let my mind wander as my gaze stays on the water outside. I count the waves crashing against the cliffs, think fleetingly of my mother and the call she never returned, wonder how Sophie and Elaine are doing, and…

"That's enough for today."

I blink, turning back to Claude, caught off guard by the subdued note in his tone. He sets down his paintbrush, shakes his fingers out, and rubs at his temples, sighing.

"Is everything alright?" I ask, standing and stretching myself.

"Mm-hmm," he says. His eyes stay on his canvas, his mouth a pinched, troubled line. "That will be all, thank you."

Chapter Fourteen

I t feels like I'm doing something wrong.

Every day I expect Claude to seem happier. Better. He loves painting, so surely it will lighten his mood. But instead, it seems to sink lower each day. He makes my breakfast, drinks from me, and passes at least an hour in the studio while I sit in silence.

But every evening, his expression seems more troubled, his shoulders drooping lower. He is slower to smile, less prone to conversation. During our session at the end of the first week, he doesn't say anything, just sets down his paintbrush, shakes his head, and walks away.

I'm so tempted to steal a peek at the canvas. It's right there, taunting me… but I respect his wishes. It's the least I can do when he's treating me like royalty. And I feel helpless to do anything else for him, as much as I try to think of ideas.

One evening, as he sits across from me at breakfast looking particularly forlorn, he says, "It occurs to me that you still haven't told me what you didn't like about my last painting."

I blink at him, taken aback. I thought he had given up on that line of inquiry from the ball.

"Why do you care so much?" I ask. He just looks at me,

awaiting a response, and I sigh. I think back to that painting, and my reaction to it, trying to remember exactly what it was that made me speak out about it. I can still recall some of his other paintings with a striking clarity—the interplay between light and darkness, beauty and ugly truth—but the last one is just a vague blur in my memory. It was a vase of flowers, I think. Just flowers. "There wasn't anything wrong with the painting, Claude. It just… seemed to lack something that your other work had," I say. "It wasn't bad. It just didn't feel like *you.*"

He looks away, his expression unreadable.

"But I hardly know you," I say. "You shouldn't care what I think."

"You're right," he says. "You barely know me at all. That's what bothers me." He rakes a hand through his curls, leaving them messy. "You barely know me, but you alone…" He shakes his head. "I hate that painting too. But most people think it's my best." His gaze slowly drifts back to me. "And the house. Ambrose had it built for me. I was grateful because he expected me to be. But you… you *knew* this wasn't the sort of place that suited me. How? How do you see these things so clearly?"

I stare at him, taken aback.

"And you, the one person who seems to understand me so well, cannot stand me," he says quietly.

My stomach twists with guilt. "What are you talking about?"

"Don't lie to me now, after all of your brutal honesty," he says. "You were the one who first insisted upon no intimacy between us."

"That wasn't about you," I say, then hesitate. "Well, it wasn't *just* about you. It was about me, my future, what I wanted from our arrangement."

"And what is it that you want, Nora?" he asks. His gaze climbs up the curve of my neck, to my lips, to my eyes. His gaze is arresting.

I swallow, and force myself to be honest. "I want to finish this year and move on to the future I've planned for myself," I say. "I want… I want to be able to walk away without a broken heart."

He smiles, though there's a sadness in it. "You think I'll break your heart?"

"No," I say, "because I won't let you."

"Mm." His gaze drifts downward again, lingering on my mouth, my neck, before dropping away. "Maybe you don't understand me as well as I thought. You were never in any danger of that from me."

I'm not sure if he's a liar or just oblivious. Even now, with all of my effort to hold myself back, it feels like he's reached into my chest and is squeezing hard. "I understand perfectly well," I say, my throat tight. "I understand how people like you love, and I want none of it." I think of my mother, of how it felt to be in the spotlight of her affection—so intense it's blinding, and then gone just as quickly. Brief warmth that only made me realize how cold I was the rest of the time. It would be better not to experience it at all.

Claude studies me in the silence. "People like me?"

"You're an artist," I mutter, poking at the remains of my breakfast though my appetite is gone. "Your art will always be what you love the most."

"Mm." He shifts in his seat, still watching me. "My art is my raison d'être, I'll not deny that, but… I'm not sure *love* is an appropriate word. To love one's own art so much would be a form of narcissism, would it not?"

A flash of memory: my mother waving away my question without ever turning her gaze from her sketchbook. Me, all of six years old, standing with a dented can of soup I couldn't figure out how to open on my own.

Narcissism. I can't manage anything more than a tiny nod of a response.

"All that is to say…" Claude leans forward. "I'm sorry for whoever made you feel that way, but I'm not them."

"No," I say. "I know." He's so much worse, because I could see myself falling for it—falling for him. And that's not something I can allow myself.

* * *

The next evening, Claude seems particularly distant. He brings me my coffee just how I like it, and a breakfast as decadent as always, but then he paces beside the table instead of sitting. As I eat, he stares off into space, fiddling with the rings on his fingers, without saying a word.

"Claude?" I venture after a few moments. "Is everything okay?"

"Of course," he says, without looking at me.

I smooth over my napkin, just to give my hands something to do. Watching his antsy behavior is making me anxious. "We could try something else today, if you want," I suggest. "Maybe you could use a break?"

He turns and looks at me, puzzled for a moment, as if he's trying to figure out what I'm talking about. Then he shakes his head. "Oh, no. Er, yes, I mean. It will be a break, I suppose."

"...Huh?"

"I mean to say, we won't be painting today. My sire is coming for a visit."

"Oh." My pulse quickens at the memory of Lord Ambrose at the ball, the hard look in his eyes when he studied me, the knee-locking power he exuded. "Should I—"

"You're to stay in your room," Claude says before I can even finish the question.

My mouth clicks shut. I raise my eyebrows at him, shocked at the way he just spoke to me, but Claude is avoiding my gaze. "But... why?" I ask. "I thought everything was fine. You said he knew about our arrangement..."

"Of course he does. Of course it's fine. I just need some privacy with him. He'll be here any minute." When I still stand, unmoving, Claude finally looks at me. "I don't have time for this right now. *Please*, Nora, just do this for me."

I press my lips together. It's obvious he's not telling me something, and I remember Benjamin's worry that there was something off about Ambrose from the start, but his *please* is enough to make me relent, for now. "We're going to talk about this afterward," I warn him, heading for the door.

He waves a hand at me. When I glance back from the doorway, he's pacing the room, running his hands through his hair, his jaw a tense line.

* * *

As I shut the door to my bedroom behind me, I stare around, uncertain what to do with myself. The walls feel restrictive, the time unfathomably long. What am I supposed to do with a full day of nothing?

There's also a nagging anxiety in the back of my mind. Claude is a mercurial man, but his behavior today felt especially off. I can't stop thinking about what Benjamin said.

After debating about it for a few minutes, I take out my phone and text him: *Did you ever find out more about Lord Ambrose? He's coming to visit today.*

His response comes quicker than expected. *Nothing. Please keep me updated. I can come immediately if you feel unsafe.*

Unsafe? I chew my lip. I'm nervous for a reason I can't quite put my finger on, but I have no reason to question my safety. I send Benjamin my assurances and tell him I'll text him after the visit to let him know my read on the situation.

I do feel better knowing Benjamin is just a text away. I'm not used to having someone so reliable in my life. So unlike my mother, who *still* hasn't responded to my anxious stream of texts from before this whole valentine situation. It reminds me that it's early enough in the evening to contact my friends. I flop onto my bed, open a video app, and call.

Sophie picks up immediately, her phone an inch from her face, giving me a lovely view up her nose. "Queen of my heart," she says. "Are you finally calling me to let me know you've fallen madly in love with your vampire beau?"

I roll my eyes. "Don't even start. You haven't even met the man, Sophie." Though I know it would only be worse if she did. Both of my roomies would probably be swooning over Claude. His pretty face, the occasional smile that doesn't reach his sad eyes, his long artist's fingers... I grimace and shake the thought away. I *cannot* be thinking of him like that.

"And whose fault is that?" Sophie asks. "Anyway, you best

believe I looked him up the second I heard his name. Not a lot of photos on the internet, but those paintings would have me dropping my panties."

"*Sophie*," I groan. "Please stop."

"Oh, right," she says. "I'm probably making you jealous, because you've already fallen madly in love with him."

I take a breath and count to five in my head. Before I trust myself to speak, Elaine joins the call.

"Hey," she says. "I'm in the bathroom at work. What's up?"

"Oh, just catching up! You can get back to work."

"No, thank you. How's the lifestyle of the rich and famous going?"

I hesitate. Part of me wants to spill everything about the strange isolation out here, Claude's moods, the situation with Ambrose. But my problems pale in comparison to what they're dealing with out in the real world, I'm sure. "It's good," I say. "It's great. He's been starting to paint again, and he cooks for me…"

"Ooh," Sophie whispers. "Say that again but slower."

I sigh.

"So are you two fucking yet or what?" Elaine asks.

"Elaine!" I hide my face and the damning blush. "No. It's not like that. I *told* you guys about the contract."

"Mm-hmm," Elaine says, doubtful.

"Mm-hmm," Sophie echoes, even more doubtful.

"Anyway…" I roll my eyes, eager to change the subject. "Tell me what's going on with you guys."

We spend a half hour chatting about everything and nothing, aside from one break when Elaine makes sure the coffee shop isn't being overrun without her. Sophie regales us with tales about her boyfriend's horrible roommates, and Elaine reluctantly admits that she's growing to love her parents' cat, even though she's long viewed it as some type of replacement for her.

By the end of it, my face hurts from smiling so much, and I hang up feeling a little less alone. Yet as soon as the call is over, the silence of the house presses in on me again.

I expect Claude to come get me sometime before dinner. A knock comes late… and I open the door to find a plate of food waiting with Claude nowhere to be seen. I frown, looking up and down the hallway, and decide it must be his way of telling me to continue staying here.

* * *

When I wake the next evening, I venture out to the kitchen. But Claude isn't here waiting to make me my coffee. I wrangle with the high-tech espresso machine by myself for the first time and make myself a quick omelet. The whole time I expect him to show up any minute complaining that I didn't let him cook for me… but he never appears.

I wander the house restlessly, hoping at some point he'll emerge, but the door to his bedroom remains closed.

Perhaps I should be glad to see a reprieve from our painting sessions. They *were* a bit of a pain in the ass. But they were also the only scheduled part of my day, and without that, I feel even more useless and bored as I prowl the house. Plus, I can't fight the growing sense that something is wrong. Even if he's not painting today, shouldn't he at least need to feed? He didn't drink from me yesterday, either.

I pause in front of the double doors leading to his room for an embarrassingly long time before working up the courage to knock. "Claude?" I call.

No response.

"Hello?" I try again. "Are you in there?"

Silence. I stare at the doors, nibbling my lower lip. Did he leave with Ambrose? Is he upset with me? I don't know what to think.

But if he isn't answering, then… I should at least make sure he's alright.

I reach for the doors, and they give easily, opening to either side to reveal Claude's bedroom.

It's my first time setting foot in here, and I hesitate on the threshold, looking around. It's not what I expected. It's luxurious, of course, huge compared to my generous bedroom. One wall is covered in floor-to-ceiling windows, though blackout curtains are currently drawn tight over them. The bed is expansive and plush, with white silk sheets, a fur throw, and a ludicrous amount of pillows. A fireplace is built into the wall across from it, though it currently sits cold and unlit.

The whole room reeks of modernity and expense, all hard lines and neutral tones. It also feels oddly empty, devoid of personality, like it's staged for a house showing. Despite Claude's love of art, the white walls are as bare as the rest of the house.

And where is Claude himself?

For a moment I look around, squinting in the dim light coming through the open doorways behind me.

"Claude?" I ask, tentative.

There's a faint stirring among the pile of pillows on the bed. "Leave me alone," a muffled voice says.

I sigh, shut the doors behind me, and approach the bed. Only after some intense scrutiny do I detect a hint of dark curls and pale skin lost somewhere in the mess of blankets and pillows.

I place one fist on my hip. "What are you doing?" I ask. "Spending all night in bed?"

"Why shouldn't I?" He stares up at the ceiling rather than at me. His face is wan, almost waxy, his dark hair in uncharacteristic disarray. "What's the point?"

I frown and settle on the edge of the bed. It's so soft that it sinks beneath me. "What is this?" I ask, trying to gentle my voice. I've seen Claude in melancholy moods, but never quite like this.

In response, Claude grabs one of the pillows and places it directly over his face.

"Claude." I lean over, poking him in the side. "Talk to me."

Nothing. Not even a twitch when I dig my fingertip between his ribs, trying to prompt some kind of response. Suppressing another sigh, I walk over to the window and throw open the curtains, letting moonlight fill the room. I'm caught off guard by the view out the window. It's truly lovely; the sea glows silver beneath the moon.

"It's beautiful out tonight," I murmur, unable to tear my eyes away. "Come here and see it."

After a few seconds, he still hasn't moved. I head back to his bedside, frowning. "Did something happen with Lord Ambrose?"

"What happened," Claude says from beneath his pillow, "is that I am a perpetual disappointment."

"But you've been painting again," I say. "Shouldn't Ambrose be pleased?"

A bitter laugh. "Oh, yes," he says. "My canvas is in the corner. Go see how much progress I've been making."

When I hesitate, a pale hand emerges from the heap of blankets and gestures to the corner. I walk over to where his easel is sitting and turn it toward the window so I can see it in the moonlight.

The canvas is blank. Or mostly blank, at least, aside from a few swathes of paint, perhaps starting to form a background. If I look closely, I can detect a hint of the window seat I usually pose in, the stone around, the window itself. But no sign at all of me.

"I don't understand," I say, staring at it. Maybe I should be annoyed, after the hours I've spent posing all for naught, but instead there's just a hollow ache in my chest. It feels like my failure instead of his. I'm supposed to be his muse. "You said you were feeling inspired."

No response from Claude. I tear my eyes away from the canvas and return to the bed.

"You don't have to talk to me if you don't want to, but you should at least feed. It's been days." I kneel on the edge of the bed and lean over to remove the pillow from his face. Beneath it, his face is as blank as his canvas is, his eyes dull. There's a twist of anxiety in my gut. Claude can be dramatic, I'm aware of that, but seeing him like this doesn't feel right. "You'll feel better with some blood in you."

"Nothing will make me feel better," he murmurs, but his gaze follows my wrist as I hold it out. His lips move slightly as his fangs slide out behind them, one pointed canine catching the moonlight.

"Try it." I shift forward on my knees, one hand braced on the bed near his side so I can hold my wrist closer to his mouth.

And suddenly I'm on my back, pinned. Claude leans over me, half of his face soft and lit by the moonlight, the other drenched in shadow. He is still expressionless, but there's a new spark of hunger in his pale eyes.

"Don't you know it's dangerous to tempt a vampire who hasn't fed in days?" he asks, slender fingers gripping the wrist I was offering.

But even after flipping me so effortlessly, his touch is gentle.

"I trust you," I say, breathless.

He brushes his mouth against my pulse, his lower lip dragging against my skin, his fangs not quite breaking the surface. "Dangerous."

I thought I was starting to grow used to the sensation of being bitten, even the nearness of Claude. But it is an entirely different situation to have him on top of me and a soft bed beneath. When his fangs pierce me, I gasp, my spine sinking into the cloudlike mattress. Claude shifts his weight as he drinks from me in slow sips. One knee comes to rest between my thighs, and heat floods my lower belly.

He was right. This *is* dangerous. The two of us in bed together, his bite smothering my thoughts in a pleasant haze. I am all too aware that all I would have to do is shift, just slightly, for his leg to brush against the aching heat between my thighs. I let out a tiny whimper at the thought, and Claude abruptly pulls away from my wrist. He looks down at me, his mouth red with my blood, his eyes locked on my lips.

"You…" His gaze flicks between my mouth and my eyes, and he blinks rapidly, as if trying to remember where he is. His tongue glides over the tiny spot of blood he missed, and he shudders slightly before releasing me, shifting back. "You should go." He catches my wrist, one fang nicking his own lip before he presses a kiss to it. "Please," he adds, when I hesitate.

For a moment I can only lie there, breathing, my legs like jelly. I force myself to sit up and slide off the edge of the bed, and head for the door, wobbling slightly.

"Nora?" Claude calls after me when I push open the doors.

I glance back at him, not trusting myself enough to speak.

"Thank you," he says after a pause.

"Of course, Lord Claude," I say, and slip through the doors. Once I shut them behind me, I lean back against them and let out a sigh that comes from somewhere deep inside.

Chapter Fifteen

T he next evening, I wake up and make my coffee myself again. But as I'm reaching for the sugar, a hand snatches it away.

"No you don't," Claude says, close to my ear. "That's my job, *mon chou.*"

Goose bumps ripple over me at the French endearment on his tongue. I bite back a smile, and only turn to face him when I'm sure any sign of it is gone. "I thought I'd have to drag you out of bed today."

He leans against the counter, pouring the perfect amount of sugar into my mug without breaking eye contact. "And I thought you might join me again if I slept late."

I roll my eyes, trying not to think of his lean body pressing me down into the mattress, and grab the cream from the fridge before he can. "Don't make it sound like that."

He grabs the cream from my hand and pours it. "Like what?" He looks down at me, his lashes lowered to half conceal his eyes. "Intimate?"

"Exactly." I grab the mug of coffee and take a sip. It tastes better when he makes it for me, which I truly cannot understand. "Because that would be against our contract."

His amusement dries up in an instant. "Quite right, of course." He turns away before I can say anything to fix the abrupt change in mood. "What would you like for breakfast?"

"Oh, I don't care. Whatever's convenient."

He stays at the stove, waiting.

I gnaw my lip. If he's going to insist, then I suppose… "Pancakes?"

He shoots an approving look over his shoulder. "Excellent choice."

It's hard to ignore the flutter in my stomach as I lean against the counter and watch him cook. I know I shouldn't get used to this treatment—this arrangement is temporary—but I suppose it can't hurt to let him do this if he wants to. Maybe it will help get him out of the sulk he's been in.

He already looks more himself today—one curl artfully swooping across his brow, smiling as though he hadn't disappeared into a mountain of pillows and made me come looking for him. He hums to himself as he cooks for me, but after serving me at the dining table, he leaves me to eat alone.

When he returns again, I stare. He's changed into a dramatic black corset vest over a ruffled white monstrosity of a shirt, a combination that looks far better than it should, exaggerating his lean silhouette into something almost uncanny. I'm not sure how he can breathe wearing that, though of course he doesn't have to.

He takes a seat at the other end of the table. He props one elbow up, holds his chin, and stares at me.

"What?" I ask, suspicious at his sudden good mood.

"Just admiring you."

I roll my eyes. "Well, stop. There's plenty of time for that when you paint later." I try to say it casually, as if I hadn't seen that nearly blank canvas and witnessed what appeared to be a mental breakdown in his room yesterday.

"Oh, I'm not painting today. It's the weekend." He pauses, lips curling. "We're going to a party."

"A party?" I falter, set down my utensils. "Do I have to?"

"Yes," he says. "It's part of your duties as a valentine."

Leaning back in my chair, I sigh. "And here I thought my job was to get you painting again."

He shrugs. "Consider this part of my search for inspiration."

In the end, there is no way for me to argue. This is, technically, part of my job, and my contract details attending events as part of the expectations of my role. I suppose I should be grateful for something to do, but the thought of a *party*, of all things, has my stomach in knots.

"What kind of party is it?" I ask. "What should I wear?"

Claude leans forward, his eyes brightening. "I'm so glad you asked."

He comes to my room after I've finished eating and peruses my closet, muttering to himself. He pulls out a flowing white cotton dress, which isn't as bad as I was expecting. But then he adds a tight black corset that nearly matches his own.

I eye it, and then him. "Really?"

"The car will be here soon. Shall I help you dress?"

"Absolutely not." I shoo him out the door and spend a while wrestling with the outfit. I'm frustrated by the end of it, realizing it's impossible to do up the laces myself and he *must* have known that.

"Of course his had the cinches in the front," I grumble. "Bastard…"

I fix it up as best as I can on my own, quickly do some basic makeup, and head out. Claude hurries me straight into a waiting limousine too quickly for me to even consider asking about my laces. The moment the door shuts behind us, the car starts moving. Unprepared, I nearly topple off my seat, but Claude holds me steady with a gentle hand on my shoulder.

"God," I huff, anxiously patting down my hair and smoothing my dress as his hand recedes. "What's the rush?"

"We're late," Claude says.

"What? Why didn't you warn me earlier?"

"It was a last-minute decision to attend."

I think about his mood yesterday and *almost* bring myself to inquire about it. But Claude has been pointedly avoiding saying anything about it, pretending everything is normal, and I don't want to be the one to ruin his good mood.

"Is it a Vulpe party?" I ask instead.

For a moment I swear Claude winces, but a second later it's covered by an affected wrinkling of his nose, like he finds the idea distasteful. "No, and count yourself lucky. Camelia parties are far more entertaining."

"Camelia," I murmur to myself, remembering Benjamin's explanation and the glimpses I got of glamorous vampires at the Valentine's Day Ball. The court of beauty with their rose-and-dagger icon. Part of me worries I'll never fit in with such a crowd, but then again, I'm unlikely to ever be in the spotlight when surrounded by such peacocking.

"Lady Viktoria de Camelia is hosting. She's a friend of mine."

My eyes widen. I *know* that name, that face, just like *everyone* knows her and her famous valentine, Jonah.

Claude's look turns sly. "Ahh. Not going to be starstruck, are we? I didn't take you for a fan."

"I'm not a *fan*," I protest. "Everyone knows who they are. They're so luxurious and… and beautiful."

Claude's eyes narrow as he notes the color rising in my cheeks. "And I am not?"

I huff a laugh, look away.

"Well, don't go saying that kind of thing in front of them," he says. "You'll only stroke their already insufferable egos." A pause. "Feel free to compliment me, though."

I studiously inspect my nails.

"Very well," Claude says, his tone further stiffening. "May I drink from you, at least?"

I look up at him, sighing. "Now? *After* we dress for the party?"

He presses a hand to his heart, mock-wounded. "Nora! When have I ever spilled a drop? Even my bedsheets were spotless, and I was in a wretched state last night."

I grit my teeth and will myself not to flush at the reminder. "Yeah, fine." I hold out my wrist. Instead of biting in to drink directly from me, he grabs a wineglass from a nearby shelf and carefully holds it under my wrist after he bites me.

It stings more than usual, but he's careful as always, and seals the puncture wounds with a quick kiss. Then he produces a bottle of sweet red wine and pours a generous portion into the glass before drinking. His eyes close with a hum of pleasure. Only when he opens them again and glances at me does he hold out the wine bottle in offering.

"I just had breakfast," I say. And then, belatedly, "This is *your* breakfast."

"We're going to a party," he says. When I still stare, he shrugs. "Suit yourself."

I watch, arms folded across my chest, as he makes his way through one bottle of wine, and a second, tapping the bottle against the rim of his glass to make sure he gets every last drop. He always tops off his drink without fully draining it, ensuring that each glass contains my blood. Each one must be progressively less blood and more wine, but it seems it's still enough for him to drink it comfortably… a fact he must have gleaned from doing this many, many times before, I gather.

As he opens a third bottle, he glances at the dregs in his cup before glancing at me over the rim. "May I have a little more?"

I sigh. "Are you sure you should be drinking this much before we even arrive?"

He gives me a surprisingly sharp-edged look, the corners of his mouth curling down. "If I wanted to be babysat, I would've invited Lord Ambrose."

I fix him with a dead-eyed stare. "Excuse me?"

He holds my gaze for only a second before dropping his eyes. "Sorry," he says. He lowers his wine glass and rakes his free hand through his curls. "I didn't mean that. I'm just on edge. It's been a while since I've been to one of these events."

There's an ember of resentment burning in my stomach—doesn't he realize I'm nervous, too?—but after a moment I relent and offer my wrist. He presses a kiss that feels like an apology to my skin before he drains my blood into his cup again, and then seals the wound with another, bloodier kiss.

After he pours himself another large glass, I grab the bottle from his hand and take a swig directly from the neck of it.

"Best to follow the party expert's lead, I guess," I mutter.

Claude grins, his lips red with blood and wine, and clinks his glass against my bottle before we both drink again.

* * *

As the car pulls up to our destination a half hour later, I'm grateful for the wine taking the edge off my nerves. I only drank about a half bottle, but I'm not much of a drinker, especially just after breakfast. My mind is pleasantly hazy.

"Oh, shoot," I say, craning my neck in an attempt to see my own back. "I forgot about the laces."

"Oh, here." Claude pulls me so I'm nearly on his lap.

I try not to squirm. "You better not mess them up because you're drunk."

"Fear not," he murmurs, close to my ear. "I'm very good with my hands."

And he is, his fingers firm and sure and far too clever as he navigates the lacing on my dress. Blushing, I try to come up with a retort and fail miserably. I'm silent as Claude eases me off his lap and steps out of the car. Thankfully the heat has faded from my face as he bends to take my hand and help me out behind him.

All other thoughts fade as I find myself on the steps to a mansion.

"Wow," I breathe, staring up at it. The place sprawls against a mountainous backdrop, all brick exterior and gambrel roofs and Venetian windows. It looks huge, and old, and intimidating.

"Lovely, isn't it?" Claude offers his arm and I accept, trusting him to lead me as I stare around the beautiful building.

The ballroom isn't as large or crowded as the venue that hosted the Valentine's Day Ball, but it is somehow even more intimidating. Not the least because I recognize several faces from my guilty-pleasure magazines. Actors, models, and musicians flow through the crowd, each of them shockingly beautiful and dressed to the nines.

It's a relief that none of them spare me a second glance, because I feel even more plain and underdressed than usual. Claude, however, earns himself a handful of curious glances and startled double takes. He seems oblivious to it as he brings me past a gathering of tables and a sprawling dance floor to a bar. I'm still a little drunk from the car ride, but when he presses a glass of wine into my hand, I'm grateful for something to hold.

He touches his own glass to mine. "Santé."

"Cheers." I sip; the taste is far richer than whatever we had on the way over. "So… what now?"

His eyes crinkle at the corners. "Have you never been to a party before?"

"Not like this." I fidget with my wine. "Not… much ever, really, no."

Claude's eyebrows rise in a silent question, but before he can voice it, a young man approaches to greet him. I stand with a smile frozen onto my face as they launch into an easy conversation about parties of days past.

The young man—a model, I gather from their discussion—is the first in a steady stream of beautiful people whose names I can't seem to remember. I spend the whole time standing stiffly at Claude's side, drinking my quickly dwindling wine, murmuring pleasantries when he introduces me before swiftly getting left behind in the conversation. Every time I try to think of something to say, my throat tightens with the sudden certainty that I don't belong here and everyone knows it.

"Sorry," I mutter, when the last of them walks off.

Claude slides closer to me, his hand brushing over my elbow. "Whatever for?"

"I'm not very good at this." Just another part of my job that

I'm failing at. I haven't been a successful muse, nor a successful party guest. What am I getting paid for?

"You're fine. These people are dull," Claude says, dropping his voice to a whisper. "Let's go find Lady Viktoria. I'll tell her what a huge fan you are."

"Don't you *dare*," I sputter, clinging to his arm as he heads to a quieter corner.

We find Lady Viktoria in a corner of the room, lounging on a plush couch with her long, long legs stretched out in front of her. Her dress is adorned with what must be hundreds of actual roses, and the thigh slit is so high, I can tell she's not wearing anything beneath. She's engaged in discussion with another Camelia vampire, but when Viktoria sees us, she dismisses the woman with a casual flick of her wrist.

"Claude de Vulpe," she says with a slow smile. "I didn't expect to see you tonight."

"Well, I know how you love a good surprise." He bends down to take her hand and brushes a kiss against her knuckles.

When Viktoria turns her smile on me, I feel a little stunned. She's even more gorgeous in person, with smooth alabaster skin and eyes like a cloud-free sky. Her short blond hair is slicked back, and diamonds glitter on her ears, her neck, her fingers. "You must be the new valentine I've heard so much about."

I drop into a slightly belated curtsy as I remember myself. "Lady Viktoria." I hope she doesn't *actually* mean it when she says she's heard about me. The thought of her knowing anything about me is terrifying. "This is such a lovely party, thank you for inviting us."

"Hmm." She gives me an appraising once-over while I try not to quiver.

"And where is your darling Jonah?" Claude asks, glancing around. He shifts subtly closer to me, his hand grazing my lower back before settling on my hip. I'm surprised at how reassuring it is. "I thought he was a permanent fixture at your side."

"He's off indulging himself, I suppose."

"Without you?" Claude quirks a brow.

"Come now, you know I have no problem sharing." Viktoria's gaze falls on Claude's hand where it rests on my hip, and his grip tightens. Her eyes glimmer with amusement. "Neither do you, usually."

"It's Nora's debut. I'm not sure she's ready for that."

I glance sideways at him, peeved at the way he's talking about me like I'm not here. And the way he's talking about me in general, like a *thing* he can choose to give out at will.

But Claude is oblivious to my glower, or doing a good job of pretending at it, as his hand slides off my hip and he settles on the couch next to Viktoria.

"Fair enough," she says. "Is it true you've been painting again?"

Claude's eyes narrow. "Word *does* get around fast, doesn't it?"

"I've no idea if it gets around, but it always finds its way to me quite quickly."

As their conversation continues in low tones, I glance around, trying to figure out what to do with myself now that Claude seems to have forgotten my existence. Maybe I should wander off, but it isn't like I know anyone else here, and I'm terrified of being around so many vampires alone. So I settle myself onto a chaise a few feet away and sit awkwardly, gazing at the crowd.

A man breaks away from the dance floor and heads our way. It takes me only a moment to place him, since I'm pretty sure he's one of the most recognizable faces in the world: Jonah Montgomery, the valentine poster boy known for his stunning good looks and, according to most vampires, the sweetest blood one could ever taste.

And clearly quite a few have been tasting him tonight. He wears a silk dress shirt with half of its buttons undone, revealing a pale chest and neck decorated in fresh bite marks and lipstick stains in various colors. His cheeks are flushed, his eyes bright, his hair thoroughly mussed but somehow still elegant.

He drops onto the chaise beside me with a sigh, lying on his back so that he takes up almost all of the space. Then he glances up at me as if just registering my presence.

"Oh," he says. "I don't know you."

I clear my throat. It's hard to look directly at him, with his sex hair and bedroom eyes and famously perfect face. "I'm Nora," I say. "Clau— Um, Lord Claude's valentine. Nice to meet you."

"Ahh." He gives me a slow, knowing smile, as though he's in on some secret that I'm not privy to. "Interesting." But not interesting enough, apparently, because he immediately turns onto his side to face our patrons on the couch. He props his head up with one hand while the other flutters at Claude in a lazy little wave. "Why, hello. Pleased to see you made it."

"Pleasure's all mine," Claude says. His eyes drift toward Jonah's open shirt, lingering for a moment before darting guiltily to mine.

I lift a brow and slowly sip my wine, making sure he knows I saw that. There's a curious warmth, low in my stomach at the thought he might want Jonah. A hint of jealousy, but… I can't deny I'm intrigued, as well.

Judging from Jonah's sultry smirk, I'm not the only one who notices Claude's interest. "I still remember when you bit me at that New Year's party," he says. "You're very good at it." Then he looks up at me, still smiling. "Isn't he?"

I flush despite myself. I can feel Claude eyeing me, too. Normally, I'd never admit to Claude having any sort of effect on me, but in this situation, in front of his friends, I can't bring myself to insult him by brushing the question aside. "Yes," I admit. "He is."

"One of my many talents," Claude says, though he looks far more pleased with himself than the offhand remark suggests.

"Well, I love to see an artist at work," Viktoria says, and nudges him. "Go on and show us, Claude."

Claude glances at me. To my horror, I feel heat climbing up the back of my neck and then across my face, undoubtedly turning me a horrible shade of red that's impossible not to notice. I don't know how to say no, but the thought of Claude biting me in front of these people, knowing what it does to my body, feels so… so *public*, almost obscene. And it's not just in front of any people, but a famous couple, and a gossipy famous couple from what I've seen tonight. I don't know if I can—

"Jonah?" Claude asks, his gaze sliding off me and to the man sprawled on the chaise at my side. "May I?"

There's a flicker of surprise on Jonah's face, followed by a smug smile. "Thought you'd never ask."

Claude stands and moves over to us. I don't move, can barely think nor decipher the tangled knot of feelings in my chest. The thought of Claude biting me in public was mortifying, but the thought of him biting someone *else* in front of me makes something in my chest burn.

Viktoria pats the couch at her side and beckons to me. "Nora."

There's a moment when I could refuse. A moment when I could say something to Claude. He wouldn't be happy about me interrupting, and it'd probably be a faux pas to refuse our host, but I think he would listen.

Yet instead I find myself moving to Viktoria's side. I sit stiffly on the couch, hands in my lap, and watch as Claude leans down over the chaise that Jonah's resting on. His fingers trail down the other man's neck, down his chest.

Viktoria is watching intently, and so am I, even though I keep willing myself to look away. It's obvious Claude welcomes the attention. Maybe the display should irritate me, but instead there's a strange and sinuous heat in my stomach.

When Claude throws a leg over Jonah's hips and sinks onto the chaise to straddle him, that heat sinks lower still. I press my knees together, heart pounding in my ears. *Look away*, I tell myself, but I can't.

Claude pins Jonah's wrist beside his head and leans down, his lips brushing the delicate skin over his pulse point. For a moment I swear I feel his eyes on me, though it's impossible to tell for sure with curls falling over his brow. Then he bites.

Jonah sucks in a sharp breath, his eyes rolling as his head lolls back on the couch.

I have to glance away after a few moments, my face hot and my chest burning with the oddest mix of jealousy and arousal. When I turn, I find Viktoria watching me, her eyes heavily lidded, her smile small but showing a hint of fang.

"They make a pretty picture, don't they?" she murmurs,

shifting closer to me.

I squeak out something that might be an agreement, over-whelmed by her sudden nearness. My pulse pounds as she leans in, brushing a lock of hair behind my ear with one painted nail.

"Claude and I tend to have similar tastes," she says, her eyes following the curve of my neck with a gaze so heavy, I feel it on my skin. "I can only imagine how sweet you must be."

"Oh," I say faintly. I'm sure she can see the movement of my throat as I swallow.

"May I…" Her tongue flicks out to wet her lips. "Try you?"

That burning in my chest slowly spreads through my limbs and belly, making me feel almost dizzy with the rush. I have an urge to glance at Claude for approval, but I can see out of the corner of my eye that he's still thoroughly entangled with Jonah on the couch.

It's just a bite, I tell myself, though it's obvious that Viktoria is offering more than that. Yet if Claude didn't feel the need to ask my permission for a bite, then why should I?

I don't trust my voice right now, so I simply hold out my wrist and nod.

Her lips are soft against my skin. If Claude's bite is a kiss, then hers is barely a breath, a brush of a butterfly's wings. As she drains my vein, that usual rush of pleasure comes in to replace the blood I've lost. It isn't quite as intense as when Claude does it, but it still feels good.

I bite my lip, swooning slightly. *Very* good. Especially when she puts her other arm around me to hold me against her. If I shut my eyes and pretend, it would almost be like being in Claude's arms. Almost.

When she pulls away, and my eyes slide open, they go

straight to him. Claude is staring at me, his lips tinged red and an intensity in his gaze that I haven't seen before, sharpening his soft blue eyes into hard chips of sapphire. The emotion on his face is far more complicated than anger or jealousy, and it gives me an odd thrill to see him so obviously affected by me.

Victoria touches a bloodied fingertip to my wrist to heal the wound. Her other arm is still around me, keeping me pressed against her side. Not an unpleasant place to be, especially if it makes Claude keep looking at me with that smoldering intensity.

"I have a lovely vintage up in our room that I've been saving for a special occasion," Viktoria says, her gaze sliding over to Claude. "The four of us could share it, if you're so inclined."

I bite my lip as I look over at Claude. His expression has shifted at the question, his long eyelashes obscuring his eyes as he looks down, and it's impossible to read him in the low lighting. Is this something he wants? Is it something *I* want? Surely it's insane to be considering it. I've never done anything like that before. I've never done *anything* with Claude, even.

But it wouldn't technically break our contract if we weren't touching one another, would it? For a moment I imagine it, all four of us in their bedroom. Someone else's hands on me, someone else's mouth on Claude, and our gazes meeting, locking, across the room. The ache that image sparks in my chest is equal parts pain and pleasure.

As Claude finally raises his gaze to meet mine, that ache deepens. Then his mouth firms, and he stands up, holding out a hand.

"No, thank you," he says. "Not tonight. We should head home."

I stare at his hand, and then up at his face. A glance at

Viktoria tells me she's almost as taken aback as I feel, though Jonah's smirk tells me he anticipated this and is somehow amused.

Claude gestures at me, impatient. "Nora."

Is he calling me to him like a dog? My annoyance breaks through the strange haze I had fallen into, at least, and I shake myself before getting to my feet. "Very well." I curtsy to Viktoria. "It's been a pleasure. Thank you for having us."

"Of course." She takes my hand and kisses the back of it. "I hope to have you in the future, as well."

I flush at her wording, and mumble a goodbye to a still-smirking Jonah before heading for the door, brushing right past Claude and the hand he's holding out to me. He trails after me silently, out the door and to our waiting car.

The stumble in my step tells me I either drank more than I thought, or was drunk *from* more than I thought, or both. I clamber into the limo and rip my heels off, tossing them to the floor.

After the door shuts behind Claude, we sit in silence. I rub my aching feet and refuse to look at him.

Claude slides closer, reaches out to close slim fingers around my ankle. "Let me..."

I swat his hand. "No."

I catch his wounded look out of my peripheral vision. "You're angry with me."

The snort that leaves me is far from dignified. "Perpetually observant, Lord Claude."

"Why?" He leans forward in his seat, elbows resting on his thighs as he stares at me. "You wanted to sleep with her?"

"I... wanted..." I'm not even sure what I wanted, except— "I wanted to have some choice in the matter."

A beat passes. When Claude speaks again, his voice is lower, with a sharpened edge. "Then you shouldn't have signed a contract to be *my* valentine."

I ignore the way it makes my heart beat faster to hear him call me *his*. "The contract didn't stop you from having your mouth all over someone else's valentine."

"All over…?" He huffs a laugh. "I bit his wrist. And Nora, you said—" He shakes his head, looking stupefied. "You said you didn't want intimacy with me. If it bothered you, you should've said something."

He's right. I didn't—*don't*—want that with him, and I've been very clear about it. But I'm too drunk to suppress my feelings right now, especially the clawing monstrosity that is my jealousy. "When should I have stepped in, precisely? Before or after he started writhing like an animal in heat?"

Claude throws up his hands, exasperated. "You're acting like I fucked him."

"Well, you looked barely a step away from it," I snap back.

"I was within sight of you the whole time, you know I didn't do anything indecent."

I let out a harsh laugh. I can't stop remembering the way Claude threw a leg over Jonah's hips, the sounds the other valentine made. There is a bubbling heat within me, and I am both annoyed and annoyingly turned on. "Oh, so you call that *decent*?"

"Yes! In fact, I know it is, because our contract is clear that biting someone *does not* count as intimacy!"

There's a pause after he speaks. A shift in the air between us as we both realize what he said. What it means.

I'm not sure which of us moves first, but all of a sudden I'm on his lap. My fingers tangling in his hair, his lips against my neck. Both of us clutching at each other with the same desperate need. This is dangerous—we're both drunk and sexually frustrated—but I need him, and this is the only way I can have him.

"Yes," I whisper, before he can even voice the question.

His teeth sink into my neck. I arch against him, crying out, as pleasure floods every nerve in my body. It's bliss, pure bliss, my body trembling against him as the ache between my legs becomes a pulsing throb. Claude moans into my neck, drinking from me like a man dying of thirst even though he's been thoroughly glutted tonight. Each pull from my veins sends a new wave of need through me. I feel feverishly hot, panting on his lap, so close to the orgasm my body has been craving all night.

Claude shifts his weight, and one of his knees slips between my thighs. The gentlest pressure where I so desperately need it. And I come apart instantly, crying out his name and grinding against his leg.

As the blinding pleasure recedes, I realize Claude has stopped drinking from my neck—has already sealed the punctures with his blood-tinged kiss—and is frozen beneath me. I pull back, pushing hair out of my face, to look down at him. His eyes are shut, his expression a pained grimace.

"Please," he whispers. "Move."

I jump off his lap as quickly as I can, scrambling into a seat opposite him on still-wobbly legs. "I'm so sorry," I blurt out. "I didn't realize— If you didn't want—"

"I did want," he says, his eyes remaining closed. His hands are braced on the seat on either side of him. "I do want. Very much. Thus the problem."

My eyes drop to his trousers, and I blush. I felt it beneath me on his lap, but seeing the size of his bulge is another story altogether. "Oh," I say faintly. I pause, swallow. Then, "Claude…"

"Please don't say it," he says.

"I want it too."

He winces. "I told you not to."

"But I… what I'm saying is, we could make an exception tonight…"

He's shaking his head already. "We have a contract."

"A contract between us." My brow furrows. Claude suggested the clause, and I agreed, but… "If you want it, and I want it, then—"

"A valentine contract is a matter of court law. We cannot amend it without approval."

I bite my lip. It does sound a lot more serious when he puts it that way, but still. "Nobody would know if something were to happen."

"*I* would know," Claude says. A muscle in his jaw twitches. "Nora, please, drop it. We can talk about it later. Not now."

I study him across the car. His eyes are still shut tightly, his usually perfect face creased as if in concentration or pain, his hands in fists at his sides. If my arousal is an uncomfortable distraction even after my release, then his must be worse. Much worse. So I relent. "Okay." I turn my head away stiffly. "It was a mistake anyway. We're drunk. Let's just forget it ever happened."

It is a very, very long car ride home.

Chapter Sixteen

I eat breakfast alone, moonlight making the silverware shine. I fully intend to talk to Claude about last night, and the matter of our contract, but I wait and wait, and he doesn't show up. When I venture to his bedroom to make sure he isn't having another one of his moods, I find it empty.

My stomach twists. He left without me. Without even telling me, after what happened last night. It's irksome that he's avoiding me, but even worse to imagine where he might be. Maybe he wants a chance to drink from pretty men and women without me there to ruin his fun. Would he have accepted Viktoria and Jonah's offer without me there? I wonder.

I know I shouldn't care. We both know—and agreed upon— the contract. There's nothing to prevent him from getting on with others, especially since he can't do anything with me. But… it annoys me that he'd leave me here alone. Like he put me up on a shelf to go play without me.

I spend the night drifting through the house, scrolling on my phone in bed, sending texts that don't receive responses.

The next evening Claude drags himself in for breakfast, looking rumpled and bedraggled in a dramatic cotton terry robe. He drapes himself over his seat at the head of the table with a groan and pushes messy curls out of his eyes.

"I need blood today," he says, looking over at me as he drags a hand down his face. "Please."

I glower at him. "You're hungover."

His lips quirk. "Am I so obvious?"

I grimace, and stab one of my eggs hard enough that my fork scrapes the plate. "Well, you can wait until after I've eaten."

"Of course." He leans further back, head lolling, one arm flung across his face as if even the dim lighting in here is too bright.

I want, so badly, to ask where he's been. But I can't find a way to phrase it that doesn't sound desperate. It's none of my business, after all. Our relationship is defined in writing, and I have no claim to his time beyond my duties.

"Are you going to paint tonight?" I ask instead.

He lets out a muffled groan. "Tomorrow, perhaps."

"Claude." I set down my utensils. "Do you *want* to paint again?"

His arm falls away from his face, and he blinks at me as if startled. "What? Of course I do." His gaze drops, brow furrowing. "I am quite useless otherwise."

"That's not true." I hesitate, struggling to find the words. "I just mean… It doesn't seem like it's making you happy."

"I would be happy if I were actually painting."

"Then why don't you just do it?"

He grimaces, massages the bridge of his nose. "God," he mutters. "Everyone tells me that. As if it's so simple. You don't understand."

"Then explain it to me," I say. "I *want* to understand."

Claude groans, dragging his hand down his face. "Fine," he

says. Then he sits silently for a moment, expression one of consternation. "When I was a human," he says, "I felt... so many things when I painted. Joy. Freedom. Fear, that I would never have enough time to put everything I wished to on the canvas, and those images would be lost with me." He pauses, his face a storm cloud.

"Then... Lord Ambrose gave me that time. He gave me *endless* time to pursue the thing I loved most. It is the best gift I could have ever imagined. And yet... when I tried again to put paint to canvas... all those things I once felt were gone. All that was left was a sense of pressure. Enormous pressure. Because the thing that I once did out of love, I was now supposed to do because it was *expected* of me. No matter what I do now, people will judge it, and judge me, and weigh it against my previous work... and it feels like no matter what I do, it will not be enough to please them, nor earn the gift I was given. So why try?"

I study his face as he stares down at the table. I expected his explanation to be ridiculous, dramatic. And maybe it is, but I can tell how much it weighs on him. I don't understand art, but I do understand how heavy other peoples' expectations can be.

"It's a lie that I never painted after I was turned, you know," he says, when the silence lingers. "I did try, in the early days. I painted a few landscapes."

"What happened to them?" I ask.

"Lord Ambrose tore them apart. He said they weren't as good as my previous work. That I had to do better so I wouldn't embarrass him." His lips twitch in a bitter half smile. "Well, that's what happened to two of them, at least. I ripped up the third myself. And then... *Then* I stopped painting."

"But you love to paint," I say. "You shouldn't do it for Lord Ambrose, or anyone else. You should do it for yourself."

He looks away. "I don't know if I remember how anymore," he says.

* * *

The next evening, he's gone again. And again, and again, until a full week has passed without a single painting session.

The sound of the doorbell startles me one night. I shuffle there with my coffee, open the door, and nearly drop my mug.

"L-Lord Ambrose," I say. After a moment of pure, frozen panic, Benjamin's etiquette lessons take hold of me and I dip into a curtsy. "What… what an unexpected pleasure. I'm sorry to say that Lord Claude isn't here to welcome you himself—"

"Oh, I knew he wouldn't be," Ambrose says. "He's my fledgling. I always know where he is." Sometimes I forget about that unseen link between them, a bond that I don't—and *can't*—truly understand. But at least I remember enough from Benjamin's lessons to know that Claude, too, knows of Ambrose's whereabouts, which means, I *hope,* he'll come home. Quickly, I hope, because Ambrose studies me in a way that makes my skin crawl. "Why don't you go make yourself presentable? I'll wait in the sitting room."

"I-I…" I swallow back anger and a prickle of fear. "Yes, of course. Come in." There's nothing else to say.

It feels ridiculous to doll myself up for a man who just showed up on my doorstep, but of course Lord Ambrose is the old-fashioned type and basically ordered me to do so. So

I apply my makeup and put on a decent dress as quickly as possible before heading to meet him in the living room. I stop in the hallway outside, take a couple of deep breaths, and roll my shoulders back before entering the room at an unhurried pace.

Ambrose's piercing gaze is on the doorway, waiting, even before I enter. Of course he must have heard me approach, must have heard me pause outside to gather myself. A slight smirk tells me he finds my anxiety amusing. Stupid of me not to think of that, but I plaster on a smile and try to act unbothered.

"Pardon me," I say, curtsying again. "I wasn't expecting company. Can I get you something?"

Despite my efforts to be *presentable*, as he put it, Ambrose still radiates disapproval as he eyes my sundress. "Is this how you dress for him? It's no wonder Claude isn't painting."

I stare. Anger chips through my icy fear. "Pardon," I say carefully, "but I'm not sure what my appearance has to do with Lord Claude's art."

"You're a fool, then," Ambrose says, as easily as breathing.

I'm bristling. Did this man show up just to insult me? I'm eager to strike back at him, but I know my tongue is going to get me in trouble if I'm not careful, and I remember the strength in his grip when we first met at the ball. "Is there something I can help you with, Lord Ambrose?"

"There very well may be." Ambrose stands, smoothing down the front of his jacket. "I had hoped to check on the progress of Claude's work. Since you're here, perhaps you can show me."

I waver. I know very well that Claude hasn't worked since the last time Ambrose was here. But telling Ambrose that, let alone showing him, feels like a betrayal. Claude can be aggravating at times, but I have no desire to see him in a state like he was after Ambrose's last visit.

"If you wait for him to return, I'm sure he could show you himself," I say, ignoring the fact that we both know Ambrose showed up here knowing he *wouldn't* be home.

Ambrose steps closer to me. Goose bumps break out all over me; it takes all of my willpower to hold my ground.

"I am asking *you* to show me," he says, his voice soft and dangerous.

Ambrose is not the kind of man who someone like me can say no to. But every fiber of my being rebels at the thought. Claude is my patron. I owe him my loyalty. "I'm sorry," I say. "I don't believe I can do that. I…" I force a wobbly, sheepish smile. "I'm afraid I don't even know where he keeps his works in progress. He is… private about it."

Ambrose's fingers dart out to grab my chin, and force my face up so he can look me in the eyes. I gasp even as I try to suppress it; he's so fast, so strong, his fingers digging in hard enough to hurt.

"You expect me to believe that's true?" he asks, eyes piercing mine. The rest of his body language is casual, almost bored, even as he grips me so hard I can feel bruises forming beneath his fingertips. "You're his one and only valentine. Yet he doesn't keep you in his confidence?"

I try to swallow my fear, knowing he will only enjoy it, but I can't keep my heart from racing. "We do not have a usual arrangement, as you likely know, my lord."

"I had wondered about that," he says. Still holding me in place, still staring into my face as though he can read it. "I felt quite a disturbance through our bond a few nights ago. And

then I heard rumors of all of these parties he's been attending…
"

A few nights ago. The Camelia party. I try to think of something, anything else, to keep the color out of my face. "As you can see, I am not in attendance at these parties," I say. Not quite a lie. "Perhaps someone else was responsible for whatever… disturbance… you might have noticed."

Ambrose studies me for a moment longer, and then releases my chin. I step back, resisting the urge to touch my face or flee.

"All for the best, I suppose," he says, sounding almost disappointed, though I can't imagine why. "Wouldn't want Claude to go breaking his contract with you."

So he knows about that. He knows an awful lot, I'm gathering, though I can't fathom why Claude's private life could possibly matter so much to him. But again, I feel the urge to defend Claude. "He hasn't," I say. "He won't. Claude is very respect—"

One minute I'm upright, and the next I'm on the floor, head spinning. It happened so fast, it takes me a moment to process the shocking pain, the crack of his hand across my face. He just slapped me.

I raise a shaking hand to touch the stinging skin, where I'm sure a red mark is forming. I taste copper from where my teeth cut into my cheek.

"It's *Lord* Claude to you," Ambrose says.

I slowly raise my eyes to him. He's standing casually, hands now in his pockets, head cocked to one side as he regards me. He doesn't even look angry, just blank, as if this is a commonplace interaction.

My legs are wobbly, but I force myself to stand. I refuse to grovel on the floor in front of this man. "My apologies," I say. My smile is sickly sweet. I can still taste blood on the back of my tongue, but manners are the only armor I have. "As I was saying, *Lord* Claude is a perfect gentleman. I have no concerns about our contract."

Ambrose looks away. For a moment I think I've just begun to bore him, but then the door bursts open, and Claude is here. He's dressed in a tight black shirt with a ludicrously plunging neckline, his eyes are smudged with eyeliner, and his hair is in disarray. He looks first at Ambrose, and then at me.

Instinct drives me to turn away, just slightly, to hide the mark on my face. "Welcome home, Lord Claude," I say, stiff and formal. "Should I wait in my room while you're with your visitor?"

A long pause. I can feel the weight of Claude's eyes on me, but I don't dare look at him out of fear of what my expression will betray.

"Yes, very well," he says finally. "I'll come and find you when Ambrose and I are finished speaking."

I dip into a curtsy and flee the room as quickly as I can. Down the hallway, gulping down my emotions. Once I'm in my room, I shut the door behind me, lean back against it, and finally let loose the sob that's been growing in my chest since Ambrose hit me. I clap a hand over my mouth and sink down to the floor, shaking all over as the fear finally sinks into me.

The way he hurt me was so casual. So effortless. And over such a small reason. He reacted so quickly, it was like he was just waiting for an excuse to punish me. But why? Does he hate me, or was he using me as a way to get to Claude?

I remember Benjamin's warning that I didn't want to get into the middle of a situation between a sire and his fledgling, and I wish I had taken it more seriously. Because if push came to shove… Ambrose has power over Claude. Would my patron even be able to defend me, if he knew?

Chapter Seventeen

I t's very late, just a couple of hours from dawn, when a knock comes at the door. Claude comes in after I call out, and is at my side faster than I can process, his hands skimming my shoulders as he looks at me. Studying my neck, my wrists. At least he's not looking at the bruise on my cheek, disguised by makeup… but it gives me a flicker of anxiety to realize he's looking for bite marks. Does he think Ambrose would bite me? *Would* he have, if Claude didn't show up when he did?

"Claude." I reach out and place a hand on his chest, gently pushing him back. I've already decided to pretend that everything is normal until I have a better read on the situation. I don't want to escalate something that I still don't understand. "Claude, I'm fine."

His eyes are troubled as he looks at me. "I should never have left you here alone."

"Why not?" I ask, silently begging for him to tell me more about what's going on.

He opens his mouth, shuts it, shakes his head. "What did he want from you?"

"He asked me to show him your work."

I'm watching him for a reaction, but all I see is a sudden stillness, his shoulders braced as if in anticipation of a blow. "And did you?"

"Of course not."

He relaxes, but at the same time his brow furrows. "You should have. You should agree with whatever Ambrose wants, especially when I'm not here."

"It wasn't mine to show," I say. "Your paintings are yours, Claude. It should be your choice to share them."

We stare at each other. I wait for him to break, to be honest with me about whatever is going on… but I'm distracted by the shadowed, wan look of him.

"Are you hungry?" I ask, my eyebrows drawing together.

He hesitates. "It's been a while." He catches my expression, and his head tilts. "Why are you surprised? You know I haven't been here."

"Oh…" I know he hasn't fed from *me,* but he's been at all of these parties without me. "I assumed you would be drinking from others."

"I haven't been."

"But… why?"

"Because it upset you when I did."

I stare at him, taken aback. He seems earnest, which perplexes me more. "You…" I start, but then stop, unsure what I even want to say to him. After a moment, I sigh and hold out my wrist.

He takes it with two fingers, peers at me as his fangs slide out. "Are you sure you're alright? You're being surprisingly agreeable."

"Drink before I change my mind."

He lowers himself onto the bed beside me and bends over

my wrist, looking up at me as he bites down. He drinks from me in slow sips while I try not to squirm. I keep thinking I'll get used to this sensation, but every time it is as fresh as if it's the first time, lighting a lovely burn of pleasure beneath my skin.

When he's done, Claude seals his bite marks with a bloodied kiss and then, to my surprise, lays his head against my shoulder. I hesitate before reaching up to touch the back of his head. This affection feels odd—*intimate,* to use the forbidden word— but Claude seems so vulnerable right now that I can't bring myself to push him away.

His hair is even softer than I expected, his curls like silk between my fingers.

"Are *you* okay?" I ask. "After your sire's last visit, you seemed, well… despondent."

Claude is silent for so long, I don't think he's going to answer. "I thought I had grown used to his disappointment," he says, finally. "But perhaps such a thing isn't possible."

"Mm. I… kind of understand how that feels. My mom could never quite shake her disappointment in me, either."

"What about you could possibly disappoint her?"

I smile, trying to fight down bitterness. "Oh, everything, really. I was just never quite what she wanted me to be. Much too plain and practical. She couldn't muster much enthusiasm in any of the things that interested me."

"She's an idiot, then." Claude leans into my touch, and I realize I've begun stroking his hair without realizing it.

"I could say the same of Ambrose," I say. "Why do you care so much what he thinks?"

His shoulders lift toward his ears. "He is my sire," he says. "He pulled me from obscurity, gave me the gift of eternal life with certain expectations. I haven't held up my side of the bargain."

"Your art, you mean?" Claude burrows his face further into my neck instead of answering. "Your art is beautiful, Claude, but that's not the only thing about you that matters."

"It is, though," he says. "Art is what I lived for. It's what I died for. It has always been my passion and my purpose. I am empty without it."

"Well, I would like you even if you weren't an artist," I say. "In fact, I'd like you more. I've always found artists aggravating."

"I almost forgot that your first words to me were an insult to my work. You must be relieved that I quit."

"So relieved," I tease. "Though you're still full of tragically artistic sensibilities, I'm afraid."

"What does that mean?"

"It means that you are intensely broody. Prone to dramatic mood swings and posing theatrically in front of windows."

"I do not *pose*." I can feel his smile against my neck, a hint of fangs making me shiver.

"Liar. Nobody stands like you do unless they're expecting to be looked at."

"Well, clearly the expectation would be a correct one, since you *were* looking."

"Only to note how ridiculous you were."

He laughs, a rare sound, softer than I expected it to be, sending a ripple of warmth through my chest. He pulls away from my shoulder and he looks at me. For a moment he is so close, looking down at me, and I hold my breath, certain he's about to kiss me. But instead he stands, something unreadable flickering across his face.

"Goodnight, Nora," he says. "I appreciate your company."

Company? Is that what he calls this? The sudden formality feels like an insult. But I swallow back the bitterness. He's only giving me what I asked for, after all. A lack of intimacy.

"Goodnight, Claude."

When he's gone, I fall asleep remembering the softness of his hair, the press of his face against my neck, the sound of his laugh.

It's almost enough to make me forget the way my cheek still throbs where Ambrose hit me.

Chapter Eighteen

It's a relief that Claude doesn't disappear like he did the last time Ambrose visited. In fact, he is more present than he's been for weeks now, staying home instead of going out to his endless stream of parties. He is there across the table at breakfast, there watching out the window when I sit on the back porch to read. Like he's afraid to let me out of his sight.

Yet at the same time he's uncharacteristically quiet, his brow furrowed whenever I look over at him. And he never asks to paint. I watch him across the table at dinner, while he swirls blood-tinged wine in his glass and frowns into the distance, chin propped up with one hand.

I sigh. "Aren't you going to paint today?" I ask. "It's been more than a week."

Claude shifts his arm aside. His eyes flash toward me, long lashes obscuring an irritated look. "I thought you said it didn't matter if I painted again."

I suppress a sigh, and a biting comment. The last thing I want to do is send him into another one of those sulks again. "It doesn't matter to me, but it sounded like it matters to you. And isn't that why you hired me? To inspire you?"

He groans, leaning back in his chair and shutting his eyes.

I study him, trying to gauge his mood, but the pale angles of his face are impossible to read. "I thought you wanted to paint."

"I do," he says. Then he frowns. "Maybe. I don't know. It's not so simple."

"I don't see why it can't be," I say. "You don't have to paint some masterpiece. Just paint… something. Anything."

He sinks further in his chair, looking half melted and very dramatic. "You wouldn't understand."

"Then help me understand. What are you afraid of?"

"Afraid?" he repeats. His eyes slowly open, fixed on the ceiling. "Indeed, what is there to fear? Aside from proving that I am and forever will be a failure. That I didn't deserve the immortality they granted me. Disappointing my sire, my court, my valentine, myself…"

I sigh, pushing up to my feet. "Well, I'm honored I made the list," I say, slowly walking down the length of the table to his side. "But I couldn't really care less about all that. I like you *despite* the fact you're an artist."

His head lolls back as he gazes up at me, a slight smile curving his lips. "You like me?" But then his eyes go distant, his expression pensive. "Perhaps I should run away and become a… a farmer. A simple man living off the land…"

"Claude, you wouldn't survive a day on a farm." I touch his chin, guiding his gaze back to me. I'm not sure why I'm trying so hard at this. My contract isn't dependent on getting him to paint. But… I want to see him happy. My mother was always happiest when she was working. "Why don't you try painting something fun?"

He makes a face.

"Oh, does that offend the serious artist in you?" I ask, teasing. "Okay, it doesn't have to be *fun* if that's so against your principles, but it can just be… I don't know. Just for you."

His brow creases in thought. "Just for me…"

"It could even be temporary. You can tear it up afterward, or burn it, I don't care. You don't have to show me, or anyone."

"Temporary," he repeats. Then his gaze turns sly. "Mm… I have an idea."

* * *

"This is not what I had in mind," I say, standing in the middle of the room while Claude mixes paints on his palette. I feel exposed in my white sundress, the hem skimming above my knees.. He's donned a deep V-neck shirt and tight trousers that are about as close to casual as I've ever seen him. But his hair is still in disarray, wild curls springing every which way. His eyes are bright, almost wild, but shadows linger beneath them.

"You'll have to trust my artistic vision," he says, looking pleased with himself. "Personally, I think it's brilliant. Maybe all this time what I really needed was a beautiful canvas to work upon."

I roll my eyes and grit my teeth. I hate when he says things like that, because I *know* it's the sort of line he must use with everyone. But most of all, I hate the way it sends butterflies through my stomach. My body reacts to his flirtations even though my mind knows better.

When he kneels on the tile, heat slowly creeps up the back

of my neck, over my ears, until it consumes my entire face in red-hot fire. I try to think of something else, *anything* else to distract me from what's happening, but it's impossible when he's on his knees in front of me.

"There has to be a better way to do this," I mutter, averting my gaze and trying to take deep breaths.

"Am I making you uncomfortable?" Claude asks, seemingly more focused on his paints. When I don't answer, he looks up at me. "Nora?"

"No," I say, my throat tight.

I should be glad I succeeded at getting him to paint again. I just didn't think he would be painting *on* me. Or that it would feel so charged. The air is practically crackling between us.

Surely he can hear the rapid drumbeat of my heart, but he gives no sign of it. His expression is open and easy, unfazed. He's probably done this a hundred times before, with a hundred women. Probably some men, too. Why should I affect him?

He reaches out and touches my ankle. I shiver at the coolness of his fingers against my skin as he leads my bare foot to rest on his thigh. Instinctively, I grab his shoulder to steady myself.

He shoots me an amused glance. "You can rest your full weight on me. I promise I can take it."

"Right." Sometimes it's dangerously easy to forget how strong he is. Those long artist's fingers could probably crush bone, yet he cradles his paintbrush with such gentleness.

"Just try to stay still," he murmurs. He dips the paintbrush into his green paint and brings it up to my leg.

He hesitates for a moment and then the brush drags over the skin of my calf in one long stroke. Cool paint, cooler fingers gripping me to help keep me in place. Goose bumps shiver over every inch of my body, and I resist the urge to squirm, staring fixedly at a wall behind Claude's head. Watching him do this feels oddly sensual… yet after a few seconds I can't resist a glance.

There's a furrow on the normally smooth skin between his brows, and his eyes are narrowed in concentration beneath his long lashes.

After a little while, though, that furrow disappears. His eyes soften. His expression of concentration fades into something different, something open and vulnerable.

I realize I'm staring and look away. There's a glowing warmth in my chest. *I'm just happy for him*, I tell myself. *He's finally painting.*

Once he starts, he's like a man possessed. He paints around my calf, my knee, my thigh, all the way up to the hem of my dress. Then he switches to the other leg, pausing only for me to find my balance again. Once I get used to it, the brush of paint becomes pleasant, a delicate tease of sensation over my skin. Claude's fingertips, too, ghost over my body, here and gone again, maneuvering me with an ease that would be disconcerting if it weren't *him*.

When he sets my foot on the floor and stands, I expect him to be finished. But instead he takes one of my arms and continues painting on my skin. Here it is easier to see his work, to watch as vines dance over my skin and petals bloom, a bouquet of flowers spreading over my body. It's so lovely it makes my breath hitch, yet my eyes keep wandering back to his face instead of his work. He seems lost in his art, his face so relaxed and open, his lips holding the slightest curve.

When he reaches my collarbone, he pauses. His eyes drag up to meet mine. Then he releases me and steps back, walking in a slow circle around me.

I stand still, flushed under the scrutiny but trying to tell myself it's not me he's staring at. He's admiring his work, that's all.

When he comes around to the front again, he nods once, approving. "You need to see the full effect." He takes my hand, stepping backward as he leads me. "Come, come."

He takes me to the parlor and poses me in front of a full-length mirror, gently brushing my hair back behind my shoulders. "Look," he says, and steps aside.

I lift my eyes to my reflection, and my breath hitches. I thought of the painting as a bouquet earlier, but it's more than that; my skin is transformed into a garden in full bloom. Red and purple and white petals burst across my skin, along with crawling green vines and leaves ripe with springtime life. Lush and vivid and wild. It seems to slide over my skin as I twist and turn to observe myself, giving the effect of a breeze rustling the petals and leaves.

I turn slowly, craning my neck so that I can see the back of my arms and legs. Every time I look, I seem to find new details.

"That's ivy," Claude says, finger tracing along the green leaves climbing my arm. "Red roses, of course. Myrtle, and dahlias…"

Dahlias. I think back to my dress at the Valentine's Day Ball, and Claude's words to me: *They symbolize eternal love, in the Victorian language of flowers.* What do the rest mean? I wonder. The words stick in my throat; I'm almost afraid to ask.

Claude steps up behind me, gazing over my shoulder. Our eyes meet in the mirror.

"It's incredible," I say. "You're incredible."

His eyes widen slightly and then crinkle at the corners as he breaks into a smile wider than I've seen from him before.

I flush, studying the art on my skin again as an excuse to avoid eye contact. Surely he must hear compliments like that all the time; I didn't expect mine to have such an effect on him. But I suppose it's been a long while since he's created something new.

"It seems almost a shame that we're the only ones who get to see it," I murmur. "You could take a picture."

"Mm, no." He steps closer, one hand brushing against my lower back as he gazes at me in the mirror. "It was created to be private. We'll let it remain private."

There is something fitting about it. Flowers on my skin, as temporary and beautiful as in life. We're both quiet for a while as we look at his work.

Eventually, I clear my throat. "I hate to ruin the moment, but it's starting to itch…"

Part of me expects him to argue, or to fall into one of his melancholy moods at the thought of losing his newest artwork so quickly, but Claude throws back his head and laughs. "We should get you cleaned up, then."

"We?" I ask, flustered.

"It seems a pain to wash yourself, no?" he asks. He tilts his head to one side, a mischievous glint in his eye belying his innocent expression. "It will be easier if you let me help."

I think of him kneeling in front of me. His fingers gripping me as the paintbrush whispered over my skin. *Dangerous.*

"Fine," I say, before I can think better of it.

His eyes widen, but he quickly covers the look of surprise as he bows and offers his arm like a gentleman at the ball. "Allow me to show you to my bathroom, mademoiselle. The biggest and best the house has to offer."

My lips quirk. "Ridiculous," I huff, but I take his arm anyway, and let him lead me toward the bathroom.

Chapter Nineteen

There's a new lightness to Claude as we move through the house together. He smiles more easily, chatters about the different flowers he used to decorate my skin.

"How did you decide what to paint?" I ask, remembering my earlier curiosity.

He pauses. "It was just whatever flowers came to mind, I suppose." Before I can pry, we enter his bedroom, and the mood shifts.

I swallow as I remember the last time we were in here, the feeling of silk sheets beneath me and his weight on top, his mouth on my wrist. But Claude doesn't pause, leading me to the attached bathroom. It's huge, all pale marble with gold accents, and a glass-walled rainfall shower that seems big enough for five people. Claude turns on the shower while I'm taking it all in.

I've been refusing to imagine precisely how this is going to happen. He said he was going to help, but that could mean a number of things. But I should've known better to think even for a second that Claude would do something as practical as getting a washcloth. Instead he steps into the shower's stream, fully clothed, and gestures for me to follow.

I bite my lip. "This is your plan?"

He smiles at me as the water slowly plasters his shirt to his body. "Why not?"

Why not? There are a thousand answers on the tip of my tongue. This is too much. Too intimate. Exactly the kind of situation I was hoping to avoid when we began this arrangement.

Now, I am torn. I want this but if one of us breaks the contract, I'll lose him.

There's no reason I should be getting into the shower with him, but I step forward as though pulled by some unseen force.

The water is like warm rain as it patters over my skin, drenching my white dress. I tilt my head back, letting it soak into my hair.

"This shower is even nicer than the one in my room," I murmur.

"You're welcome to use it whenever you wish." Claude takes my arm and begins to scrub at the paint, his fingers working in slow circles. The colors bleed under his fingers, dripping a kaleidoscope into the drain at our feet.

It's easier to scrub off than I expected. I definitely could have done this on my own. But Claude's fingers feel dangerously good as they massage my forearm, his thumbs providing perfect pressure as they work my muscles. I sigh, head lolling back, as his hand moves up over my bicep and to my shoulder.

His fingers ghost over my collarbone before making their slow way down my other arm. Then he turns me around—I'm putty in his hands at this point—and massages my shoulders.

"Mmm." I shut my eyes. "Do I have paint there?"

"Oh, yes," he murmurs, his voice low and soft. "It's everywhere, I'm afraid."

His thumbs rub slow circles on either side of my spine, working his way down until he's on his knees behind me. My heart starts to pound, but my body is loose; I brace one palm against the shower wall as his hands skim over my ass before beginning to work on my thighs. My dress is soaked through at this point, clinging to me. But his hands don't wander anywhere untoward as he washes the back of my legs.

He turns me again, and my eyes drift open to see him kneeling on the shower floor, soaked through, gazing at me through strands of wet, dark hair. His white shirt is smeared with paint, and his eyes are heavy-lidded, pupils huge and dark. The air is thick and hot between us, steam filling the bathroom.

He takes one of my feet into his lap, just like he did when he painted me. It draws my eyes to the obvious bulge where his wet trousers cling to him.

My heart races, my breath hitching. I have a thousand dirty thoughts that all violate our contract… and one that doesn't. "Claude…"

His fingers slide up my calf, over my knee. "Yes?"

"Are you… thirsty?"

He stares up at me, pupils growing.

I lean back against the wall and lift my foot, trailing it over his chest before placing it on his shoulder.

He turns his head, just slightly, and I feel the faint press of fangs against my thigh. "Here…?" he murmurs against my skin, barely audible.

"Yes."

I cry out as his teeth sink into my inner thigh. My heel hooks around his shoulder, pulling him closer.

"Oh, God," I whimper, shaking. When my other leg gives out, Claude grabs it and lifts it onto his other shoulder without pause. He holds me effortlessly against the wall, hands cupping my ass, still drinking from me.

It's too much, too good. Each pull of his mouth sends throbs of pleasure through my thigh, straight to my core. I grab a fistful of his dark curls, fingers digging into his scalp, not to push him away but to hold him there against me.

With my eyes shut, I feel when his fangs recede, when he closes the punctures with a soft kiss. I keep my grip on his hair, unwilling to let this be over yet.

"Nora," he groans after a moment. "I can't…"

I loosen my grip until he's able to disentangle himself. He moves, and without him supporting my legs, I slowly slide down the wall until I'm seated on the shower floor. I open my eyes to find him still kneeling in front of me with an agonized expression. My dress is soaked through, my legs still parted, so I'm sure I'm giving him an eyeful, but I'm beyond the point of caring.

"This is torture," he whispers.

My head thumps back against the wall. "The damn contract," I whisper. In this moment, when I feel wild and wanton and entirely unlike myself, I'm finally willing to admit I might have made a mistake.

"The damn contract," he agrees. His hand brushes over the front of his too-tight trousers as he adjusts himself, and my gaze follows the motion.

It gives me another idea. An idea I shouldn't have, let alone voice, but…

"Would it break the contract," I say slowly, "if we were to… only touch ourselves?"

Claude pauses. "You mean…"

I slowly slide my hand down my stomach without breaking eye contact. He's the one forced to look away, his Adam's apple bobbing in a hard swallow, his eyes on the ceiling as he considers. "The contract forbids intimate contact, excluding biting," he says slowly, as if struggling to remember.

"So as long as we don't touch each other, we're not in breach of the contract."

"I suppose not," Claude says. "But—" His eyes drop to me, and he stops as he sees my hand between my legs. "Nora," he says hoarsely.

"What?" I whisper. "You don't want to?"

"We shouldn't."

"That's not what I asked."

His hand drifts to the button of his trousers but pauses there. "I'm not sure I can control myself."

"You can," I say. "I trust you."

The blues of his eyes are almost entirely swallowed by his pupils as he stares at me. He slowly unbuttons his trousers and slides his hand into them, groaning as he wraps a fist around himself. "You don't understand," he says, "how badly I want you. How badly I have wanted you, since the first moment I saw you."

The sight of him is obscured by his briefs still, but my eyes follow the movement of his wrist, trace the blue veins in his forearm as they bulge beneath his pale skin.

"Then tell me," I whisper. Then— "No. Show me."

A small shudder goes through him. He removes his hand from his briefs to push his trousers down his thighs. The white fabric of his briefs is soaked through, nearly translucent, the delicious bulge of his arousal on full display. He watches the way my breath hitches, the way my hand slides over my panties, and then he pushes his briefs down, too, letting his stiff length spring free.

"Oh," I whisper.

I watch his fingers slide from tip to base and back up again. My tongue darts out to wet my lips as I imagine how it would feel to take *all of that* in my hand, my mouth, inside of me. When I look back up at his face, he's smiling at my reaction. It's a knowing smile, aware of his own impressiveness, and it should aggravate me but instead it turns me on.

I bite my lip and push my panties to the side. Claude's smugness turns swiftly to a winded look, as though I've punched him in the stomach.

"God," he says, his voice strangled. *"Belle, si belle.* You're beautiful." He leans over slightly, his eyes between my thighs, the movement of his hand quickening. "Spread your legs," he whispers. "Wider."

A delicious flush spreads through my body, all the way from a bloom of heat in my cheeks to a tingling in my toes, as I let my knees slide to either side. Claude lets out an almost wounded sound, leaning forward to brace his free hand against the tile between us until his face is nearly level with my core, his heavily lidded eyes locked on me. My fingers glide across my own wetness before circling my clit, the movement quickening to match the frantic pace of Claude's hand pumping between his legs.

"Such a pretty pussy," Claude whispers. "God, I want to taste you." He doesn't appear to realize he's cut his lip on his own fang, a bead of dark blood swelling and running down over his lush mouth. I imagine licking it off him, and let out a quiet whimper, pressing my shoulders back against the shower wall.

"Are you close, *mon chou?*" he murmurs.

The lush French words send a pleasant shiver through me. I nod, not trusting myself to speak. My thighs are starting to quiver, my stomach taut as pressure builds within me.

"Come for me," he says.

I am helpless to do anything but obey. The orgasm rocks me from head to toe, making me cry out and grind against my own fingers, mouth hanging open and eyes fluttering in ecstasy. Claude gasps, his hand sliding over his length in short, frantic pumps before he follows me over the edge, hips jutting forward as he spills himself onto the wet tile between us.

Then we are both still. There is no sound but my own heavy breathing, and the pitter-patter of the shower raining down on us both.

Claude slowly pushes himself up to rest on his heels again, his curls plastered against his forehead. There is a desperate sort of heat in his face, making it difficult to hold his gaze. I rest my head against the wall instead, shutting my eyes and focusing on breathing. After a few moments, I hear Claude stand and button his trousers again. When I open my eyes to look up at him, he holds out a hand, and I grab it and let him lift me to my feet. His fingers are warmed by the water we've been soaking in, but still feel cooler than my own feverish skin. Our hands linger together for a moment before we simultaneously pull away. Our faces are inches apart, and for a moment I swear he's about to close the distance between us, contract be damned. But then Claude turns away and runs his fingers through his hair, shaking out his curls.

I stare at his back, where his wet shirt clings to his shoulders. It seems so strange, that things could be awkward between us after what we just did, but… we still haven't really touched, *can't* really touch, under the terms of our contract.

Which is what I wanted. Right? It all seems so fuzzy to me now. My head feels light; it must be all of the steam in here, boiling my thoughts into useless sludge.

"I'm… going to go get dressed," I say, after a moment.

"Very well," he says without turning to me. "I need a minute."

I step out of the shower, feeling ridiculous in my sopping, paint-stained dress. After a glance over my shoulder to confirm he's turned away, I shimmy out of the clinging material and wrap a towel around myself instead. Then I hurry to my room, to gather my clothing and my thoughts.

Chapter Twenty

When I emerge from my room again, the house smells of butter and garlic. My nose leads me to the kitchen, where Claude is hard at work on another meal that is too big for me to eat. A ludicrous amount of spaghetti fills a pot, while tomato sauce simmers on the stove.

I expect it to be awkward between us, but when Claude shoots me a glance and a crooked smile, I relax against the counter. This is normal, I tell myself in an attempt to calm my racing heart. Most valentines do more with their patrons than we just did in the shower.

Yet I'm surprised by how much I'm craving *more*. Not just sex, but… affection. Touch. I have an urge to walk over and run my fingers through Claude's still-mussed curls, to massage the muscles of his neck and shoulders the same way he did for me in the shower.

But that way lies danger. I know that. I'm the one who insisted on the intimacy clause, and I have to remember that I did it for a reason. I may have been momentarily overtaken by desire today, but I'm not here to fall in love. Even falling in lust feels like teetering on the edge of a steep cliff.

I'm not going to let this year ruin my future.

I clear my throat, trying to pull myself out of my thoughts. "Anything I can do to help?"

"No, no," he says, waving me away, as I expected. "You're welcome to go wait in the dining room."

I sigh, hopping up to sit on the edge of the counter. "I'd rather not." Sitting here and watching him cook without doing anything feels awkward, but not as awkward as waiting alone in the dining room. Especially because the meal he's making is for me, and only me.

Which reminds me…

"Why don't you ever cook for yourself?" I ask.

He looks up from the sauce he's stirring. "What's the point?"

"I know you get sustenance from blood, but food still tastes good, right?"

He shrugs.

"And I would feel a lot better if I wasn't eating alone every night with you staring at me," I say, folding my arms over my chest.

"I like staring at you. Watching you enjoy the food I make you."

I roll my eyes. "Sure. But it's not great for me. I'm sure I look like a slob."

"Never," he says, without looking up from his work. "You're always lovely."

I suppress the urge to squirm under his flattery. "Come on, please, for me? Try some tonight. You can add my blood to the sauce. It's the right color already. And… the thing about vampires and garlic is a myth, right?"

He looks up at me, one corner of his mouth curling. "I truly cannot believe how many humans fell for that particular lie from the Solomon Court. Why would *garlic*, of all things—"

"Don't try and distract me," I say, though in truth I am *very* tempted to hear more about the idea that Solomon intentionally spread false information about vampire weaknesses. "The point is that you'll have no problem joining me for dinner."

His lips twitch. "If you insist…"

"I do."

* * *

Claude still watches me eat the first few bites of my meal, waiting for me to make the usual appreciative noises. Then he grabs his own blood-infused pasta with an elegant little twirl of his fork and hesitates before taking a bite.

Surprise blooms across his face. He chews thoughtfully, and swallows.

I watch him, eyebrows raised. "Well?"

He looks down at his plate. A smile slowly spreads across his face, not one of his amused smirks but something broad and joyous that takes me by surprise. "I *am* still a good cook," he proclaims.

I force an eyeroll, trying to ignore the butterflies causing a ruckus in my stomach. That smile. My God. "You're insufferable," I mutter. "But, yes. You are."

There's something comfortable about eating together at the dinner table. Almost like we're a normal couple—or a couple at all, though I chastise myself at the thought. Because we're not that. I don't know *what* we are, but that much I know.

"Thank you," he says at the end of the meal, dabbing at his

lips with a napkin.

"For what? You're the one who made the meal."

"For insisting," he says. "For thinking of me."

My stomach does another flip, and then sinks way down, as I drop my gaze to my plate.

Oh, no.

I thought that avoiding sex was the secret to keeping my heart safe in this arrangement. But… it isn't, is it? It's too late already.

Our inability to be intimate—well, *more* intimate than we already have—isn't doing anything to protect me. It might just be making it worse. Giving me this idealized view of Claude.

Maybe it's better if we just… get it out of our systems.

Heat rolls slowly through me as I think of the idea. As I let myself *imagine* it. Surely Claude wouldn't be entirely opposed to it, after what we already did today. He just needs a little push to realize that I'm fine with it, too, despite my insistence on the contract.

When I drag my eyes up from my plate, Claude is staring at me across the table, his brow furrowed.

"That's a wicked look," he says. "What are you scheming up over there?"

I smile, take another bite of food, and shrug oh-so-innocently. "Nothing," I say. "Nothing at all."

Chapter Twenty-One

Claude is so focused on his paints that he doesn't even glance at me when I walk into the room. I excused myself to freshen up and change after our usual breakfast together—both mine and his, from my wrist—but I know he won't be expecting what I've changed into.

I walk slowly to my usual seat on the alcove and arrange myself carefully, tugging down the hem of my silk robe so it isn't *too* scandalous. Even so, it still reveals a generous amount of thigh… and dips low between my small breasts. Beneath it, I'm bare, and every time my thighs rub together it feels deliciously naughty.

The longer it takes for Claude to notice me, the more my self-consciousness grows. But there's no use in being shy now. I wore this for him to look at me.

When he finally does glance up, he stops short, his brush frozen in hand, his lips forming a small "o" of surprise.

"I thought I might try to inspire you today," I say, looking up at him through my eyelashes.

"Oh," he whispers. He can't seem to look away from my thighs. "Consider me… thoroughly inspired."

I resist the urge to cross them. Instead I part them slightly, emboldened by his gaze upon me, so heavy I feel it like a physical touch.

"Claude," I whisper.

"Yes?" He sounds pained.

"You're going to break your paintbrush."

He glances down, and seems surprised to notice that the wood is bending in his fingers. He readjusts his grip, clears his throat, spins the paintbrush between his fingers. "Right." He lifts it to his canvas, but it just hovers there. His eyes keep drifting back to me, again and again, even as he seems to be making a concerted effort to look away.

I bite my lip. I wasn't expecting him to be quite so affected. I also wasn't expecting him to actually try to paint me like this, and now that it's happening, I'm strangely nervous.

"We talked about, um, making paintings only for yourself," I say, after a moment. "This would have to be another one. Just for you. Not public."

His smile is strained. "As if I would ever share this sight with anyone else," he says softly, his eyes still raking over me, as if he can't get enough.

The intensity in his gaze sends a pleasant shiver through me. "In that case…" I take a deep breath and reach for the belt on my robe.

Before I can undo it, Claude is suddenly there, his hand over mine, the other still holding his paintbrush. I startle back, shocked by how quickly he moved.

"Don't," he says. He's staring down at me with something like agony, his pupils blown wide and his fangs out.

"Why not?"

He hesitates a moment, and steps back, his fingers brushing against mine before he lets go.

"We can't," he says. "The contract."

"I know. But…" I shake my head. "Look, it's clear there's… something between us." Claude raises a brow, spinning his paintbrush in his fingers again. "I think it'll be easier if we get it out of our systems."

"Get it out of our systems," he repeats, each word slower than before, making it sound thoroughly ridiculous.

I clear my throat and try to ignore the color rising to my face. "Yes."

"Be plain, *mon chou*. What exactly are you proposing?"

"I am proposing that we have sex," I say. "One time."

"Hm." He looks me over, from eyes to feet, his gaze moving as slow as a drip of honey. "Once isn't going to be enough for me, Nora. I'm going to want more. And so will you."

I flush, half annoyed and half turned on, which only irritates me further. "Will I?"

"Yes." He doesn't sound smug or cocky, just matter-of-fact. He sets his paintbrush down and closes the space between us in measured strides, until he's leaning over my place on the window seat, one arm braced on the wall. "If I could get my hands on you, Nora…" He touches the inside of my knee with a single finger, nudging me and, after a moment's resistance, I let my legs slide apart. "I would have you desperate," he murmurs. "Begging." His finger traces up my thigh, and his touch is a cold fire on my skin, leaving goose bumps in its wake. When I look up at him again, his lips are parted, revealing the tips of his fangs. "I would unravel you piece by piece, and you would love every moment of it."

I swallow hard. My skin is on fire, my heart beating wildly. I lean back against the window, reach up to push my hair off my neck and reveal the bare curve of it. "Prove it."

He leans in closer. Closer. I feel the prick of his fangs, touching my skin but not breaking it. But then his nose brushes up the curve of my neck, and he whispers in my ear, "No."

As he pulls back, I stare at him, lips parted in wordless, growing outrage. The sting of rejection is harsh, but worse is my anger, because… "*Why?*" I snap. "It's obvious we both want this." I cast a pointed look at his tented trousers, which he does nothing to hide. "Why should we deny ourselves?"

"Because we are under contract. And there is a certain intimacy clause that is quite explicitly laid out."

I sigh, brushing my hair out of my face. The damn contract. "Is that what this is about? You want me to admit I was an idiot for claiming I didn't want intimacy?"

"No," he says. "I'm sure you had your reasons. And…" He hesitates. "If you recall, it was me who insisted on putting it in the contract."

I fold my arms across my chest. It pushes my breasts up, which I notice him noticing. "Then *why*? Explain."

"The contract," he says. He reaches forward and carefully pulls up the sleeve of my robe where it's fallen. His fingers graze my bare skin, and I shiver. "Like I said. It's important."

I frown. "I understand, but… Do you think I would go running to Benjamin and tattle? You think this is all some ploy by me to… get out of our agreement, or something?"

His gaze drifts back to me, slowly, as if against his will. "No," he says.

"Well, I'm sure you wouldn't tell anyone, so what's the problem?" He hesitates, and my eyes narrow. "*Would* you tell someone?"

"You are aware of the relationship between a vampire and

his sire, yes?" he asks.

"Yes," I say, impatient at the apparent non sequitur, but then I pause. "You would tell Lord Ambrose?"

"Ambrose could… *compel* an honest answer out of me."

"But why would he ask? Does he know about the intimacy clause?"

"Of course he does. He's the one who suggested it." I try to wrap my mind around that. I thought Claude suggested it because he thought it was the only way I would agree to this, but it came from *Ambrose*? "He thought it was for the best. He was worried that you would distract me."

I roll my eyes. "What, distract you from all of the painting you were doing before?" He winces, and I bite my lip. "Sorry. I'm just trying to understand why Ambrose is involved in this."

"*Lord* Ambrose," he says, a gentle chastisement, "is involved in everything I do. He made me, and he had such great hopes for me. He is always trying to find new ways to… inspire me." He rakes a hand through his hair, and his shoulders slump. The humor is gone from his expression now, leaving him somber. "But inspiration has not found me today, I'm afraid," he says. "I should go. I'm sorry."

He leaves me there, half naked with my head spinning.

Chapter Twenty-Two

I'm too embarrassed to leave my room for dinner. Instead I lie in bed, all bundled up in pajamas after shedding that sexy robe, staring at the ceiling and feeling... I don't even know how to put a name on it. Hurt, confused, disappointed. *Rejected*.

It seems so unfair that Claude and I can both want each other so badly, but be held back by the contract I *thought* I wanted. Now we're trapped in a way I still don't fully understand, with *Lord* Ambrose somehow involved.

My ceiling holds no answers, so after a while, I scroll through my phone instead. I want to vent to someone, but who? My mom still hasn't been in contact for months. I don't want to talk about the details of my sex life—or lack thereof—with Benjamin. And Sophie and Elaine... they have real problems to deal with. I won't burden them with an issue that is entirely my own fault.

But a memory bubbles up from the depths of my brain. A certain valentine blog that went viral recently. An *anonymous* blog, that takes *anonymous* confessions and offers advice. I roll onto my stomach as I open the web page. It feels odd to pour my heart out to a stranger. But that's what *Anonymous*

Confessions of a Valentine is for, after all. A place to vent to someone who might understand, even just a little bit, how I feel.

It's hard to get started. But then my fingers start darting over my phone screen. *Dear Anonymous Valentine*, I say. *My patron sees me as his new muse, but I want to be more than that...*

By the time I hit *send*, it feels like I just purged a poison from my soul. I sigh, drop my phone, and rest face-down on my pillow. It's good to get it out, but I still feel hopelessly at a loss.

Now that my embarrassment has faded, I can admit that Claude was right to reject my half-baked proposition. One night of casual sex isn't the solution to this confusing mess of feelings.

Especially since I was the one who insisted that I didn't want our relationship to be romantic. I hate to think I would've woken up regretting what we did.

Would I regret it?

I don't know anymore. But I need to think about my future. My career. My entire life, I've sought stability, and it's finally within reach. I'm not going to throw it all away for a man, no matter how badly I want him.

Because I do still clearly recall what Benjamin said would be the consequences for me breaking a contract: dismissal without pay, and being blacklisted from ever being a valentine again.

* * *

As days pass, the strangeness between us lingers. Claude seems just as determined to pretend the other evening didn't happen as I am. But it's impossible to ignore the new tension between us.

When I start waking up earlier to make my own coffee and breakfast, Claude doesn't comment. I hate the part of me that misses him spoiling me, but… it's better that I don't get used to it. This situation is temporary, after all.

Claude still feeds from me, still cooks for me and sits at the dinner table, though he doesn't always eat. That is the only time we spend together, and our conversations are polite and distant.

He doesn't try to paint again, and I don't push him to.

I drift from night to night, uncertain about my purpose here, until…

"We're going out tonight," Claude announces at breakfast.

I set down my fork. "Another party?" I ask, unable to conceal my reluctance. I knew attending events would be a part of my job when I signed up as a valentine, but I'll admit I had hoped Claude wouldn't be attending many. Attending one with things so awkward between us sounds disastrous.

Stress renders Claude's expression in hard lines. "It's a Vulpe event."

"Oh." I frown. "But… I thought you said you're never invited to Vulpe parties?"

"I'm not. But Ambrose wants me there." He hesitates. "If you would truly hate to go, then I can attend on my own." His brow furrows. "Maybe that's for the best, anyway. It'll be—"

"No," I say, before he can go on. "I'll come."

It's only because I'm studying him that I note the way his shoulders relax, the ease of tension from his jaw. He hesitates, and then says, "Very well. We'll depart in an hour and a half.

CHAPTER TWENTY-TWO

The dress code is formal."

As I head to my room to shower and get ready, I'm not sure what possessed me to insist on going. It's just that for a moment, Claude looked… sad. And it made me remember how he was after Ambrose's first visit, those long nights of despondence. My feelings about Claude confuse me, but I know for certain that I don't want to see him like that again. Maybe I can't help either way, but the least I can do is stand at his side when he's going into a nest of vipers.

I choose a floor-length, pleated chiffon dress in pale green, hoping it's enough to satisfy Claude's vague dress code requirements. But when I meet him near the door around the time we're set to depart, he barely spares me a glance. It's odd for him not to have a kind word for me, but as we get into the waiting car, it becomes all the more obvious that he's not himself. He stares out the window, arms folded over his chest, uncharacteristically silent. Even his outfit is understated, just a gray suit and a white shirt beneath—perfectly fine, but perfectly ordinary, which makes it quite unlike his usual style. He doesn't even reach for the wine, though I can't decide if that's a good sign or a bad one.

"Are you nervous?" I ask.

He blinks as if just remembering I'm there, and shifts on his seat, leaning back against the plush cushioning. "*Nervous* is not precisely how I'd describe it."

"Then how would you describe it?"

"Mm…" He tilts his head from side to side. "I don't know. Perhaps a deep and pervasive sense of dread?"

"Ah." I'm not sure what to say to that. I've never been very good at this whole comforting thing—I'm more of a "practical solution" person than a "talk it out" one—which makes me all the more aware of how poorly suited I am for this kind of job. "Is there anything I can do?"

He purses his lips, shrugs, looks away. "No," he says. He fiddles with his rings, a couple of plain titanium bands rather than his usual ornate ones. "I'm still not sure I should have brought you."

"Well, I'm happy to be here with you." I scoot closer, and after a moment's hesitation, place my hand on his knee and squeeze. "I'm sure it'll be alright. We'll get through it."

He looks at my hand, and then at me, and offers a wan smile. "You're being kind. I must really seem pathetic."

"Mm, maybe a little," I say, teasing. "But in an endearing way. Like a cat who fell in a bathtub."

He huffs a laugh. "Now that's more like the Nora I know." He reaches down and takes my hand, twining his fingers with mine. "Does this count as intimacy?"

I bite my lip, hating the way my heart races at the simple touch. His thumb rubs slow circles on my hand, sending electricity tingling all the way up my arm. "I don't think so."

He lifts my hand to his lips and kisses my knuckles. "How about this?" he murmurs against my skin, his eyes still locked on mine

The sparking spreads beneath my skin, turning my insides warm and bubbly. "You're on thin ice," I whisper, finding it suddenly hard to breathe.

Claude smirks and flips my hand over. He presses a slow kiss to my palm that feels far more sensual than it has any right to, and then returns our clasped hands to his lap.

He holds my hand the entire ride to the party, and even by the time we arrive, my heartbeat still hasn't slowed.

Chapter Twenty-Three

As we step out of the car and I gaze up at the venue, a new kind of anxiety fills me. I turn to Claude, who is shutting the door behind me.

"This is a gallery," I say. "It's… an art exhibition?"

"Indeed." He stops at my side, his expression flat as he stares at the tall, boxy building with its walls made almost entirely of glass. Within are glimpses of moody lighting and large portraits, and a small crowd wandering throughout. "A big opening for one of the younger Vulpe vampires."

"You said it was a party."

"I said it was an event."

I chew my lip. Maybe I did assume, but he also hid the truth from me. I understand his behavior on the way here, now, because I can only imagine the kind of emotions an event like this would stir up in him.

I wish he had given me a chance to better prepare myself. But we're here now, I suppose. And I *should* be able to do things like this for him, even though I feel unqualified to be any source of emotional support.

"Well, then." I slide my arm into his. "Let's get it over with, shall we?"

His lips quirk before dropping again. "Give me a moment."

I wait by his side, unsure what to do or say. After a couple of moments, he clears his throat, nods, and leads me up the stairs and through the doorway.

Inside, the dark walls and dim lighting lend everything an almost sensual air. As I catch my first glance of a painting, and then do a double take, I realize that *sensual* is an understatement. As I glance from painting to painting, all I see is skin. Skin of all colors, displayed on bodies in all manner of interesting, intertwined positions. The art is hyperrealistic and hypersexual. Looking at it makes me feel voyeuristic, bringing a heat to my face that makes me thankful for the dim lighting.

I probably shouldn't be feeling this odd heat in my belly. It's art, after all. It's probably supposed to be meaningful, and symbolic, and highbrow, not...

"Remarkably horny," Claude mutters into my ear. I stifle my startled laugh with a cough.

"Don't be inappropriate," I whisper. "We're supposed to be admiring the art."

"I'm not sure it's possible to admire it *appropriately*."

"Sure it is," I say. "And it starts with being silent."

He manages it for a couple minutes, but then speaks up again to say, "One *must* wonder at the artist's process. Is it all from memory? Or photograph? Or perhaps they arrange an orgy and set up the canvas nearby—"

"*Shh!*" I elbow him in the side, blushing furiously, and his eyes brighten in mischievous delight.

But as we continue to wander through the building, that amusement fades. He studies the paintings with more care, his brow furrowed. As the shock of all the nudity wears off, I find myself doing the same. It's certainly not the kind of art I'd choose for myself, but I can appreciate the care that went into them. The artist has a great eye, and every body has been so lovingly recreated in paint that it feels like an act of worship.

We stop in front of one and spend a while just staring up in silence. This one feels different. Almost private, like I'm looking in through a window. A couple is entangled on a bed so thoroughly that their skin blurs together, and it is impossible to tell where one begins and the other ends.

It makes my heart ache in a way I can't explain.

"They're quite talented," Claude says. "The Vulpe Court must be very proud."

His tone is impossible to read, obscuring the heavy emotions I'm certain are warring within him. When I glance at him, his face is stony too. But his eyes… his eyes always reveal his sadness.

I squeeze his arm. "I prefer your work."

A brief twitch of a smile. "You hate my work."

"I do *not!*" I bump my shoulder against his. "I'm never going to live this down, am I? I like your paintings, I really do. All I said was that the last one wasn't your best."

"Mm-hmm." He sounds unconvinced. "So the issue is that you dislike me as a person?"

I know he's teasing, but a small, frustrated huff escapes me. "Please. I think I've made it quite clear by now that's not the case."

"Well…" He's starting to smile, the slow curl of his lips peeling away his aloof expression. "I suppose that's true after…" But the sentence dies, along with his smile, as he looks toward the other side of the room.

I follow his gaze to see Ambrose, dressed all in exquisite

white, surrounded by a small coterie of beautiful vampires who are all looking our way. When Ambrose catches Claude looking, he beckons with two fingers, and my stomach drops.

Claude stiffens at my side before heading over, crossing the room in slow, measured steps.

"Wait," I whisper, tugging on his arm. Claude turns to me questioningly, and I fumble in my purse, past painkillers and extra tampons and all the other things I carry *just in case*, until I find a pair of sunglasses. I stand on my tiptoes to place them on his face, smoothing his curls back behind his ears before pulling away.

He tilts his head, his eyes hidden behind the lenses. "It's nighttime," he says. "And dark in here besides."

"It's a fashion statement," I say. "Or perhaps a way to disguise a hangover." Or a way to hide that sadness in his eyes. Something tells me the vampires of the Vulpe Court will be eager to see it, and I don't want them to.

After a moment, he dips his chin in the slightest nod, and we continue ambling along to Ambrose and his coterie, taking our sweet time to get there.

"Claude," Ambrose says, his voice a drawl that makes my skin prickle. "I'm surprised to find you here tonight."

"As if I could ever decline an invitation from you," Claude says, his tone deceptively mellow.

"Such a dutiful little fledgling. If only you were as mindful of the rest of my expectations." He swirls a finger, gesturing to the gallery around us. "This could all be yours, if only you weren't so stubborn."

I bite the inside of my cheek to hold back a retort. He isn't even bothering to be subtle about why he invited Claude here. Even the sexual nature of the display feels… pointed, now that I know Ambrose is aware of *that* clause in our contract. Another jab at something that Claude *could* have but *doesn't*.

I glance around the circle at the other vampires, who are quiet but watching with thinly veiled amusement. There's a flicker of hot anger in my chest at the thought that this is part of tonight's entertainment for them.

"Is the artist here tonight?" I ask, butting in as if unaware of the tension crackling through the exchange. "We'd love to meet them."

Ambrose's lip curls as he looks at me as if he just realized I'm there and is displeased by it.

"Lady Elizabeth is in the back lounge," one of the other vampires offers, perhaps taking pity on me. But then Ambrose turns his gaze on her, and she shrinks back, as if realizing she made a faux pas.

"Oh, we should go see her, Lord Claude, please," I say, tugging on his arm.

"Very well." He dips his head in a small show of respect to Ambrose. "Lovely to see you, as always, sire."

I only manage to relax once we're out of eyesight of that horrible little group. "God," I say. "Sorry, we don't really have to go see the artist, but I couldn't stand being there a moment longer."

Claude squeezes my hand. "I'd like to meet her."

The back lounge is filled with the low chatter of a small crowd of vampires and valentines. A bartender serves drinks in one corner, both blood-infused and otherwise. It's easy enough to find the star of the night, since people keep approaching to congratulate her. She's a petite Black vampire who appears to be in her early twenties, and quails under the attention each time, deflecting compliments with an embarrassed smile.

Something about her seems strange, though it takes a few minutes of studying her to put my finger on it. Most vampires are so *still*, but she's fidgety, and— "She's… breathing? I thought she was a vampire."

"She is. Very freshly turned, though." Claude's hand rests idly on my side, fingers tapping my hipbone. "It takes a while to forget that muscle memory."

Claude waits for a break in her line of admirers before heading over.

"I'm sure you're getting tired of hearing this, but the exhibition is delightful," he says. "Truly extraordinary. Congratulations."

"Oh, thank you," she says, smiling. If she could blush, I'm sure she would.

"Is this your first gallery showing?" I ask.

"My first of this size, definitely," she says. "And my first since being turned. I confess, I'm not so used to all of the attention. Usually I get less compliments and more weird looks."

"Well, I hope there are many more to come," I say, smiling. "Gallery showings, I mean. Not weird looks."

She laughs. "Right. Thanks. I'm Elizabeth, by the way. Er, Lady Elizabeth? You probably know that already, but it feels so strange not to introduce myself, so…"

"I'm Nora," I say, shaking her hand. "Pleasure."

Claude, in an unusual show of what could be mistaken for shyness, only steps in when we both look at him. "Lord Claude de Vulpe," he says, with a small, self-mocking bow.

"Oh," says Lady Elizabeth.

"Oh," he echoes, rising from his bow with a sardonic ghost of a smile.

I look back and forth between them, not sure what to make of the pause in the conversation. At that point, I realize that the room's attention is on us, a rather alarming number of heads turned in our direction.

Elizabeth clearly feels the spotlight too. "I…" she starts uncomfortably. "I'm afraid I have to…"

"No need," Claude says, holding up a hand. "We'll go. Just wanted to extend my compliments."

He leads me away while I'm still trying to make sense of what just happened. His mouth is a stiff line, his shoulders tense.

"What was that?" I ask.

He pauses to sink into an unoccupied armchair, tugging me down to share the plush seat with him. A man sitting on the couch next to it abruptly stands and walks away. He heads to the bar, so he could have just been getting himself a drink, but I'm starting to get the sense that there's more than that going on here.

"As I've mentioned, I'm not exactly popular with the Vulpe Court," Claude says.

My brow furrows. "I didn't realize that meant they'd treat you like a *leper*."

"Perhaps they fear my lack of inspiration is contagious," he says, leaning his head back against the chair.

But we both know that's not the truth. "It's Lord Ambrose, isn't it?" I ask. "They're afraid of him."

Claude shrugs, but he squeezes my shoulder in a way that feels like a warning; it's not safe to talk openly here. Because of course it isn't. We're surrounded by snakes.

"Surely you must have some friends within the court," I say.

Claude's smile is strained. "I used to. One by one, they've

been chased away." He breaks eye contact. "Or bribed away. One or the other."

I study him, struck by what a lonely existence it must be, being shunned like this by his own court. Living in that house by the seaside, with no one for company before I came along. Ambrose *made* him come tonight, just so he could be reminded of how alone he really is.

I take Claude's hand in mine and stand. "Well, there's no use wallowing about it. Let's go look at the art some more."

He stares at me quizzically but lets me urge him to his feet and lead him out of the room.

We walk through the gallery together. People keep looking at Claude, but no one approaches him. Conversations have a habit of quieting as we walk past.

Claude seems resigned to it, but there is a spark of anger in my chest that grows every time I notice the way they're snubbing him. I don't let that show, though. Instead I talk loudly about the art, and laugh, and tease Claude. If these assholes want to see him miserable, then I refuse to let it happen.

Every time I coax a smile out of Claude, it feels like a victory. Yet every time that victory fades, and I catch him staring in silence—not at the vampires who are snubbing him, but at the artwork on the walls around us—with an expression like heartbreak.

* * *

On the ride home, Claude stares resolutely out the window.

He looks especially broody, still wearing my sunglasses, but I can't seem to find a good moment to ask for them back. Especially when the silence stretches out like this, bubbling with tension.

"That was awkward," I finally say.

Claude doesn't turn, but I catch his grim smile in his reflection on the window. "It was not much fun for me either, I'll admit."

"I can see why you don't like to attend Vulpe events." I chew my lip, trying to think of how to broach the subject. "I knew you had a strained relationship with Lord Ambrose, but I didn't think the whole court would be so…"

"Oh, the Vulpe Court despises me," Claude says, saving me from my fumbling.

"But why?" I press. He shrugs, still turned away. "Claude, please look at me."

He turns slowly to face me. A smile is plastered across his face; with his eyes hidden behind dark lenses, it's much harder to read his actual feelings. "I'm a blemish on their reputation. A drain on their coffers. An embarrassment and a nuisance."

"If that's true, then why haven't they kicked you out yet?"

His smile is strained, but his voice is still light as he says, "I'm sure they'd be rid of me if they could. But it's not so simple. There are laws about these kinds of things, and no matter how much Vulpe wishes it were, refusing to paint is not a breach of vampire law."

After a moment, I slide closer on the seat. Claude doesn't move as I reach up to remove my sunglasses from his face, revealing the soft blue of his eyes and the sad depths they contain.

I study him as I tuck the glasses away. "Do you even want

to be in Vulpe?" I ask. "Surely you can't be happy as a part of a court that openly snubs you."

He shrugs. "Better that than courtless."

"Benjamin is courtless, and he seems to do well enough for himself."

"Benjamin is a rare case, and he has not made enemies of half the Vulpe Court."

"You think they'd come after you if you were courtless?" I ask, taken aback. He seems so flippant, I figured he was exaggerating. "They hate you *that* much?"

His eyes flicker. He looks away. "I'd rather not find out."

"But…" Surely there has to be a better answer than him existing in perpetual misery in Vulpe. "Couldn't you join another court? You have friends in Camelia, don't you?"

He pauses, stares at me. For a moment I think I've said something helpful, but then he says, "You think I'm beautiful enough for the Camelia Court?" He splays a hand over his chest. "I'm touched, Nora."

"Claude, I'm being serious," I say. "You can't be happy with the way things are now."

He drops his hand. "Of course I'm not," he says. "But it's… it's complicated, Nora. Even under better circumstances, it's extremely difficult to change courts like that. In my situation, nigh impossible. Camelia and Vulpe don't have the best relations as it is, and Ambrose would never allow such a thing."

"Ambrose has that much power over you?"

"He is my sire," Claude says, as if that explains everything. Then he presses his hand across his eyes. "I'm tired of talking about this."

Chapter Twenty-Four

The next evening, I make myself coffee. Claude doesn't emerge from his bedroom. Maybe it would be best to leave him alone… but I hate the thought of him wasting away in there again, so after bolstering myself with my evening dose of caffeine, I knock on his door and enter at the sound of his voice.

He's still wearing last night's clothes, but at least he's sitting up in bed. "Do you need something?"

"Well…" I clasp my hands behind my back, feeling awkward. I've never been very good at comforting people. "I was wondering if we could go to the beach today."

He frowns at me dubiously. "The beach?"

"We're so close to the ocean and haven't gone this whole time, so…" I shrug, feeling foolish. "It's fine if you're not feeling up to it, though, we can go another time."

Claude hesitates, and then swings his legs out of bed one at a time with slow determination. "No. We'll go today. Give me an hour to get ready."

* * *

It turns out to be a short walk to the beach, down a path descending the cliffs behind the house. I probably didn't need to ask Claude to accompany me, but at least it's gotten him out of bed. He even has me feeling underdressed in my shorts and hoodie, since he's donned what I can only describe as a belted silk kimono.

It's too rocky to take off my sandals, but still pleasant to walk along the shoreline. The sea glows under the movement, and the sound of the waves is soothing. We walk for a while, side by side, while I try to think of something to say.

Claude surprises me by breaking the silence first.

"What do you plan on doing after our contract is up?" he asks. "I mean, I know you want to go to school, but for what?" His brow creases. "I realize… I've never asked. I've been so caught up in myself that I…"

I nudge him with my shoulder. "Don't worry. It's not very exciting, anyway. I want to study engineering. Not sure which kind yet."

He glances sideways at me, frowning. "Really?"

"What? Is it so surprising?"

"It just doesn't seem like you, somehow."

"Well…" I shrug, shoving my hands into my pockets. "I don't see why not. The job market is great, and the pay is good, so…"

"Ah," he says. "So it's the practical choice. That *does* sound like you."

"Mm-hmm." Before all of this happened, that future was all I could think about. But now it almost hurts to imagine, because it'll mean being done with my contract and away from here. I'll have all the money I need for the future I've always planned on. All the independence I need.

And I'll be alone, with no one to care for me, just like I've spent most of my life. I'll leave Claude alone, too, all by himself in this too-big house.

"What if you could be anything?" Claude asks, pulling me from my thoughts. "If it wasn't a matter of money or practicality."

"Well…" I brush my hair behind my ear as the wind stirs it. "When I was younger, before I realized how poorly it paid, I wanted to be a teacher."

"Mm." Claude smiles. "Now, that I can imagine. *Miss* Rivers. Did you want to teach children?"

"Yeah. I, um…" I clear my throat. "I didn't have the best mom, growing up. And I had this one English teacher who was so kind to me. She would share her lunch when my mom didn't pack one, wait with me after school when my mom was late to pick me up…" I trail off, remembering it with a twinge in my chest. "Mrs. Castro. When I was younger, I wanted to be like her. To make a difference for kids like me."

Claude nods along, his eyes on me the whole time, but my face heats. It feels like I'm rambling. Talking too much about *me*, when this is supposed to be about cheering him up. "What about you?" I ask, eager to change the subject. "Did you ever want to be anything other than a painter?"

Claude frowns down at the sand, thoughtful. "I guess… when painting seemed like a far-off dream, sometimes I thought I'd like to become a cook."

The word choice throws me off until I remember that Claude's youth was a long, long time ago. *One hundred and fifty,* Benjamin once told me, and it's still hard to wrap my mind around the idea. Even so, I'm left confused. "A cook?" I say slowly. "Weren't you… well… rich?"

Claude laughs, the sound catching me off guard. "I was a

kitchen boy."

"A *what?*"

He laughs again at my surprise. "A servant, Nora. I was a servant."

"I…" I shake my head, baffled at the mental image. "I guess I always imagined you as… nobility, or something."

"My deepest apologies for ruining your idea of me, but no. In life, I was no one. An orphan, a servant. I would spend my paltry wages on art supplies; it was my only escape from the drudgery of my life." His smile fades. "When I say that Lord Ambrose made me, I don't just mean as a vampire. I was nothing before him. He saw one of my paintings and pulled me up from the dirt. He gave me a home, an education, all the art supplies I could need… and eventually the bite, and its gift of eternal life." He stops walking, his expression clouding. "And I… In return, I've—"

I stop as well, turning to him, and wrap my arms around him before I can second-guess the instinct. He startles, and then softens against me, resting his chin atop my head.

I press my face into his chest. I can't look him in the face when I ask, "You loved him?"

Claude holds me tighter against him. "Sometimes I'm afraid I still do."

* * *

When I'm lying in bed that night, I find myself staring at the ceiling, unable to stop thinking about Claude and his predicament. That sadness in his eyes, the resignation in his voice when he spoke about the situation, the way he looked at those paintings yesterday…

My chest aches in an echo of his sorrow. I would do anything to soothe it, if only I knew how. It hurts to imagine him alone in his own room, up tossing and turning like I am. For a moment, I'm struck by an urge to go to him, to slip through his bedroom door and into his bed, weave my fingers into his hair, and kiss him.

And that realization leads me to finally confront an uncomfortable truth: what I feel for Claude has gone beyond attraction. Beyond lust.

I have feelings for him, and they're growing.

Groaning, I roll over and press my face into my pillow. Even alone in my room, my cheeks are flaming hot as I think about it. About how embarrassing it will be to admit to him, after I was the one who insisted on making our contract non-intimate.

But I'm not going to let my pride prevent me from talking to him about it. We're only a couple of months into our contract. Maybe there's still a way to salvage things, if I'm willing to try.

* * *

The next evening, I sit at the table for breakfast with my heart pounding. "I think we need to talk about our contract," I say.

Claude glances at me. "What is there to discuss?"

My cheeks are burning. "You know what I want to talk about, Claude. Stop being deliberately obtuse."

Claude sighs. He leans back in his chair, regarding me from beneath his long lashes. "I'm not," he says. "The contract is set,

Nora. I thought you understood that."

"But I thought the contract was between *us*," I say. "If we both want to change it, then…"

His brow furrows. "You want to change it?"

"I…" It's embarrassing to admit it. "Yes. I do."

"Hm." I expect him to leap at the chance to tease me, if nothing else, but instead he regards me in silent consternation. "But you wanted it for a reason. I don't want you endangering your future for me."

"It's my choice to make," I say.

He shakes his head. "I'm afraid it isn't at this point, though. Nor mine. You're represented by Benjamin. I'm represented by my court. They'd both be involved in any potential changes to the contract."

My mouth has gone dry. "But…" I frown down at my half-eaten plate. "Surely they wouldn't care? It can't be that serious?"

"Oh, Nora." He says my name like a sigh. "I suggest you talk to Benjamin. I'm sure he can answer any questions you may have." He pushes out from the table and leaves the room without feeding from me.

Chapter Twenty-Five

The conversation leaves me with my gut in knots. It's obvious I'm missing something, and Claude doesn't seem willing to explain it to me. So I take his suggestion and invite Benjamin over for tea. I emphasize that it's not an emergency, but still, he agrees to meet me that very night.

I meet him in the foyer with a curtsy and a smile. "So glad to have you, Lord Benjamin."

His returning smile is warm and tinged with relief as he looks me over. "Look at you. A proper lady of the house. I take it you're settling in, then?"

"Better than expected. Thank you." I lead him to the sitting room, where a pot of tea is waiting along with cups and saucers. I found the lovely set of floral-decorated porcelain in one of the cabinets, along with an outrageous amount of tea just ready to be made. I'm not sure whether to be relieved or worried that Claude let me set it all up myself without coming in to insist on helping.

"You seem well," Benjamin says, pouring himself a cup and drawing me out of my thoughts.

"I am," I say, sitting across from him at the table. "Truly. I hope you didn't rush here thinking I was in trouble."

"The thought crossed my mind, but really, I had been meaning to visit. I wanted to see for myself how this arrangement was working out. Especially since you and Claude have an… unusual agreement."

"Right." I bite my lip, looking down at my cup as I stir sugar into my tea. "That… *is* what I wanted to talk about, actually."

I can feel him watching me, but I can't bring myself to make eye contact. It's embarrassing to have this discussion after how insistent I was about adding the intimacy clause. More embarrassing still because Claude clearly indicated that I don't understand something. But Benjamin did once tell me I should ask him whatever questions I want.

"Go on," he says, after a few moments of silence trickle past.

"Benjamin," I begin, "is it possible to change my contract with Claude? If… both of us wanted that?"

It's difficult not to squirm under the weight of his gaze. "It's not impossible," he says, "but it's not as easy as an agreement between you and him. It would require my agreement, and that of the Vulpe Court, as your representatives."

I nod, considering. I'm sure that Benjamin would agree if I asked him, though he might not be thrilled about me changing my mind after all of the trouble. But the Vulpe Court… that might be a bit more problematic, given Claude's tumultuous relationship with them.

"And what would happen if the contract was broken?" I ask.

Benjamin sets down his cup rather heavily. "Has something happened?"

"No," I say. "I'm just curious. I realized I made all that fuss about the intimacy clause and I don't actually know how it would be enforced. Are you the one responsible for it?"

Benjamin's gaze is heavy, suspicious, but after a moment he leans back in his chair. "Partially. But a vampire's court is responsible for enforcing any contracts under their name, and the Solomon Court would also step in to render aid if requested."

"I see." Or at least I'm starting to have an inkling. "It's… pretty serious, then. If a contract were breached."

"Very," Benjamin says. "Valentines are cherished and protected by vampire society. Who would ever want to be one if they weren't? It's paramount that we have humans willing to provide blood for us, and also vital to our relationship with humans as a species that we treat them well. Valentines are the embodiment of the deal our species made long ago, and the trust that keeps us in balance now."

"I… hadn't thought about all of that," I say, feeling dizzy as the realization starts to set in. "So you're saying the punishment would be severe, if a vampire broke the contract." I glance at Benjamin, who nods, his expression grave. "They would be… what? Imprisoned?"

"Mm." Benjamin holds up a hand, waves it vaguely. "Imprisonment is considered a light sentence, given our infinite lifespans. Unless it's a *permanent* imprisonment, but that's a rare cruelty usually reserved for traitors to one's own court."

"So what?" I ask, my voice tight. "They'd hurt him? They'd… kill him?"

"It's up to the court," Benjamin says. "It'd be a severe punishment, but…"

I think of Claude saying *the Vulpe Court despises me*. How I thought he was being dramatic. But then, what I witnessed at the art gallery, the way they all shunned him.

"In Claude's case," Benjamin continues, "since his sire is alive, the final decision would fall to him…" He pauses, expression shuttering as some realization seems to hit him.

I remember, all at once, that Claude mentioned Ambrose was the one to suggest the intimacy clause. The final piece of the puzzle slots into place. I shut my eyes, fighting a wave of nausea as I realize exactly what situation I've found myself in.

Claude. The contract. The Vulpe Court. Ambrose.

Me.

I'm sure they'd be rid of me if they could, Claude once said.

"I'm a trap," I whisper. "Aren't I?"

* * *

The moment Benjamin departs, I search for Claude. He's out on the back porch, flipping idly through an art magazine, dappled moonlight casting his face in hard angles.

I stop, wrapping my arms around myself and staring at him. How much does he know, or at least suspect? Before I can think of how to begin the conversation, he looks up at me, and his stoic expression gentles.

"Come sit with me." He scoots over on the small sofa, making room.

I walk over and take a seat at his side. It's small enough that our shoulders brush. When he flips the page on his magazine, the backs of his fingers brush my knee. The contact sends a familiar tingle down my spine, followed by a lurching sense of dread as it reminds me just how dangerous this situation is.

"Lord Benjamin and I were just discussing our contract," I say, my voice tight.

"Oh?" Claude flips another page, picks the magazine up, and frowns as he studies some of the artwork within.

"We talked about what would happen if it were to be broken."

"I see," Claude says, still staring at his magazine. I reach over, place a hand over it, and lower it back down to his lap. He looks up at me.

I study his face. "You know what will happen if you break it." It's not a question; I can see the answer already in his expression. "Why on earth would you agree to that? The intimacy clause especially…"

He shrugs. "You wouldn't have signed otherwise."

"But why take on a valentine at all?" I ask. "You would have been safer without me."

"And without me, you would've been in danger."

My breath hitches. "What?"

"I… noticed you at the ball," he says. "Ambrose noticed me noticing." He smiles, but there's a bitter twist to it. "My mistake, to think I could have a single moment of joy without him finding some way to use it against me."

I shake my head. "But… he couldn't have *hurt* me. The vampire courts would never have allowed him to get away with it."

"Old-fashioned vampires like Lord Ambrose don't consider humans to matter," he says, with a terrifying matter-of-factness. "And he is powerful enough that the court likely would've covered up." His smile is wry, bitter. "Or, more likely, pinned it on me."

My lower lip trembles. "I'm so sorry," I whisper. "I didn't know what it meant. How serious it would be."

He slowly lifts a hand to cup my cheek, swiping a tear away before it can fall. "I did."

I shut my eyes, unable to look at him. "Then *why?*"

"He would have used you against me either way. But as a valentine, you'd be safe."

"But you'd be in more danger," I say. "And you barely knew me at the time."

"Even so."

"You thought I hated you."

"Even so."

I open my eyes and suck in a breath, chest aching at the softness in his gaze. "Claude," I whisper, even though I know I'm about to break my own heart. "We can't keep doing this. It's too dangerous, and it isn't fair to either of us."

His expression shutters, and he lowers his eyes. His hand slips away from my cheek. "No," he murmurs. "I suppose not."

* * *

We go through our contract line by line, with Benjamin on the phone to provide clarification, to determine what exactly is required of each of us. Aside from the intimacy clause, the contract is pretty boilerplate, outlining the usual duties of a valentine. I must reside at the house, give blood regularly, and attend events as Claude's guest when requested.

In a moment of quiet when I'm jotting down notes, Benjamin says, "Lord Claude, I must apologize. I never realized the severity of your situation, or else I would've…"

"There's nothing you could've done," Claude says. "It's not your fault."

"I hope you know it isn't yours, either," Benjamin says.

After we've been through the contract, we hang up and look down at my bullet points. Claude is pressed close against my shoulder; he's remained close to me ever since our conversation, like he expects what I'll soon ask of him.

"Most of these requirements are left open to interpretation," I point out. "There's no specification that I have to give blood every night, nor that you have to only drink from me. No exact number of events we have to attend together. We both have to reside in the house, but that doesn't mean we have to be together all of the time."

Claude puts an arm around my waist and draws me against his side. "But I like being together," he murmurs in my ear.

I can't bring myself to pull away, even though I should. "That's the problem," I say. "It's dangerous. I think we should have a rule not to touch each other at all. Except when you bite me."

He goes still. He's so close, I can feel the flutter of his eyelashes against my skin. "Living here without being able to touch you will be agony."

"It's agony either way." I shut my eyes, will my resolve not to break. "But this way will be safer."

A pause. "You're sure?"

No. "Yes."

He pulls away from me slowly, his hand grazing over my skin, giving me every opportunity to change my mind, but I don't. I bite my tongue and keep my eyes shut until I'm sure I'm not going to cry. Then I take a deep breath and open them. "It's better this way," I say, unsure if I'm trying to convince him or myself. "We won't be tempted to cross a line. And maybe when the year is up, then… things can be different."

He nods. "Maybe. If I can only paint, then maybe… maybe

Lord Ambrose and the rest of Vulpe would be more amenable to a change in the contract, or a new one at the end of the year, at least." But his sad smile tells me he doesn't believe it. And even though I want to, neither do I.

Chapter Twenty-Six

Days pass, then weeks. Life settles into a rhythm that is bearable, if only barely so.

Claude drinks from me most evenings. Sometimes he cooks for me. But often he is gone, leaving me alone in the house with nothing but the sea for company.

I've never been a person with real hobbies before. I never had time for them, always busy with school, work, and taking care of myself. All of this empty time is uncomfortable, but I find myself seeking escape in books, which I used to enjoy during spare free time. It's been years since I picked up a novel for pleasure, but I find them surprisingly soothing now.

So I read, and talk to my friends, and try not to think about where Claude is. I asked for space, and he's giving it to me. But I can't help but imagine him off at a party somewhere, laughing and talking with people who aren't me, drowning his sorrows in blood and wine.

I wish I had such easy escapes. Instead, I'm often left sitting in the seat by the window where he used to paint me, staring out at the dark waves, bitter in the knowledge that I've gotten everything I asked for. It's hard to imagine that I thought I wanted this… but back then, I suppose, I didn't know what it was like to feel the weight of Claude's attention, his fingers brushing against me; to see him on his knees in front of me as if in prayer.

But that only leads to spiraling. I try to think of other things. To lose myself in my books and self-care. But Claude haunts the house when he isn't here. Such a short time together but already I have so many memories of him, in the kitchen, in the dining room, in the studio. Inescapable.

I told him I wasn't going to let him break my heart, but sometimes I fear I've broken my own by pushing him away.

Then, one night, I wake to a missed call from my mom.

I stare at it, and stare some more. Do a quick search online to ensure I haven't missed some huge news, but the internet has no answers. Why would she call me now, of all times? Finally receiving my attempt at contact from months ago, when I needed help with my rent?

I shouldn't call back. I should be furious that it took her this long to deem me worthy of a response. But... I so badly need someone to talk to right now, and against my better judgment, I press *call*.

She picks up, which is unheard of. On the second ring, which is even *more* unheard of.

"There she is! Hi, Nora."

Again, I want to be angry at the fact she answers like nothing is wrong, like she didn't ignore me for months, like we haven't been low-contact ever since I was eighteen and left home without a word. Instead, I find myself getting choked up at the sound of her voice.

"Hi, Mom."

"It's been too long, sweetie. I was wondering when I'd hear from you. How is everything?"

"It's…" I take a deep breath, blink away tears. "Well, complicated. Didn't you get my text a few months ago?"

"A text?" There's a sound of shuffling on the other end. She's distracted by something else. Either her art or her van, I expect. "…Oh, yes! Yes, sorry, darling, I was without a phone for a while. You know how it is."

"Right…" Pushing my glasses up to rub at my eyes, I try to think of what to say. How much to tell her. But just as I open my mouth to launch into it, she speaks first.

"I was thinking I should come visit soon. I miss the West Coast."

It takes me a second to process. "…Really? You haven't been here in years." I should say no, but it's tempting right now, the idea of having company in this big, empty house. "You should probably know, um, I don't live in LA anymore. I'm up north a bit, and… well, I'm with someone."

"I was wondering when you were going to tell me the news!"

"What?" I pause, brow furrowing.

"You know, I was looking through an art magazine the other day, and it was covering some new vampire's opening show—interesting stuff, though not to my tastes…" Another pause as she rustles something on her end, though I have a sinking suspicion where this is going. "And as I was looking through the pictures, who did I see? My lovely daughter! On the arm of Lord Claude de Vulpe, nonetheless! It gave me quite a shock, I'll tell you."

Shit. I shut my eyes, bracing myself. "I'm…"

"I can't believe you didn't tell me. My own daughter, a valentine, and I didn't know! I mean, no judgment, of course. I just didn't think you had it in you, quite frankly."

I clear my throat. "It… was a surprise to me, too."

"Sure, sure." I'm not sure she's even listening to what I'm saying. "But anyway, as I was saying, I'd love to come visit and meet him."

Realization is a cold pit coalescing in my stomach. "...That's why you finally called."

"Hm?" She's half distracted, as always.

"You didn't call because you were checking in on me," I say. "You called because you wanted an introduction to Claude. I should've known."

There's a long pause. "Honey," she says. "That's not—"

I hang up before she can finish the sentence. Before she can hear the sob tear out of my throat. I fling my phone to the other side of the bed and sink down, head in my hands. The weight of grief settles on me again, heavier than before.

I'm so alone, and such a fool. I've always known that the only person I can rely on is myself, but for a while, I had almost started to think...

A knock at the door startles me. I gulp back tears, trying to steady myself enough to answer.

"Nora?" Claude's voice comes through the door. "May I come in?"

"N-not right now, Claude," I say, my voice thick with tears.

There's a long pause. Then, "Please?"

I wipe my face with the sleeve of my hoodie. "...Okay," I say, in such a small voice I'm not sure if he'll hear, or if I want him to.

But of course he does, with his vampire senses. He probably heard me crying from across the house too. And a moment later, he's pushing through the door, approaching the bed where I sit in a miserable, tear-stained lump.

I must look awful, my face blotchy and eyes swollen. But

Claude's face is tender as he sits on the edge of the bed. He reaches for me, but hesitates, his hand falling to the comforter between us.

"I know you asked me not to touch you," he says. "But…"

I throw myself onto his lap before I can second-guess the instinct. My arms around his neck, my face buried in his chest. He holds me close and rubs circles on my back, murmuring soothing words. I feel horrible for taking comfort in touch when I was the one who asked him to stop, but I need it right now.

"Talk to me, *mon chou*," he murmurs. "What's wrong?"

It takes a while until I'm able to speak. But when I do, it comes as an outpour. I cry about everything: my mother and the way she always loved her art more than me, my childhood where I was forced to learn to take care of her instead of the other way around, the years she seemed to forget my existence, that goddamn phone call and what an idiot I was for thinking she actually cared.

"She's the *imbécile* for not seeing your worth," he says, stroking my hair. "Her failure to be a mother is not your fault."

I pull away, sniffling and wiping at my eyes. "I'm sorry," I say. "I shouldn't be dumping this on you."

"Why not?" he asks. "I want to listen. I want to be here for you, Nora."

"But you have real things to worry about," I say. "Ambrose and the court… My problems are stupid. I should be able to deal with them."

"Your problems are no less real than mine." He cups my face as I try to turn away. "Nora. If they matter to you, then they matter to me. They're not stupid."

Our eyes meet. His gaze is so soft I can hardly stand it, his hand still on my cheek, his mouth so full and inviting.

I press my face into his shoulder again so I won't give in to temptation. My hand fists in his shirt. The texture is odd, stiff, and when I pull back and look at it, I see drying splatters of color.

"Were you painting?" I ask.

"Making an attempt. I thought… I might as well try." His lips twitch in a half-hearted smile. "Lord Ambrose was right, in a way. Dangling the contract over my head *was* enough to get me to try again, after all these years."

"I'm sorry." I wipe my face again, freshly annoyed at myself. "I interrupted. You didn't have to drop everything and come, I would've been fine—"

"No. I'm glad I did. It doesn't matter." He shakes his head, that fragile smile fading. "You make me happier than I've been in a very long time. But I still can't do it. I'm starting to think that that part of me is… is well and truly dead."

My heart seizes. I try to brush my tears away, but they won't stop coming. "I'm sorry," I whisper again. "I should've been checking on you instead of making it about me—"

"Nora, stop that at once." He pulls me close and presses a fleeting kiss to my forehead. "Your feelings matter." His lips brush my nose, barely there before they're gone. "They matter to me." The corner of my mouth next, while I stay perfectly still. "You matter to me." He hovers just in front of me, so close. Dangerously close. "More than painting. More than the contract."

My voice is hoarse and barely audible. "Your *life* is staked on that contract."

"More than that, too." When I speak, I catch a glimpse of

fangs. His eyes are on my mouth, too. "Tell me to kiss you and I'll do it. I don't care what they do to me."

I have to shut my eyes to clear my head. Force myself to think of the contract, the stakes. "No," I say. "I'm sorry, I want to, but we can't." I shake my head and pull away from him, even though it hurts to put space between us. "Thank you for being here. But… this is exactly why you need to keep your distance."

It's for my sake as well. Because right now, I want nothing more than to seek comfort from him. I want to be held, to be kissed. I want him to spend the night with his body wrapped around mine, making me feel less alone.

But instead, after a brief goodbye, I curl up in my sheets by myself.

Chapter Twenty-Seven

After a sluggish night and a day of fitful sleep, I wake again to a phone notification, though this one is far more welcome: a video call from Sophie and Elaine. I'm still half asleep, with bedhead and puffy eyes from all of the crying I did yesterday, but a cold call from my friends is rare enough that I scramble to answer.

"What's wrong?" I ask, holding the phone a couple inches from my face and squinting, since I didn't even bother to grab my glasses first.

"Good evening, madam," Sophie says. "Why do you look like you just woke up?"

"Probably because I just woke up," I grumble, fumbling for my glasses on the nightstand.

"Oh, shit, that's right. You're like, nocturnal now."

"Yup." I find my glasses and push them up my nose. Sophie's face comes into focus, grinning. "Why do *you* look like you're up to no good?"

"Me?" she asks, too innocently. "I'm always up to good!"

"She lies," Elaine says, poking her face into the frame.

Seeing the two of them together without me gives me a strange surge of mixed emotions. Fresh loneliness, an undeniable tug of envy… but mostly, happiness to see them, and gratitude that they thought of me even though I'm not there.

"Aww, look at you two," I say, smiling. Heat pricks the back of my eyes, but thankfully, I think I cried too much last night to manage any embarrassing tears now. "What are you up to?"

"Just a little weekend trip," Elaine says.

Again, I fight back a tug of bitterness. I miss those little trips away, going to concerts or the beach, like a weekend-long sleepover. "Where to?"

"Well…" Elaine taps her chin thoughtfully, and spins the camera. "Any guesses?"

It takes me a second to realize what I'm looking at: a house, modern and square and gray, and all too familiar.

"Wha…" I sit straight up and then scramble out of bed, almost falling over in my haste. "Is that…?!"

I rush to the front door, fling it open, and there they are, giggling like the evil masterminds they are. My best friends. I screech and throw an arm around each of their shoulders, yanking them in for a group hug. They embrace with just as much fierce affection, and then there's yelling and excitement and a few tears shed.

"How are you here?" I ask, pulling back to wipe my eyes. "How did you know where to find me?"

"Well…" Sophie starts, exchanging a look with Elaine. "Your loverboy contacted us."

"I'm pretty sure you're not supposed to refer to actual vampire nobility as *loverboy*," Elaine says.

"*Lord* Loverboy," Sophie corrects in a mock-snooty tone.

I barely hear their playful bickering, though. "Claude…? Claude did this?"

"Well, I guess Claude contacted Benjamin, and Benjamin got him in touch with us," Sophie says. "He wanted to surprise you, so he offered to fly us out. All expenses paid. Car service from the airport and everything."

"He didn't get into specifics," Elaine says, "but it sounded like you needed company."

"But what about work?" I ask. Another wave of tears is threatening to overtake me. "And… I'm sure you had other things to do this weekend, you didn't have to do this…"

"Babe," Sophie says, grabbing me by the shoulders and shaking me. "We're here because we want to be."

"I mean, I'm glad you're here, obviously! But you didn't have to drop everything and fly out." I bite my lip to stop it from wobbling. "I'm fine. Really. And I know you both have your own stuff going on, so…"

"Nora," Elaine says, somehow gentle and stern at the same time. "We're your friends. Stop pushing us away."

The words catch me off guard. Pushing them away? That's never what I intended. I just didn't want to be a burden. But… looking at them now, I imagine how I'd feel if they were intentionally concealing details of their lives from me. I'd be hurt, because I *want* to be there to support them. I see myself as a burden when I talk about my problems, but I'd never view them like that. I'd be offended if they thought I did.

I thought I was being selfless by keeping everything to myself. But really, all I was doing was keeping my friends at arm's length.

After a deep breath, I nod and manage a watery smile. "Let me make some coffee," I say, "and I'll tell you everything."

* * *

A note by the coffeemaker, written in Claude's slanted handwriting, informs me that he'll be away for the weekend and I should enjoy my time with my friends. It's agonizing not to be able to thank him right away, but as soon as I settle on the couch with Elaine and Sophie, I know he was right; I needed this time alone with them.

It takes hours to explain everything to them, especially with breaks for tears and snacks. But it's such a relief to be able to share it. I don't get into the details of the situation with my contract and Claude's court—I'm nervous at the thought of involving them too deeply—but I tell them the gist of it. I also vent about the phone call from my mom. And most of all, my growing—and impossible to act upon—feelings for Claude.

Sophie actually tears up when I admit it. "Oh, Nora," she says.

"I know it's hard right now," Elaine says, "but once the year is up, you can be together, right?"

I curl up with my knees to my chest. "I don't know," I admit. "We haven't talked about it. I get the feeling it will be more complicated than that."

"Such bullshit," Sophie says, still teary.

"Until this is resolved…" I stare down at the floor, the words sinking in as I speak them aloud. "We're safest apart." I clutch the blanket closer to me. "But… it may never be resolved."

Silence is thick after I speak. Both of my friends cuddle in closer around me.

"I don't have any answers," Elaine says, "but I'm sorry this is happening."

I nod, leaning my head against her shoulder.

"Yeah," Sophie says. She wipes her eyes and takes a shaky breath. "It must be hard, spending all this time around an undead hottie but never getting that vampire di—"

Elaine smacks her on the back of the head before she can finish, and despite myself, I laugh, and keep laughing until I end up in tears again.

* * *

The weekend passes too quickly. We eat and vent and laugh and cry, watch movies in a cuddle puddle on the couch, splash each other on the beach, order in my first taste of fast food since I started living here with Claude. They tell me what's been going on in their lives: Elaine groans about work, and Sophie about getting accustomed to moving in with David.

It feels like so much time has passed since we were last together like this, and yet now that we're reunited, nothing has changed. It eases something in my heart, to know that distance won't take our friendship. To know that they don't just love me when I have something to offer, in the form of rent or cleaning the apartment or cooking for everyone. They'll be here during the hard times, too, as long as I let them in.

They can't fix my problems, but they can help shoulder the load. At least I know that I'm not alone in this anymore. And if the worst happens, if Claude and I truly can't be together… I know I'll have them to support me through that, too.

Chapter Twenty-Eight

y heart is full after the visit, but the house feels especially empty once Sophie and Elaine leave for the airport. I keep myself busy to stop myself from wallowing. Claude is supposed to be back sometime today, and I want everything to be perfect when he does. I spend hours cleaning the place from top to bottom, and then acquaint myself with Claude's kitchen, since he's not here to stop me. There are still loads of fresh groceries, given his tendency to overbuy, so I have plenty to work with.

I smile when I hear the front door open. Perfect timing. I light the candles on the dining table, open the wine to breathe, and go to greet him at the door.

Claude's eyes are shadowed and his mouth downturned, but his expression lifts when he sees me. "Nora," he says. "How was your weekend?"

It takes every ounce of my willpower not to throw my arms around his neck and kiss the weariness off his face. "It was perfect. I can't thank you enough, but… I tried to do a little something for you in return."

"You didn't have to do anything for me," he says.

Something in my chest twinges at an echo of words I've

said so many times before. In return, I echo him. "I know. I wanted to."

I ease his coat off his shoulders and hang it up before leading him to the dining room, where everything is set out.

"Coq au vin?" he asks, eyes lighting up.

"Yes." I bite my lip. "I'm not expert at French cuisine or anything, but I did my best."

"Well, it smells heavenly."

I lean against the table next to his seat, pouring him a glass of wine. "I haven't added my blood yet," I say. "I figured you'd want it fresh."

He looks up at me, his fangs already out and his pupils growing as he looks at me. "You figured correctly."

The meal is good, the company better. The night is almost perfect.

Almost.

I missed spending time with Claude like this, and yet… every second together is just a reminder of what we can't have. That distance between us, impossible to cross for our safety. And it is impossible to miss Claude's exhaustion, even as he does his best to keep the mood light when we eat.

After I clear away the dishes—refusing to let him help—I return to find him sitting in his seat with his elbows on the table and his head in his hands. I hesitate for a moment, and then walk over, grazing a hand over his slumped shoulders.

"What's wrong, Claude?" I ask in a soft voice, my thumb circling over a tense muscle on the side of his neck. "Where were you this weekend?"

He leans into my touch but doesn't lift his head. "You don't have to worry about it."

"If it worries you, it worries me," I say. "Talk to me. Please."

After a moment, he drops his hands from his face. "I was visiting Ambrose. Trying to mend things between myself and the Vulpe Court, see if there was any possibility of altering our contract."

My stomach twists. No wonder he seems so tired. I wish he had told me beforehand, but… what's done is done. "And?"

He shakes his head. "Lord Ambrose only took my begging as a sign that this tactic is working," he says. "He was exceedingly clear. So long as I'm unable to paint, he will make it so I'm unable to have you. For the duration of our contract, and… in perpetuity."

A part of me suspected it, but it's something else entirely to hear it aloud. I brace myself against the table, since I suddenly don't trust my legs to support me. "There's nothing we can do?" I ask. "He'll never let us be together?"

There is one thing, of course—he could paint, like Ambrose wants. But somehow I know that wouldn't be enough. It will never be enough. I will never be anything but a tool to him to use, for Claude's reward or punishment, and the threat of that will never let us be together in peace.

"I'm sorry," he says. "I never should have drawn you into this."

"Don't say that. I'm…" I shake my head, struggling to express myself. "I'm glad I can be here to support you, if nothing else." No matter how badly it hurts, that will be true.

But the idea of never being together is agonizing. Even if I walk away at the end of the year, how can I live the rest of my life never knowing what it would've been like? How can I abandon Claude to suffer Ambrose's cruelties alone?

Claude takes my hand and squeezes, conveying a thousand unspoken words in that one gesture. "There's one more thing," he says, after a moment's quiet. "Ambrose was getting on me about the rest of the contract. We need to spend more time together, be *seen* spending time together."

The thought of pretending to be happy in the public eye feels like swallowing glass, but there's no avoiding it. "Right."

"I secured an invitation to a Celeste gathering from a mutual friend," he says. "We'll be seen without being too much in the spotlight. I figured that would be most bearable for you."

Even now, he's thinking of me. I force a smile. "We'll get through this, Claude."

He nods, but he doesn't meet my eyes. Because we both know the truth: there is no getting through this, because there will never be a happy ending for us.

Chapter Twenty-Nine

After another week of uncomfortable distance between us, Claude and I endure a long and painfully silent ride to the Celeste event he asked me to attend with him. Between our subdued black semiformal outfits and the somber quiet, it feels like we're on the way to a funeral instead of a party.

I sit staring out the window, Claude's words from our last conversation still ringing in my head. *In perpetuity.* Ever since he said those words, I lost a flicker of hope that I wasn't aware I was still holding on to. Part of me thought that if we made it through a difficult year, everything would be okay. But now it looks like the only way this ends is with us walking away from each other.

It's exactly what I said I wanted. One year, a great salary, and then I'd be out of this lifestyle, moving on to the future I've always worked for. But now I know what I'll be walking away from. *Who* I'll be walking away from. And the idea of leaving Claude to this eternal solitude makes my chest ache.

On the other side of the car, Claude clears his throat, looking down at his ring-laden hands. He hasn't touched the wine. "I've been thinking about your safety," he says.

I turn to him, frowning. "Shouldn't you be thinking about your own?"

He gives his head the smallest shake. "After our contract is up, I mean… Of course I won't fault you for walking away, but…" He shifts in his seat, brushing hair out of his face. "It would be safest for you to continue to be under the protection of a contract and a court."

My brow furrows. "So… stay under contract with you?"

"No." He hesitates. "With someone else."

I can only stare.

"I could introduce you to some other vampires who would be amenable to—"

"No," I say. "I don't want that."

"It would just be for your protection," Claude says, "until Lord Ambrose's attention wanders elsewhere."

It makes a certain amount of sense, but that doesn't make it hurt any less. I can't imagine being someone else's valentine. The mere thought of it… I shake my head, turning to gaze out the window. "I don't want to talk about this."

"We have to talk about it," Claude says, with a gentleness that makes my eyes burn. "I don't like it either, Nora, but I will do whatever it takes to protect you."

I shake my head again, unable to find the words. It seems so unfair, so impossibly cruel, that the best we can hope for is him protecting me by letting me go. "We'll talk about it closer to the end of our contract," I say, finally. "But not now. Maybe there will be another option." Even if it seems impossible right now.

* * *

Claude told me this party would be different, but I didn't realize just how different. The mansion hosting this event is just as lovely as any of the others, with an old-school Victorian charm, but it's so *quiet*. Only a few dozen vampires and valentines are in attendance, spread throughout the open space in small clusters of conversation.

It's intimidating in an altogether different way than the other events, yet at least I don't feel so out of place here. Still, I won't ignore the opportunity to hold tightly to Claude's arm as he offers it. Any excuse to touch him, to be near him, to spend time with him, even though I'm the one who insisted we shouldn't do those things.

He, as always, seems oblivious to any stares or sense of being incongruous. He leads me straight toward a pair of women standing near a marble bust.

"Ah, Claude," the vampire says with an easy smile. "You made it."

"You know me, never one to miss a party," he says, and gestures to me. "This is my valentine, Nora. Nora, this is my old friend, Lady Georgiana de Celeste, and her valentine Farah."

We make polite conversation, but it's hard for me to keep up with social niceties with Claude's words from the car weighing on me. After a short while, I excuse myself to go to the bathroom. I take my time finding my way back, admiring some of the portraits adorning the walls. I stop short when I recognize one of them as Claude's, and stare up at it, struck by a nameless surge of emotion as I look at the painting of a lake under the setting sun.

I'm not sure how long I stand there before Claude finds me. He stops silently at my side, staring up at the portrait, and I jolt guiltily as if caught doing something wrong.

"I'm sorry," I say. "I was distracted…"

He slips an arm around my shoulders. "It's alright." His gaze flicks to me before wandering slowly, almost unwillingly, back to his painting. Those endless blue eyes show every little thing he's feeling: sorrow, pride, a deep and terrible yearning.

"I love this one," I say quietly. "It feels… nostalgic, somehow."

"It's a place I used to dream about," he says. "Maybe a memory from before the orphanage, or maybe someplace I made up. I've never been sure."

"You don't dream about it anymore?"

He shakes his head, his gaze still locked on his artwork. "I can't remember the last time I dreamed." We stand in the quiet for a long moment before I slip my arm through his. "We should get back to the party."

He finally tears his eyes away. "Right." He places a hand over mine and squeezes, and we wander back into the main ballroom.

We've barely entered when a voice halts us.

"Are you Nora?"

I blink, turning around to see a human woman smiling at me. She has a head of gorgeous curls and is wearing a butter-yellow dress, unusual for a valentine, but she's so glamorous she couldn't be anything else.

I blink a couple times. I'm not used to people approaching to talk to me instead of Claude. "Yes?"

"Hi! I'm Amelia. We have a mutual friend, Lord Benjamin Acharya? The Valentine Society helped pair me with my patron as well."

"Oh! Lovely." I shake her hand, smiling. "He mentioned you. You're with a Celeste vampire?"

"Yup!" She points across the party at a dark-haired gentleman in all black. He glances over as Amelia gestures to him, and his somber disposition softens. "I'm here with—"

"Lord Sebastian de Celeste?" Claude leans forward, his eyes locked on the other vampire with an expression I can't decipher. "The hero of the last court war?"

"Oh, well, yes. But he doesn't really like to talk about that."

I side-eye Claude, unsure what to make of his sudden interest.

"I thought he hardly ever emerged from his estate."

Amelia smiles. "*Slightly* more often, these days."

"Could you introduce us, perhaps?" he asks.

"Oh, um, sure? I don't see why not. It looks like he's having a terrible time over there right now, so I was looking for an excuse to pull him away…"

Claude pulls free from me and offers his arm. "Happy to be of service."

As she leads Claude away, I hear Amelia saying, "If he seems like he hates you, don't worry, that's just how his face is most of the time."

She returns a couple of minutes later, sans Claude.

"Sebastian probably isn't thrilled about me setting him up on a playdate like that," she says, chuckling. "But truth be told, I wanted an excuse to talk to you alone. Can we sit?"

I blink, taken aback. "Sure." We sit at a table tucked away in the corner, away from the other conversations. "You wanted to talk to me? Why?"

"Well…" She hesitates. "Not to be weird, but I've heard about your, um, situation. I wanted to see if you were okay, and if there was anything I could do to help."

"My situation," I repeat, confused. Does she know about

the problem with the contract, somehow? But how could she possibly help with that?

"Yeah," she says. "I mean, I can't imagine it's easy being with an artist like Claude, and all that pressure to be his muse..."

"Oh. Right." In light of everything that's happened, I had almost forgotten about that particular aspect of our relationship. "It is difficult, yes. I never really wanted a public-facing situation, so..."

"Right," she says, nodding. "Yeah. I'm sure. And I'm sure you don't want to be seen as *just* a muse, either. You probably want to be more than that to him."

"Mm-hmm." Something about that phrasing twinges something in my memory. I shift in my seat, taking a closer look at her. "Wait a second," I say slowly. "You're... are you...?"

She stares at me, wide-eyed. "What?"

I lean in, lowering my voice. "*Anonymous Life of a Valentine*, huh?"

"What! I'm... not... shit." She sighs, shoulders slumping. "I'm really bad at this whole anonymity thing. Sorry if it was weird to approach you like this, I just... I know what it's like to feel alone as a valentine. I wanted to help."

"No, I'm glad you did." I smile. "Seriously. Though I'm not sure there's anything you could do for me. Things have gotten complicated since I wrote to you."

"Complicated how?"

I take a deep breath. "Well..."

* * *

When I'm done explaining it all, about the contract and the court and Claude's sire, I lean back in my chair and let out a long breath. It feels like a weight off my chest, but saying it all aloud—to Amelia's gasps and sympathetic murmurs—also makes me realize just how crazy this is.

"It feels like I'm caught in this tangled web," I say. "And I can't even *see* it all, let alone know how to escape it. And I can't tell anyone in my life, because I don't want them freaking out. My old roommates would probably drag me out of Claude's house in the middle of the night if they thought I was in danger."

"Do you feel like you're in danger?" Amelia asks.

After a moment, I shake my head. "Not really. But Claude is, and I don't want to leave him to deal with it alone."

Amelia nods. "Right." She looks off into the distance, nibbling her thumbnail. I follow her gaze to see Sebastian and Claude still embroiled in conversation. Claude is having a conversation, at least, his slender hands gesticulating wildly as he speaks, while Sebastian listens with a furrowed brow.

"I'm not sure how much I can help," Amelia says, drawing my attention back to her. "But I can ask Sebastian. He's in a different court, obviously, but maybe he knows something that could help."

"I wonder if that's why Claude wanted to talk to him in the first place," I murmur, still watching them. They make an odd duo, and I can't imagine what else they might be discussing. But as Amelia pointed out, Sebastian is in Celeste; how could he do anything about a situation with Vulpe? He probably doesn't want to touch the political issues of another court with a ten-foot pole.

Amelia reaches over and touches my arm as if sensing my dismay. "Sebastian may not be able to help directly, but maybe he has some insight into all of this. He's been through wars and…" She waves a hand. "All manner of things, I don't know. He's old as hell."

I crack a smile. "Well, I appreciate it. Even if he can't do anything, it's nice to be able to talk to someone about everything."

Chapter Thirty

After the brief reprieve of the Celeste party, it hurts anew to wander out of my room the next evening and find that Claude is gone again. I make myself coffee and breakfast; neither tastes as sweet as when Claude makes them for me. I resisted his insistence on serving me for so long, but now I miss it terribly. I suppose it was my mistake to get used to such treatment. It always would've ended eventually, wouldn't it have?

Because this life is not forever. It's just for a year, which is both a comfort and a different sense of pain at this point.

The long, lonely nights blend into each other over the following weeks. Claude is absent even more than he was before the Celeste party, and when he's here, he's only half present. He seems distant, his mind wandering and his face marked with shadows of exhaustion. He barely seems like the man I know. But I suppose I'm a shadow of myself as well, so I can't blame him.

Still, it seems extreme. Sometimes it seems like he can barely keep his eyes open. On one rare night he joins me for dinner, he falls asleep in his chair, his head tilted back and his mouth slightly ajar.

"What in the world have you been up to, Claude?" I mutter to myself. I cross the room and take his shoulder to gently shake him awake.

He flinches at the barest touch, and suddenly his hand is gripping my wrist hard enough to hurt. At my gasp, he releases me.

"Sorry," he says, expression pained. "Are you alright?" He shifts in his seat, adjusts his shirt, but not before I catch a glimpse of a bruise near his neck. I didn't know vampires *could* bruise.

I raise my eyes to meet his, studying his face. "Are *you*?"

He smiles wanly. "Of course. Just tired. I apologize." He takes my hand, presses a kiss to my knuckles, and leaves me there at the dinner table with my thoughts whirling.

What could he be off doing that would leave a mark like that? I had assumed he was off distracting himself with parties and wine, but maybe the truth is something else. Something worse.

Yet the following night, he's gone from the time I wake up until the time I go to bed, leaving me without any way to ask him.

* * *

More time slips by. Long days and longer nights spent alone, or with only minutes of Claude's time. In the early days I check in with Benjamin frequently, hoping that he may have found a way to free us from the contract. He visits multiple times and we pore over it together, but there's nothing to be done without the cooperation of the Vulpe Court. Benjamin sends multiple formal requests to meet with Ambrose and other prominent vampires, but the letters are returned unopened.

I spend time talking to Sophie and Elaine, and become better acquainted with Amelia as well. It helps to be able to lean on them for support, but they can't offer much other than sympathy and friendship.

As time goes on, my hope dwindles. I busy myself looking into attending university once my contract is over, researching apartments near campus that are now well within my budget. I'm making great money as a valentine, despite all of this, and hardly spending any of it; I'll have more than enough to cover tuition, rent, and other expenses, even if I decide not to work while I'm attending school.

It should be everything I wanted… yet I can't summon much enthusiasm. Whenever I imagine my life after this year, there's a blank space where Claude should be, an emptiness I can't ignore. At the beginning of this arrangement, a clean split was exactly what I hoped for; now, it seems impossible that it might be the only option.

Then one evening, I wake up to the smell of breakfast cooking. Crackling bacon and the sweet sizzle of pancakes lead me to the kitchen, where I find Claude at the stove again. A once-common sight, now shocking enough to make me halt in the doorway and stare.

It takes a moment for him to notice me. He looks up and smiles, but his eyes are tired.

"*Bonsoir, mon chou,*" he says.

I'm gripped by the urge to cross the kitchen and fling myself into his arms, to just hold him and be held, but that would break the rules that I, myself, put in place. The distance is best for both of us, even though it makes my heart crack open.

I force a smile. "You're home."

"Indeed. And happy to be here." He plates the breakfast feast, adding thick slabs of butter and a drizzle of syrup to the stack of pancakes.

I hesitate, questions on the tip of my tongue. I want to know where he's been, and what he's been doing, but I'm afraid the answer will only make this harder. I know Claude and trust him not to hurt me, so if he's keeping the information for himself, he has to have a good reason. "Is everything okay?" I venture instead. "Why are you here?" I bite my lip. "Not that you need a reason to be in your own home, I mean... it's just..."

"Nora." He crosses the room to me, holding my plate in one hand. The other smooths an unruly strand of hair behind my ear. "I know. Come, eat breakfast with me."

I watch him head to the dining room, my brow furrowed as I realize that was no answer. There's nothing for me to do but trail after him to the dining room table and sit in my usual chair.

I eat my food while he watches me. Once a usual event at the house, but now odd enough that I'm not sure how to feel.

As with all of his food, it's delicious, the perfect balance between buttery and maple-sweet, but still I find it hard to swallow.

Claude props up his chin with one hand and smiles at me across the table. Still, he looks exhausted, his eyes shadowed and his usual charm dimmed.

"Back to watching me eat, I see," I tease, trying to lighten the mood.

"I missed it," he says. His head tilts slowly, his eyes never leaving me. "I missed you."

I set down my fork. "I missed you too."

Yet him being back here is almost painful. The way our eyes lock across the table only serve as a reminder that we can't touch, can't be together in the way we want to. Looking at him is like pressing on a fresh bruise, but I can't seem to tear my eyes away.

"Why are you here?" I ask again. "Do you need blood?"

He must have been getting it elsewhere over the last couple of months. And I know, I *know* he wouldn't do anything to hurt me, but even the thought of him casually drinking from someone else's wrist makes me hot with jealousy. It's not fair— he needs blood to live—but I am jealous of whatever skin has felt his fangs, his bloody kiss.

"I would like to drink from you," he says. "And I would like to try to paint, again."

I blink, surprised. "I thought you had given up on that."

He rubs a hand across his face and sighs. "If I could just bring myself to paint *something*," he says. "Ambrose would be pleased. Maybe pleased enough to let me alter the contract, and then... none of this would be necessary."

Somehow, I doubt that's the case. Ambrose seems like a man who will always find something to be disappointed about. He'd find some reason to be dissatisfied, some reason to continue to keep Claude under his thumb, and it would only make Claude feel worse.

But I bite my tongue. I don't think it will be helpful to say that. And anyway, I can't resist the excuse to spend time together. "Let's try it, then."

* * *

We take our usual places: Claude at the easel, me posed at the window seat. We've been here so many times before, but today my pulse races and my gut twists. As much as I doubted him earlier, it's difficult not to seize the dangerous hope he offered. Maybe he *will* paint, and maybe Ambrose *will* be pleased, and maybe he will let us change the contract…

Maybe, maybe, maybe.

The last thing I want to do is put further pressure on Claude. There's already so much on his shoulders, I fear his spine will break beneath the weight. So I stare out the window, trying to lose myself in my thoughts.

Yet I can't help but steal the occasional glance at him in the silence. And now that I know to look for it, I can tell he's not really painting at all. Instead, he just stares at the canvas, brush in hand, like he's trying to work out the answer to a complex problem.

After an hour of silence stretches out, Claude sighs and says, "That's enough for today."

"Did you—" I turn toward him, but he's already leaving, the tense line of his shoulders providing enough of an answer to my question.

Chapter Thirty-One

To his credit, Claude doesn't give up easily. He is still here the next evening, and the next. He cooks for me again, talks with me at dinner, drinks my blood and tries to paint.

It's almost like it was at the beginning of our time together, except that everything between us has changed.

And every time, as I study Claude from my seat at the window, I can't help but wonder at how miserable he looks. He gazes at his easel with an expression of despondence, his blue eyes stormy and his shoulders slumped. He claims painting makes him happy, but all it seems to do is bring about these dour moods.

I know it's not really about the painting. It's about the situation with his sire, and the Vulpe Court, and all of the expectations weighing on him… but still. How can he ever expect to get anything done when he's so obviously in pain?

And more than that, it hurts to watch. I don't want to see him like this. I want him to be happy, whether that means creating something beautiful or walking away from art forever.

But I'm not sure how to put all of that into words, and I'm not sure if he's ready to hear it either. So instead, when it becomes too much for me to bear, I settle for some good old-fashioned teasing in an attempt to lighten the mood.

"Must you always take yourself so seriously?" I ask, folding my arms over my chest.

"Someone has to do it," he says, barely paying attention to me.

"I guess so, because I don't."

"Certainly not."

I bite my lip, watching him. There's an ache in my chest despite my attempts at lightheartedness. How can I help him? How can I make him happy, even for a tiny moment? I'd do anything for a chance to make him smile, but I've never been very good at that.

I think of my roommates, and take a deep breath to steady myself. Then I slowly cross the room toward him. I wait until he looks up at me and then I dip my fingers into his paint and smear it across his face.

He gapes, looking taken aback. "Wha— Nora!"

A smile slowly creeps over my face. "Yes?"

"I—" He sputters, so shocked, he seems like he's not sure if he should be affronted. I'm shocked at myself, too, but there's a fizzing, giddy feeling beneath it, bubbling up in my veins. I feel unlike myself, and it's exhilarating. When's the last time I let myself be playful like this? "I was going to—"

"What, paint?" My daring growing, I dab some on the tip of his nose. "Does this not count as painting?" When he doesn't move, I drag my finger down over his cheekbone, leaving a smear of sky-blue. "Perhaps I'm an artist myself."

He stares at me for a moment. "You..." he says. "You ridiculous little..." Then he laughs, drops his paintbrush, and slaps an entire hand onto the palette, gathering a generous dollop of paint. I shriek and run, not nearly fast enough, and he soon catches me around the waist and palms my entire face.

"So *cold!*" I sputter.

"You have no one to blame but yourself," he says, grinning as he removes his still-dripping hand.

I rub my face against his, and he yelps in protest. He nearly drops me, but I cling to him, and soon we're both a mess on the floor, wrestling and smearing paint all over each other. Finally he pins my wrists beside my head. I lie beneath him, breathless and smiling.

"You look ridiculous," I inform him. Though even with paint smudged all over his face and shirt, he still looks more handsome than he has any right to be.

"You insult your own artwork, mademoiselle," he says gravely.

I laugh. As the sound dies away, he's still staring at me, his face just inches away from mine, and the brief joy dies away, leaving a familiar hollow in my chest. "I miss you, Claude," I admit.

His expression turns somber. He releases my wrists, but stays with his arms braced on either side of my head, holding himself over me. Close enough to kiss, though I know he won't, no matter how badly we both ache for it.

"I've missed you more than you know, *mon coeur*," he says. "But I have been..." He pauses, lifting his head and looking toward the door. He whispers a curse in French and pushes himself up from the floor.

"What?" I look toward the door, but try as I might, I can't hear or see anything amiss.

Claude grabs me and lifts me to my feet. "Go," he says, urging me toward the door. "Go clean up in your bathroom."

"What? What's going on?"

He ignores my questions, propelling me out the door with his hands on my hips. With a huff, I shake him off and stride into my bedroom. I'm not sure what has him acting this way, but the look on his face, his sense of urgency, leave me frightened enough to obey.

I scrub myself off as quickly as I can in the shower. As I'm getting re-dressed in paint-free clothes, I freeze at the sound of shouting echoing through the house. A familiar, cruel voice.

Ambrose is here.

My hands shake as I remember the crack of his hand across my face, his horrible smile. My sense of self-preservation urges me to stay here. But… there's a hot rush of anger through the fear. Claude and I finally had a *good* night, a night where I succeeded at making him smile for the first time in ages, and of course Ambrose has to show up and ruin everything.

I shake my head and force myself to continue buttoning up my dress despite my trembling fingers. I need to make sure Claude is okay. I don't know what happens between them, but I know that every visit from his sire leaves Claude despondent, and I know that the man is at least partially responsible for the precipitous situation we've found ourselves in. Maybe I can find a way to defuse the tension, or at least shoulder some of the burden of his presence.

So I quickly do my hair and makeup, square my shoulders, and stride toward the sound of the shouting even as my instincts cry for me to cower away instead.

I find them in the studio. Claude managed to clean his face off before his sire arrived, but he's still wearing his paint-stained shirt, and the room bears evidence of the playful mess we made.

Claude stands stiffly in the middle of the room, his hands clasped behind his back, and his expression blank in a way that frightens me. It's like he's gone somewhere far away, deep within his own head, leaving behind a shell.

Ambrose stands barely a foot away, one finger jabbing into Claude's chest, his features twisted in an expression of fury that renders him almost animalistic.

"What is this?" Ambrose is as cold as a snake as he jabs him again, his other hand gesturing wildly to the room around them. "Is this your idea of a joke, Claude? You wish to make a mockery of the very purpose I turned you for?"

Claude's eyes drift past his sire and then fix on me and widen. He shakes his head, but it's enough to make Ambrose turn to me, his snarl turning into a sneer at the sight of me.

I bob in a curtsy. "Good evening, Lord Ambrose," I say, coldly polite despite my heart pounding in my ears. "We weren't expecting you. Can I get you anything?"

"You..." Ambrose takes a step in my direction.

A blink, and Claude is in front of him, his back to me and his chin lifted as he stands between me and his sire.

I stay behind him, heart pounding, unable to fight the surge of fear in front of a dangerous predator. "Your quarrel is with me, sire," he says, his voice soft and measured.

Ambrose's eyes narrow. "You think I have forgotten?" He gestures, again, to the paint-smeared room. "You still haven't answered. Is this meant to mock me?"

"No, sire," Claude says. He brings his hands behind his back again, and gestures with one of them toward the door, urging me to go.

I plant my feet in stubborn refusal. The mess of the studio, which has so enraged Ambrose, is my fault. I don't know if I can do anything to help the situation, but the least I can do is be here for Claude so he doesn't have to face it alone.

"And yet that is exactly what you do," Ambrose says, coming to a stop a couple of inches in front of Claude. "Do you know how they laugh at you? At me, for bringing you into the court? Do you realize I have not been allowed to create another fledgling because of *you*?"

Claude is quiet for a moment.

"Speak," Ambrose snaps.

"I am aware, sire," Claude says. "I am sorry for it."

"Not sorry enough." Ambrose steps closer. Close enough that I can see him over Claude's shoulder. He looks right at me, and fear shivers down my spine. I have to resist the urge to step back or flee the room. "I would never have allowed you to take a valentine if I thought you would give in to such trifling desires," he says. "Have you broken your contract, Claude?"

"No," Claude says.

"Speak truly."

"That is the truth."

Ambrose's hand darts out, quick as a viper, to grab Claude by the chin. He forces his head up, exposing his throat, and hisses around his fangs, *"Tell me the full truth."*

"I have not broken the contract," Claude chokes out. The words sound like they're being pulled from him, rather than him speaking of his own volition.

A command. I press one hand to my mouth, trembling under the weight of the tension in the room. Part of me thinks Claude would not want me to witness this, but how could I possibly leave him?

Ambrose's gaze slides to me again, his lips pursing in

disappointment. "Hm." As I suspected—he *wants* Claude to break it. Wants the excuse.

"Please stop this, Lord Ambrose," I say, my voice quivering. It grates on me to address him so respectfully, but I know the consequences of doing otherwise. "Lord Claude hasn't done anything wrong."

Claude's eyes flash to me in clear warning, but Ambrose is still laser-focused on him instead of me, his fingers digging grooves in Claude's face.

"Nothing wrong?" he repeats, face twisted in a snarl. "Is that what you think, Claude? You think you don't deserve this? As if you haven't made a mockery of me and the Vulpe Court for years, haven't wasted the gift that I bestowed upon you?"

He shoves Claude back against the wall with a hard thump that makes me wince.

"You pathetic, useless *waste* of my blood and my time—"

My fear is so great that stepping forward feels like fighting against a strong current, but I do it anyway, forcing my shoulders back and my head high. "How dare you speak to him like that," I say.

Ambrose pauses. His head turns slowly toward me, his mouth curved into a small, dangerous smile that doesn't reach his dark eyes. "How dare I?" he repeats. "How dare you speak to me *at all*, little valentine?"

"Don't," Claude grits out, though I'm not sure which of us he's speaking to. As Ambrose turns fully in my direction, Claude raises a hand to grab at his sire's sleeve. But Ambrose's hand moves faster, reaching out to close around Claude's fingers—those long, gentle artist's fingers—and twists them sideways with a swift, cruel *crack*.

I cry out. So does Claude, though he tries to muffle the

sound.

"Silence," Ambrose orders, and Claude's mouth clicks shut. His eyes burn, shifting frantically from Ambrose to me as his sire releases his broken hand and steps toward me.

"Lord Claude is a better man than you will ever be," I say, refusing to back down. Having his attention on me is terrifying, like a snake's head swinging in my direction, but it means his focus is off Claude. Still, as he takes a step toward me, I take an automatic step back. "He deserves better than you," I whisper.

Ambrose smiles, slow and dangerous. "I made him," he says. "*I* decide what he deserves."

"He doesn't belong to you."

Ambrose arches a brow. "Claude," he says, "get on the floor."

Claude grits his teeth. His expression is pained as he slowly lowers himself onto his hands and knees.

"Lower," Ambrose demands, his eyes on me instead of his fledgling.

Claude then lowers himself until he's flat on his stomach against the floor. He presses his cheek to it as he looks over at me and gives the slightest shake of his head, his eyes pleading.

"Need I further demonstrate my power over him?" Ambrose asks, smiling like this is a game.

"You're only demonstrating your cruelty," I say. I take a deep breath. "And how pathetic you are, to take advantage of someone helpless against you."

Ambrose's mouth flattens, the humor disappearing in an instant and leaving something cold behind. "Clearly, teaching you manners is yet another thing that Claude has failed at."

"I only give respect to those who deserve it."

In the blink of an eye, Ambrose is in front of me, pushing

me back against the wall. I swallow a gasp as he grabs my chin. "You little brat," he hisses. When he's this close, and this angry, the pretense of manners falls away. His face twists into something hateful and inhuman. "Clearly you have forgotten your place. If you were in my household, I'd have you whipped."

His grip on me is iron, his fingers digging bruises into my face. "But I'm not in your household," I grit out, refusing to back down. "You have no power over me."

He smiles, and it is somehow more dangerous than his fury. "You think so?"

His fingers slide down to my neck and squeeze harder.

I choke. Try to gasp for air that doesn't come. My feet kick uselessly as Ambrose lifts me off the floor, holding me against the wall one-handed without any effort. He studies my face as I struggle and claw at his hand, and his grin broadens.

I try to speak Claude's name, but I can't and he can't help me. He's bound by his sire's commands to grovel in silence, to do nothing but watch. Ambrose could kill me, and Claude wouldn't be able to do anything about it. Would he go so far? Fear swells in my chest as my vision starts to go dark.

I pushed him to get him away from Claude. I didn't think he'd really hurt me, not badly. I'm a valentine, I'm supposed to be protected. But perhaps I underestimated his power, or at least his rage...

My eyelids flutter shut. My struggles weaken.

"Ambrose!"

The grip on my neck weakens, and I gasp, sucking blessed air into my raw throat. Ambrose drops me as he turns, and I catch myself on my palms and knees before I fully hit the floor. Panting, I look past Ambrose to see what has caught his attention: Claude, somehow speaking despite his sire's command. As I watch, he presses himself—slowly, painstakingly—up to his knees and lifts his head. It looks as though he's straining against an enormous weight, his head and shoulders bowed beneath it, but he grits his teeth and lifts his head to fix his sire with a look of murder.

"You…" He forces out each word as if it's painful. "Harmed. My. Valentine."

"Oh, boo-hoo," Ambrose drawls. "Go ahead and report it to Vulpe, see if they believe you."

"No. I demand… the oldest right." Claude's shoulders square, the words coming easier now. He lifts one foot beneath him, and then pushes up onto the other so he stands tall before his sire, defiance in his eyes. I can't see Ambrose's face, but I can sense the sudden tension in him as he watches Claude shake off his orders.

"You can't be serious," Ambrose says.

"Trial by combat," Claude says. "With the court as witness."

My gasp hurts my still-raw throat. *No.* He can't. "Claude…" I try to speak, but can't manage more than a whisper.

Ambrose's laughter drowns me out. "Oh, you little fool," he says. "I accept your challenge. When do you wish to meet your demise?"

"Why hold off?" says Claude. "Tonight. Midnight."

No, no, no. I want to scream it, to beg and plead for Claude to stop this, but I don't have the air or the strength, and this has a horrible sense of inevitability.

"Very well," Ambrose says, still grinning. "If you're so eager. I'll see you shortly, Claude."

He leaves us there in the parlor without another glance back.

Chapter Thirty-Two

In the back of the car, Claude fusses over my bruises, though he's the one with a still-broken hand. "You shouldn't have done that," he says, pain in his eyes, like the wounds hurt him more than they hurt me. He brushes his lips over the circle of bruises on my wrist, so gentle I don't even feel it.

"It seemed almost like you wanted it to happen," I rasp. He was so ready to duel. Eager for it, almost.

Claude shakes his head. "I…" He grimaces. "If only I could have just painted, maybe it could have been avoided. But… I was ready for a duel, it's true," he admits. "Yet not for you to be harmed. Never that. It could've gone so much more badly, Nora."

"I'm a valentine. I'm protected by the contract." I touch his cheek. "So I wanted to protect you. But…" My lower lip wobbles as I think, again, of how badly this all backfired. "I didn't think you'd challenge him like this, Claude. My intent was to *stop* you from getting hurt. I didn't want… this."

He smiles, brushing away my tears with the thumb of his good hand. "It's been a long time coming, *mon chou*. You can't take responsibility." His expression sobers. "And he hurt you. I can't forgive that." A gentle palm cups my cheek. "Tell me… has he done anything like that before?"

With his hand caressing me, I can't turn away even if I wanted to. "Once," I admit. "When you weren't home, he hit me."

Claude's expression darkens into something dangerous. "You should've told me."

I study his face. "He's hurt you like that before, too," I say, not even bothering to make it a question. His gaze slides away from mine, and I sigh. "You should've told *me.*"

"There's nothing you could've done," he says. "I didn't want to burden you."

His hand slides from my cheek, but I reach to grasp it, twining our fingers.

"I think we both need to stop thinking of ourselves that way," I say. "We can both rely on each other without being burdens."

We sit with that in silence for a moment, but as seconds tick by, I realize how precious they are. How little time we have.

"Claude, tell me…" I hesitate, unable to fully form the question. "He's your sire. Is it possible for you to beat him?" Tonight I saw him defy Ambrose's commands, but it's obvious how difficult it was. In a duel, there will be no time for that. A second's hesitation could mean death.

"Would I have challenged him if it weren't?"

"To save me? Yes." I don't understand his riddles or his smiles. How can he take this so lightly? Is this some sort of self-sacrifice?

"Mm," he agrees. "Sometimes I forget how well you know me." He leans in, presses his forehead to mine. "Will you kiss me? For luck?"

"But the contract…"

"Fuck the contract," he says, still smiling. "Soon enough it won't matter."

My stomach twists as I study him. That gleam in his eye, is it confidence or a manic sort of resignation to whatever's going to happen? It scares me, and so do his words. "Then you can kiss me after you've won."

"As cruel to me as ever, I see."

My smile is wobbly. "I can offer you more than luck, anyway." I slide into his lap and brush my hair from my neck. "Take my strength."

His nose brushes along my jaw as he kisses my bruised neck, ever so gently. "Not here," he murmurs. "You're hurt."

"I don't care. I want you to."

He sighs against my skin, but pulls away, reaching instead for my wrist. "I'll bite you there after I've won," he says, looking up at me, before sinking his fangs into my skin. He's only echoing my words from earlier, but still, it makes my stomach twist. We both know there may not be an *after*.

He drinks until his broken fingers straighten. I spend the rest of the ride in his arms, my face pressed into his shoulder, and wish I could stay here forever. Just earlier today, I thought the worst possible thing would be to walk away from Claude at the end of this year… but now I know there are worse things that can happen.

When the car comes to a stop, it's painful to extricate myself from his embrace. He smooths down the front of his shirt before he steps out, and turns back to offer his hand, helping me from the car.

His fingers linger on mine, his thumb rubbing slow circles against my knuckles. "I have to go in alone," he tells me. "They won't allow a human in the room when they're ironing out the official details. I'm sorry."

I swallow and force myself to nod. There's no use in wailing and carrying on; I'm sure he'd have me at his side, if there was a way to. "Will I be able to see you before the duel begins?"

He smiles sadly, shakes his head.

"Oh." A hot rush of tears threatens to spill over all of a sudden, but I take a deep breath and blink them away. I won't cry in front of him. I won't do anything that might make this any harder than it already is. "Then… I'll see you after."

He lifts my hand to his lips and kisses my knuckles. Once, twice. "You will," he says, and lets me go, and leaves me.

I force myself to breathe as I look around. I'm at the bottom of a set of great stone stairs, leading up to an ancient-looking mansion. It's all red brick and dark gable roofs, spires foreboding against the night sky, unnervingly quiet despite the violence that I know is about to occur within its walls.

I don't know what to do or where to go. Surely I'll be allowed inside to watch, at least. It's the last thing I want to do, but I can't abandon Claude among his enemies. Still, the thought of standing in the crowd alone, watching it unfold, makes another wave of tears threaten to overwhelm me. Claude said he wanted the Vulpe Court as witnesses, and I've seen how they treat him. Will I be the only one here not rooting for his death?

Then footsteps approach. "Nora."

I gasp, and the tears finally spill over as I turn toward the familiar voice. "*Benjamin.*" I throw my arms around his neck. "You came."

"Of course I did." He's stiff in my embrace, clearly unused to such physical affection. But he wraps one arm around me and pats me on the back with the other, which is surprisingly reassuring. "God, Nora. What happened? Is it true that Ambrose hurt you?"

"Not badly," I say.

His expression darkens as his gaze falls to the bruises around my neck. "Assaulting a valentine," he murmurs. "I didn't think he'd have the gall."

"I'm more afraid of what he'll do to Claude." I'm sick with it, now that we're here. My heart is pounding so hard, I'm dizzy. "Is it possible for Claude to win?"

"I…" Benjamin's grip on me loosens, and I slip free, trying and failing to catch his eye. "I really don't know, Nora. I'm not sure why he demanded the old right instead of letting Vulpe handle the transgression against you. I wish I could offer more hopeful news, but…"

Anxiety is a jagged thing in my chest, digging shards into my insides. "I don't understand why he would do this either," I say. "Claude isn't a fighter."

"He wasn't."

I start at the half-familiar voice, and Benjamin and I both turn to see a vampire approaching. Dark hair, dark eyes, fine black clothing.

I curtsy after a startled pause. "Lord Sebastian?" It comes out a question. I glance at Benjamin, but he seems surprised, too, though he covers it with a bow.

"Miss Nora." Sebastian inclines his head. "Amelia sends her support. She wanted to come too, but I abhor the thought of her witnessing this kind of violence."

"I'm surprised that was enough to dissuade her," Benjamin says as he straightens.

Sebastian's lips quirk. "It wasn't. But I told her I would have an easier time keeping an eye on Nora if I didn't also have to worry about her safety."

"That makes more sense."

"But…" I burst out, looking between the two. "Sorry. I'm glad you're here, but why are you? And how did you know to come?"

"Claude didn't tell you?" Sebastian asks, but nods himself a moment later as if answering his own question. "No, I suppose he wouldn't have wanted you to worry."

"Tell me *what*?" He's even worse than Claude. Are all vampires this unforthcoming?

"Claude has been visiting me quite frequently," Sebastian says. "To train."

"Ah," Benjamin says. They share a knowing look.

It takes me a moment longer. To train for…? But then I look at the building ahead of us, and remember what's to come, and I understand. He's been training for *this*. He knew this fight with Ambrose was coming, sooner or later. Over this last week he tried to paint again, to see if there was another way, but… he was prepared for this outcome.

I wish he had told me. I wish I had kissed him in the car. I am so full of wishes and hope and fear that my head is spinning and my knees feel weak.

Benjamin touches my shoulder, bringing me back to this moment.

"Lord Sebastian was a general in the last vampire war. He is a legend among our kind," he tells me, while Sebastian looks away, clearly discomfited by the praise. "Claude could not have asked for better tutelage in dueling."

"Does that mean he can win?" I ask. "Even against his sire?"

They exchange a look. Neither seems eager to answer me.

"How strong is the bond?" Benjamin asks me. "It is… a

difficult thing, to defy that connection. There is a natural attachment, an instinct to please. It's not just a matter of strength, but whether or not Claude can bring himself to finish it." He pauses, expression grim. "And… if Ambrose were to issue a command…"

"I… I saw Claude defy him tonight. But…" I shake my head. "Surely Ambrose can't be allowed to command him in a duel, can he?"

"A vampire is allowed to do whatever they see fit with their fledgling," Benjamin says, shaking his head. "A duel is no exception. It's archaic, and many will see it as distasteful, but it's law."

"But that's not fair," I say. It makes me so angry, I can hardly breathe.

I try to shut my eyes and think through it. Claude isn't an idiot. He's been training for this for months now. Surely he wouldn't have challenged Ambrose if he didn't think it was possible to beat him.

"Maybe that's why Claude insisted they fight in front of the court," I say, opening my eyes. "Perhaps Ambrose would be too proud to use a command to win in front of them."

"Might be so," Benjamin says. "Speaking of which…" He nods toward the entrance. "We should head in. They'll be starting soon."

"Right." I stare up at the double doors ahead. Despite my agreement, I can't bring myself to move. When I walk through those doors, this will be real. There will be nothing left to do but sit and watch whatever happens.

When Benjamin offers his arm, I take it, and let him lead me inside. He squeezes my trembling hand where it grips him. I'm grateful for his presence at my side, and for Sebastian, stony-faced as he is, here to support Claude along with us. They keep me from panicking as we step inside the Vulpe mansion, but only barely. Still, I feel lightheaded as I look around the room at what seems, to my eyes, to be a pit of vipers.

This wide-open space, with white marble walls and tile, could only be a ballroom. But the furniture has been pushed to the sides to open a space in the middle. Under other circumstances it might be for dancing, but now it looks, to me, like nothing so much as an arena. Archaic, barbaric. Perhaps it was what the room was first intended for, and all the glamor and manners have just been constructed around it to conceal the ugly truth. Like with everything in the vampire world, glitz and politeness cover sinister truths.

The Vulpe vampires look more casual than I expected, almost like normal people. But this is no glamorous party, and they must have rushed here last-minute to witness the duel. Because of that, perhaps, they're less intimidating than I imagined. I thought they'd all be like Ambrose, all vipers in suits and smiles, but instead I see an eclectic bunch. Some are dressed finely, but others bear paint stains, clay-crusted elbows, fingers smeared with graphite. I see Claude in them more than I see Ambrose. And the crowd is marked with lowered voices and shifting eyes, a sense of unease.

"They don't approve of this," I note in a low voice to Benjamin as I glance around.

"It is a shameful matter," Benjamin agrees. "A valentine hurt. A sire challenged by his fledgling. Even if Ambrose has power here, it isn't something the court can overlook."

"It's brought his ugliness into the spotlight," I say. That must be what Claude wanted. He'll force them to stare it in the face.

CHAPTER THIRTY-TWO

"And it makes Claude look brave," Benjamin says.

"He *is* brave," Sebastian says. He rarely speaks, but when he does, his voice is sure and strong. "And he is right, to stand up for his valentine. No one can deny it."

But none of that means he will win, and neither of my companions can tell me otherwise. Still, at least I'm not alone as I take my place in the crowd surrounding the open floor with Benjamin on one side and Sebastian on the other. There's no sign of Claude or Ambrose yet; they must be elsewhere, discussing the terms. Or perhaps finding some way out of this that doesn't involve violence. Maybe Claude has found a way to negotiate…

A door at the back of the room opens, and the crowd turns that way, silent and watchful. Vampires part as three people make their way to the empty center of the room: Claude, Ambrose, and a stern-looking vampire with a snake pinned to his breast pocket, clearly some kind of Vulpe representative.

My heart sinks at the look on Claude's face, serious and resigned. I've never seen him look this somber before, even in his dour moods. He's stripped down to a plain undershirt and trousers, his fingers bare of their usual rings and his hair combed back. He looks so unlike himself.

Ambrose, on the other hand, is smiling as he shrugs off his jacket and hands it to the man from Vulpe. They exchange a quiet word, and Ambrose laughs like all of this is a joke to him. I dig my nails into my palms to release some of my building anger, and focus on Claude.

He meets my gaze across the room. I can't read his expression this far away, but he touches one hand to his heart briefly and nods at me before returning his attention to the other vampires.

I let out a shaky breath. Benjamin's hand slides into mine, and I squeeze him, grateful not to be alone.

The Vulpe man raises a hand, and the murmurs of the crowd die away, leaving a room full to the brim with silence.

"I, Henry de Vulpe, stand today as witness to a blood duel within the court," the man says, his voice deep and clear. He holds Ambrose's jacket draped over one arm, which seems an outrageous show of favoritism given the circumstances. But Claude knew the court would be against him. He challenged his sire here, in front of them, where none could dispute the outcome. I have to believe he knows what he's doing. "Lord Claude de Vulpe has challenged Lord Ambrose de Vulpe, his sire, on the grounds of an attack against his valentine. Lord Ambrose, do you dispute the claim?"

"I do not," Ambrose drawls, shameless. "I punished her insolence, and now I shall punish my fledgling's." There's a flash of murmurs within the watching vampires, and Ambrose bears his fangs. "Do not pretend any of you would do otherwise. Claude has been a bane upon me since the day I turned him. An embarrassment and a waste. This tantrum will be his last."

The murmurs intensify but die away quickly as Henry raises his hand again for silence.

"And Lord Claude, you wish to claim your right to a trial by combat?" he asks.

Claude never looks away from Ambrose. "I do."

The witness nods. "So it shall be done. A duel to first yield, or death, whichever comes first." He looks at Ambrose, and then at Claude, gaining a nod of approval from each. Then he steps back to the edge of the crowd, leaving the two vampires in the center of the open ring.

Benjamin grips my hand. Sebastian leans forward, ever so slightly, his gaze intent.

"Begin," says the Vulpe witness.

Chapter Thirty-Three

Ambrose lunges for Claude without a word. That's all I can see before both vampires move too fast for me to follow, a blur of motion in the center of a completely still crowd. It is eerily silent, both the fight and the crowd; I fear everyone can hear the frantic drum of my heartbeat, my shaky breaths as I cling to Benjamin's arm. Dark blood splatters against the stark white floor, and I press a hand to my mouth to stifle my gasp, but the fight is such rapid chaos that I can't even tell who's bleeding.

I tear my eyes off it to look at Sebastian, whose face is unreadable as his eyes flicker over the duel, and then at Benjamin, who gives me a grim, tight-lipped smile.

"They're closely matched," he murmurs. Someone nearby hisses in disapproval of the noise, and he says nothing more but squeezes my hand. I cannot tell whether or not I should be reassured.

Then all at once there's a stir in the crowd. A group on the edge of the room scatters, and a half second later a body thumps against the wall there and slumps to the floor. My heart surges—*Ambrose*. A moment later Claude is standing over him. His shirt is torn, and he's bleeding from a half dozen bite wounds across his neck and torso, but he's still standing and Ambrose isn't.

Yet his shoulders are trembling, with exhaustion or emotion, as he stares down at his sire. "Yield," he says.

"*No,*" Sebastian says, barely more than a breath. "Finish it, Claude—"

Ambrose tilts his head back, long hair falling away from his face. His bloodstained lips curl back.

Claude lunges for him. But Ambrose speaks first.

"Don't move," he rasps.

Claude goes still. One hand is still outstretched, his grasping fingers a mere inch from Ambrose's neck. Ambrose pushes it aside and stands on shaky legs.

A murmur ripples through the crowd, along with low hisses of outrage. Ambrose glances sidelong at the watching court and bares his fangs, but he doesn't step away from Claude.

"He is *my* fledgling," he says, loud enough to be heard above the clamor. He circles around the still-frozen Claude, his steps measured and his expression calculating. "And it is *my* duel, which I have not yet lost."

The vampires watching are shifting, their disapproval palpable. But nobody steps in to stop this. I lunge forward to do it myself, but Benjamin catches me around the waist and pulls me back, shaking his head.

"I'm sorry, you can't interfere," he says. "They'll kill you." And then, slightly louder, "Nor can you, Sebastian. Unless you wish to incite another court war."

Sebastian hisses under his breath, his fangs out and his eyes locked on Ambrose. But he doesn't move.

"Kneel," Ambrose says, and Claude's knees hit the floor with a *crack* that seems to echo in the silent room. His hands sit limp on his thighs, his head tilted down so dark curls obscure his eyes.

Ambrose seizes a fistful of Claude's hair and pulls his head back, exposing the pale column of his neck.

"All of this could have been avoided," he murmurs, looking down at Claude with palpable distaste, "if you had only done as I said." He strokes one fingertip down Claude's cheekbone, almost tenderly, before his hand wraps around his neck.

Benjamin pulls me closer. "Look away," he murmurs.

But I refuse. Push him away. Continue to watch, even as tears start to fill my eyes.

This can't be happening. It can't be the way it ends. But if it is, the least I can do is watch.

And as Ambrose's fingers tighten and start to pull, I can't keep quiet. I don't care that the room is silent enough to hear a pin drop, that everyone else is merely standing by and watching as though this is some sick form of entertainment.

"Fight him!" I cry. I strain against Benjamin's arms again, heedless that heads around the room are turning to look at me. Ambrose turns too, his lips curving into a horrible grin as he sees my emotions spill over. I don't know if this counts as interfering with the duel, and at this moment, I don't care. I just want Claude to have a fair chance. *"Fight him!"* I know he can. He has to.

Through the blur of my tears, I see Claude's fingers twitch.

Ambrose turns back to him, catching the movement out of the corner of his eye. And suddenly, Claude is on his feet, twisting out of Ambrose's grip as his fist swings to deliver a swift jab to Ambrose's sternum.

Ambrose staggers back, eyes wide with shock and fury. Claude tackles him to the ground, wraps both hands around his neck.

Vampires don't need to breathe, but when I see Ambrose's lips move without sound, I realize his purpose: they still need air to speak. Ambrose struggles against his grip, but Claude keeps him pinned with his full weight.

A drop of blood splatters against Ambrose's shocked face. Another. My stomach drops but Claude lifts his head, and as I see the red trailing down from his eyes, I realize he's not wounded. He's weeping.

The room is silent, so I know he'll hear when I whisper his name, a single word containing all of my sympathy and all of my pleading and all of my love.

Claude shuts his eyes. Then, with a shout, he tears Ambrose's head off.

As Claude releases him, Ambrose's head thunks against the tile. His eyes stare at nothing.

I stand frozen, mouth hanging open, shocked at both the sudden violence and that this is real.

It's over. Ambrose is gone. And Claude...

Claude tries to rise once and falls back onto one knee, his hand clutching at his chest. I strain to break free from the cage of Benjamin's arm, terrified that there is some wound there I cannot see, but Benjamin murmurs reassurance into my ear, and after a moment to gather himself, Claude manages to stand. He turns to the crowd, searching until he finds my tear-streaked face. Then, absurdly, he bows. And, just as absurdly, there is a scattering of applause from the watching vampires.

Benjamin and Sebastian don't join in. Neither do I. I'm too busy sobbing in relief, held up only by Benjamin's grip.

"Victory to Lord Claude de Vulpe," calls the observing vampire, which feels unnecessary. But then nothing else matters, because Benjamin releases me and I run across the room to throw myself into Claude's arms.

He stumbles back a step before hugging me back, and I loosen my grip, reminding myself that he's wounded.

"You're hurt," I say, frantic. "Should I…?"

"I'm fine." He pulls me closer, and I can feel him trembling, from exhaustion or adrenaline or both. "Don't you dare let go."

I swallow hard and clutch him closer, glad for the excuse to cling to him. "What happens now?"

Claude smiles at me, and then turns to slowly survey the Vulpe Court. My stomach twists as I realize that they're all staring at us. We're surrounded by a sea of still faces. It's difficult to read their expressions; most of them seem shocked by what's just occurred. That includes the man who was acting as witness to the duel. He seems to have dropped Ambrose's coat at some point; it lies in a velvet heap at his feet.

He clears his throat as Claude's gaze falls on him, and steps forward. "Congratulations on your victory, Lord Claude," he says. "It was… well-fought."

"Why, thank you." Claude's smile is sharp, his eyes narrowed.

"As for the matter of your valentine interfering…"

The man—Henry—turns his sharp gaze on me. My stomach drops. Claude's grip on my shoulders tightens.

"What interference?" Claude asks icily when I find myself unable to respond.

"We all heard her yell for you," Henry says. "She clearly snapped you out of Lord Ambrose's command—"

Claude releases me to take a step closer to the other vampire. "If you doubt my ability to win a duel without so-called interference, you are welcome to challenge me yourself."

Henry stares at him. Claude stares back.

Only the former flinches when there's movement nearby. A vampire steps away from the crowd, watching the conversation. It takes me a moment to place her as the painter whose exhibit we visited.

Claude casts her a wary look, shifting his stance as if to hide me behind him. His shoulders brace like he's preparing to face the whole of the Vulpe Court. And maybe he is, I realize with a burst of terror. How many of them were in Ambrose's palm? I vividly recall how Elizabeth was reluctant to even speak to Claude at her exhibition.

But the painter—Elizabeth—lifts her chin and fixes her glare on Henry. "Lord Ambrose is gone," she says. "And there is no one left to enforce his threats. I think you'll find that many of us are not eager to be pressed down under someone's heel again, Lord Henry."

The rest of the room is silent. But when I glance around again, I'm shocked to see that a number of other vampires have stepped forward from the crowd, standing in a small half circle behind Elizabeth, and Claude, and myself, in silent support.

Claude turns to look, too. The shock is plain on his face, and then his features crumple in relief. I reach forward to squeeze his shoulder, silently conveying the same thing these other Vulpe members are saying: *You're not alone anymore.*

"I suppose," Henry says, "your valentine's actions do not, strictly speaking, go against the letter of the law. And—" He clears his throat. "It's rather a moot point. I'm willing to overlook it."

"How *generous*," Claude says, the word ending in a hiss

around his extended fangs. "And while I am here… I would like to bring up a change to my valentine contract. The removal of a certain clause."

Henry smiles wanly. I'm certain he would be sweating, if vampires could sweat. "Ah, yes, we can certainly begin discussing it, but I'm afraid it won't be possible on such short notice, or without Miss Nora's representative…"

"Lord Benjamin?" I call, and he peels away from the crowd to come to our side. I blink innocently at Henry, smiling. "I believe this gentleman had a question for you."

"And we have plenty of time to discuss whatever needs be discussed," Claude says, his hand resting on my lower back. "But quite frankly, *sir*, I do not intend to leave this building until my valentine and I are free from that godforsaken clause in our contract."

Chapter Thirty-Four

I t is a wondrous thing, to walk out of the Vulpe Court knowing that Claude and I are free to do what we please. It feels like I'm floating; I can still hardly believe it, even when he grabs me by the hand in front of everyone and leads me to the car. His fingers are tight as they twine with mine, like he's afraid I'll slip away if he relaxes. His grip would be uncomfortable if I wasn't grateful for the anchor right now. I clutch him just as tightly.

Once, I would've imagined we'd be all over each other the second we had the chance. But as we climb into the car, I'm exhausted, and Claude must be even more so. We cuddle together in a single seat, my fingers stroking his hair, my legs across his lap.

"Here," I say, offering my wrist. "You should heal."

He drinks from me in slow sips, and I watch the wounds on his neck and chest heal. It's satisfying to know I can help in at least this small way, after everything he's done for me.

"That must have been difficult," I murmur. Ambrose was a monster, but he was also his sire.

Claude closes the bite wound and leans into my touch, shutting his eyes. "It was," he says, and he sounds wearier than I've ever heard before. "Like cutting off a piece of myself." He lifts one hand to his chest, fingers pressing hard into his sternum. "It hurts."

"I'm sorry it came to that."

"Don't be sorry. He's the one who forced me to it." He opens his eyes and gazes at me. "I would cut off my own hand before I let it harm you."

"I know," I say with a sad smile. "But... I can't help but feel guilty. I know you're better off without him, but... you could've lived an eternity with Ambrose. I feel like I can't possibly offer enough to make up for losing him."

"I would spend an eternity with you, if you want it," he says.

My heart beats faster. I'm not sure what to say. We've never discussed this before; I've never even give serious thought to whether or not the change is something I'd want.

Claude's fingers brush my cheekbone. "You don't have to answer now," he says. "And if you say no, I would gladly take a human lifespan with you over eternity with him."

"Claude..." I start, and stop. If I say more, I'm going to burst into tears.

He smiles. "I know, *mon coeur*." He kisses my cheek. "We can discuss it all later, after I love you so thoroughly, you won't be able to walk straight. But..." He yawns. "First, I need a nap."

* * *

A *nap*, it turns out, was an understatement. Claude is soon out cold with his head against my shoulder. When we reach the house, it takes me three attempts to stir him enough for him

260

to stumble inside. It's nearly dawn, and he can barely keep his eyes open, but I pull him by the hand into the bathroom. I unbutton his bloodstained shirt, toss it aside, and do the same with his trousers.

"I don't think I'm in a state to properly ravish you, *mon chou*," he mumbles, barely able to keep his eyes open.

I laugh, pulling him into the shower. "I'm just getting you cleaned up, Claude. You can ravish me after we get some sleep."

He mumbles half-coherent confessions of undying love while I scrub the dried blood off him. When I finish toweling him off, he pulls me in and kisses me. Slow and sweet, his thumb caressing my jaw as his tongue coaxes my lips apart. My legs turn to jelly beneath me, so that only his grip on my waist keeps me upright.

"I mean it," he whispers, his mouth still mere centimeters from mine.

"Mean what?"

"All of it." He kisses the corner of my mouth, the soft spot under my jaw, the side of my neck. "I love you."

I touch his chin to guide his face back up to mine. "I love you too." I kiss him again, quick and chaste, and pull away before it can deepen into something hungry and mind-melting. He sways on his feet as he tries to chase my lips, smiling like a drunk man. "Let's get some sleep before you collapse on me," I say, and lead him to bed.

He collapses onto it completely naked while I discard my wet clothes and put on my silk robe.

We curl together beneath the sheets, barely clothed but far too tired to do anything about it, although Claude mutters a couple of things under his breath that sound like half-formed promises of what he's going to do to me tomorrow. He's asleep before I can answer. I watch him for a while, gently brushing damp curls off his forehead and studying his face before I, too, doze off.

Chapter Thirty-Five

I wake slowly, arms lifting above my head in a luxurious stretch. Silk whispers over my bare skin as I move, and I gradually remember that I am wearing only my robe, and I am not in my own bed. I open my eyes and turn to my side, and Claude is there, already awake and watching me.

I smile. "Hi," I say, suddenly shy.

"Hi," he murmurs back. He slides closer, cups my face, and kisses me.

The *way* he kisses me quickly chases away any self-consciousness about morning breath. His mouth is soft but hungry against mine, slow and deep, like nothing I've ever felt before. I sigh into his mouth and he devours the sound, devours all of me, kissing me so thoroughly that my entire body goes liquid. Barely giving me time to breathe between each press of his lips, each stroke of his tongue. By the time he pulls away, I am breathing hard and flushed, and he looks as drunk on pleasure as I feel.

He watches my face as his hands travel down over my body. His palms ghost over my curves through the thin covering of the silk. A pause, a flick of his eyes to mine, and he undoes the robe's tie.

He gently eases the fabric off my shoulders and away so I am bare before him for the first time, and stares at me like my body is a holy revelation. He gazes for a long time, so long that I can feel myself flushing, lips parting as his fangs emerge behind them. Finally he leans in, and his lips press against my mouth, my cheek, the pulse point at my neck, the hollow above my collarbone. He nuzzles his face between my breasts with a pleased groan.

"Touch me," I beg.

He obliges, teasing my nipple with first his fingers and then his tongue, lapping at the sensitive bud until it stiffens under his attentions. Then he bites me so swift I'm still mid-gasp as he pulls back and soothes it with his tongue. He lavishes the other breast with the same treatment—fingers, mouth, fangs—and slowly works his way down my stomach. He marks me a half dozen times with his fangs, each time taking only the smallest taste of my blood. It leaves me throbbing with pleasure, aching for more.

I arch beneath his touch. He looks up at me as he pauses, face hovering over my stomach, his fingers traveling south. As his knuckles graze the heat between my thighs, I suck in a breath.

"Oh, *mon chou*," Claude murmurs. "You're soaked."

He parts my thighs and lowers himself between them. But instead of giving me what I so desperately need, he kisses my calf, and then higher, mouth traveling up the inside of my leg. I cry out as he sinks his fangs into my inner thigh. So *close* to where I crave him, but he swaps to the other thigh and bites me again, even higher. He sucks hard this time, and I arch my back with a gasp as the sensation zips straight to my throbbing core.

I'm shaking, chest heaving, hovering on the precipice between agony and pleasure. I'm dizzy with it. "Claude," I beg, my voice faint. "Claude, please."

I reach down and tangle my fingers in his curls, tug him up to where I want him. He chuckles, sending cool air over my hot core. Then he finally tastes me—short, gentle strokes of his tongue over my sensitive skin. He moans, a sound that vibrates against my skin, and then grabs me by the hips and drags me closer, forces my thighs wider, lifting my ass off the bed as his tongue explores every inch of me before swirling around my clit.

In mere seconds I'm crying out and clutching at the sheets for dear life, falling apart beneath his clever mouth. Sparks go off behind my eyes as my entire body trembles with bliss.

His fingers dig into my hips, holding me in place as I shake, each flick of his tongue making my brain short-circuit. I've never had an orgasm like this—it seems to go on and on, endless rolling hills of pleasure. Just when it seems it's about to stop, he sucks my clit and curls two fingers inside of me, and I'm back in it, eyes rolling, whimpering helplessly, unsure if I'm coming a second time or if the first is never-ending. He laps at me until the shakes subside, and then lowers me onto the bed, looking down at me with my wetness glistening on his lips. He licks it off and hums in satisfaction.

I'm still breathing hard, weak with pleasure. My head lolls back and my eyes close.

"Look at me," Claude demands.

I open my eyes and drag them up to meet his. His gaze is burning as he takes in every inch of me—sweaty, panting, half unraveled.

"*Très jolie*," he murmurs, pushing a strand of sweat-damp

hair off my forehead. "So pretty as you come apart for me." His fingers are cool against my feverish skin, and my eyelids flutter, my nerves so raw that even the slightest brush of his skin gives me pleasure. "But you can take more."

I'm not sure if it's a statement or a question, but either way there's nothing to do but nod, half senseless with bliss. His smile is dazzling. He leans in to press cold lips to my cheek.

"That's my girl," he murmurs. He grabs my thigh with one hand, lifting it to position me; with the other, he guides himself to my entrance. I'm wet and ready for him, and he enters me in one long, slow stroke, stretching me out inch by inch until he is fully seated within me. For a moment he holds himself there, dark eyes locked on mine. His pupils are blown wide, his expression a mirror of the first time he drank from me: a little wild, a little stunned. I feel much the same.

"Oh, God," I whimper. It's almost too much, too good, the way he fills me up.

"Breathe," he says, nuzzling his nose against mine. "That's it. Relax for me, *mon chou.*"

I dig my fingers into his back, so I can feel the way his muscles shift and contract as he pulls out and thrusts into me again, harder. I cry out, and he kisses me to swallow the sound, his mouth slow and soft and sensual against mine as he grinds slowly into me.

"Claude," I whimper against his lips.

"Yes," he breathes, his eyes on mine. "Say my name again."

"Claude," I beg. "C-Claude— More—"

He picks up speed within me, each thrust a little harder, a little faster, until each slap of his hips against me has the bed shaking beneath us. I arch beneath him, and he groans, whispering French words between kisses, his mouth never far from mine as he pounds me into the mattress.

I gasp as he smoothly rolls me onto my side, his mouth against my neck as he pushes into me from behind. One hand grips my hip, pulling me back against his chest, while the other slides between my legs to rub slow circles on my clit.

"*Oh.*" I gasp, pushing my hips back to meet each thrust and take him deeper. "Please…" I arch my neck as he mouths me, teasing with lips and tongue and the slightest prick of teeth. "Bite me—"

I've barely finished the demand when his fangs sink into my neck. My eyes roll as pleasure shudders through my entire body. I feel—*everything*. His teeth in my neck, his hand between my legs, his cock still pumping inside of me.

I come apart. Crying out, my body shaking with an ecstasy I've never known before. Blinding, all-consuming. Claude moans against my neck and follows me over the edge with a few frantic thrusts. He holds me tightly as I tremble through the waves of pleasure. Even when I finally go limp, eyes shut, breathing hard, he stays inside of me, peppering my neck and shoulder with slow kisses. He licks at the trickle of blood from my neck, heals the various marks he left on me with his bloodstained lips.

"*Mon coeur,*" he whispers. "*Mon amour.*"

I cuddle against him, gripping his arm where it holds my waist, unable to form coherent words yet. I don't know if I *have* words for what I just experienced.

After we lie together a while, Claude insists on slipping out of bed to make me breakfast, worried about my blood loss.

"It felt like you hardly fed from me," I protest, touching my neck, where he's already healed the puncture wounds.

He flashes me a smile, fangs lending the sweet expression a

hungry edge. "Oh, but I intend to eat plenty more today, *mon chou.*"

Even after my *thorough* pleasuring, that look still sends a coil of heat through me. I mirror his wicked grin. "Promise?"

He returns a short while later with a tray, still naked, to serve me in bed. A decadent feast is laid out for me: golden French toast with dripping butter and a dusting of powdered sugar, heaped with whipped cream and fresh berries. He watches me eat for a while, smiling as I hum in appreciation. Then he slides between my legs and enjoys his own breakfast from my thigh. When I move the tray aside and grasp his hair in wordless demand, he pulls his fangs out and eats me again, two fingers curling inside of me while his tongue strokes me relentlessly toward another world-shattering orgasm.

"This isn't fair," I pant, lying back on the bed. "I'm all sweaty and disgusting and you're... perfect."

He licks sweat from my stomach as he climbs back up my body. His kiss is salty and sweet, tasting of my own pleasure. "Never disgusting," he murmurs. "But I'm happy to clean you up, if you like."

True to his word, he soon carries me to the shower in a boneless bundle. It starts off innocent as he gently massages shampoo into my scalp and holds me against him beneath the warm water. But soon enough he's on his knees in front of me, one of my legs hooked over his shoulder as his fingers work inside of me.

I press myself against the wall, whimpering. "Claude... I can't... I can't possibly..." I can't even finish the sentence. My body is weak, my head spinning.

"Of course you can, *mon chou.*" I hate how even his voice is, his smile sharp and mischievous as he makes a mess of me again. "But maybe this isn't enough for you?" He slides a third finger over my slickness. But instead of pushing it inside of me to join the others, he glides it back, teasing at the tight rim of my ass before pushing inside.

I cry out at the new sensation, my body shaking as he begins to pump his fingers again.

"Come for me," he whispers.

And I do. Again as he fucks me against the shower wall, again as he carries me to bed, again and again until I'm delirious with pleasure.

I must have passed out at some point. When I stir again and reach for Claude, the bed beside me is empty. I rub my eyes and lift myself up on my elbows with a pang of concern, but it doesn't take much searching to find him. He's still in the room, situated beside the window with his easel and his paints. He is concentrating so fully, he doesn't even notice me stir, and his face is open and relaxed in a way I haven't ever seen before as his brush glides across the canvas.

I lie quietly in bed, watching him for a while, the delicate way he holds the brush, the slow and decisive strokes of paint. I doze off with my heart full.

* * *

Not all nights are as perfect as that one. As the weeks pass, there are times when Claude is up all day painting in a manic frenzy, and evenings when he can't drag himself out of bed. Sometimes I catch him pressing his palm to his chest without seeming to realize he's doing it, as though his heart is in physical pain. Maybe it is. I can't pretend to understand the bond between a sire and a fledgling, but it's obvious that it is painful to lose, no matter what a monster Ambrose once was.

"It didn't have to be like this," he mumbles one day, burrowing beneath the covers long past the time we usually get out of bed. "If I could have just painted something, then…"

"It's not your fault," I tell him. "I know you're not a violent man, Claude. He drove you to this. He would have killed you if you hadn't killed him. He would've killed *me* if you hadn't stopped him."

I run my fingers through his hair, trying to soothe him, but when he gets in these moods, he feels impossible to reach.

Henry and other vampires from the Vulpe Court come to visit the house a few times over the following weeks, and Claude spends long, tense hours with them and then emerges from the room looking exhausted and strained.

"Will you stay with the Vulpe Court?" I ask him one night after they've left, when I'm massaging the tension out of his long fingers in bed. "With Ambrose gone, I doubt you have to fear retaliation for leaving, right?"

"I could leave if I wanted to," he says. "But…" He sighs, rolls over to lay his head on my lap. "Lady Elizabeth and some of the younger vampires have asked me to stay. To help change things from within, now that Ambrose is no longer here to force his ideals upon the rest of the court."

"And is that what you want?"

He considers it for a few moments. "I'm afraid I'm not up to the task," he says, "but I think I'd like to try."

I lean down to kiss his brow. "Then try."

I take care of him as well as I can: rubbing his back, urging him to feed from me, coaxing him down to the beach when he retreats into the bedroom for too long. He doesn't want to talk about it, but I know that killing Ambrose left a wound in him that I fear may never heal.

Plus, the end of our contract is coming up, a subject I don't know how to broach.

I love Claude. The thought of leaving him makes me physically ill. And yet… I still have my future to think about. As lovely as this year with him has been, I never intended to be a valentine forever.

Claude and I have overcome so much, but now I'm stuck in precisely the situation I was afraid about from the start: so deeply in love that I'm considering giving up on the future I've always wanted for myself. Part of me thinks I could be happy here, passing slow nights in this house by the sea, watching Claude paint and spending an absurd amount of time in bed enjoying one another.

But another part knows that eventually I will grow restless and crave more than this. I want—I *need*—to do something with myself, to be more than a valentine prized for my looks and my blood. And I know I *can* achieve more than that, if only I can bring myself to reach for it.

* * *

I finally muster the courage to bring it up at breakfast one evening, when Claude is in a decent mood and has made me another decadent spread of fluffy ricotta pancakes with lemon curd. I insisted on eating in the dining room today, because although he loves to serve me breakfast in bed, we always end up thoroughly distracted.

"We need to talk about the contract," I say, looking across the table at him.

His face dims. "Yes. I suppose we do."

Now that I've broached the subject, I find myself tongue-tied. There's so much I want to say, so much I'm *afraid* to say. I'm scared of losing him; I need to start school; I don't know what any of this will mean for us.

"We're going to have to move," Claude says, before I can figure out what I want to say.

I blink. "What?"

"Yes… that is to say…" He fidgets, looking rather sheepish. "The house, I believe I once mentioned, actually belongs to Ambrose. And in a turn of events I rather should have anticipated, he did not leave it to me."

"Oh." I sit for a moment, processing that. "Well, you hate this house anyway."

He smiles. "I really do."

I take a breath. "I… would've needed to move, anyway. Because I want to go to college. At UCLA."

"Right. Studying engineering."

"Well…" I smile. "I was thinking of majoring in education, actually."

He beams at me. "Good. Wonderful." But then his expression creases in thought. "Los Angeles, then? I'll have to look at what's on the market there, but I'm sure we can find something."

I stare at him for a moment, and then break into a small, incredulous smile. "That easy?"

He looks at me like I've gone mad. "Well, yes? Of course I'll be coming with you."

"I… don't think I can fulfill the duties of a valentine while I'm in school," I say, brow furrowed. "All the events, the parties…"

He shrugs, unbothered. "I'll take as much as you can give, and be happy with it."

"I'll be gone a lot, with school and studying," I say, though I can't stop smiling. "And my classes will be during the day. Our schedules will be opposite."

"Ah, however will I fill the hours?" he teases. "It's a good thing I've picked up painting recently, no?" His smile broadens. "And I will cook for you every night."

There's a nervous drum in my chest, a buzz of fragile hope beneath my skin. He makes it sound so simple, but can it really be? Is it possible I can have both things I want at once? It's hard to imagine Claude in some apartment in grimy LA, waiting for me to come home from class. Far from the fairy-tale life we've lived together here and all the glitter and decadence of the vampire balls. He thinks he can handle it, but what if he starts to hate it? "I know it's not a normal arrangement for a valentine…"

Claude only laughs. "*Mon chou*, when have we ever been normal?"

Epilogue

The moment I step into the apartment, the scent of freshly baked bread and garlic envelop me like a warm hug. I sigh happily as I shrug off my coat, tension from the long day already melting from my shoulders.

I follow the smell to the kitchen. It's not a long trek—our apartment is pretty small, a single bedroom with a tiny patio out back. I was worried that it wouldn't be enough for my gorgeous, glamorous vampire boyfriend, but he's taken to it surprisingly well… as evidenced by the fact that he's currently waiting in our cramped kitchen, wearing an apron that says "king of the kitchen."

I grin, leaning against the doorway to watch him stir the bubbling tomato sauce. "Hi, baby."

"Welcome home, *mon chou*." He sets aside the wooden spoon to come kiss me. "How was your day?"

I sigh, leaning into him and breathing in his familiar scent. Beneath the apron, the collar of his shirt is stained with paint. "Good. Yours?"

"Better now that you're here."

"Cheesy."

"I'm French, I don't consider that an insult." He kisses

me again, this one deeper and slower. I let myself fall into it, running a hand through his silky curls, until I'm a little breathless.

Then I pull away, biting my lip. "You're going to burn dinner," I say. "Again."

"And it would be worth it. Again."

The wicked look on his face reminds me of a dozen times I've been bent over this counter, or spread out on the table, or pinned down on the floor. He chases my lips, steals one last kiss before I laugh and playfully push him away.

"Elaine and Sophie say hello," I tell him, leaning against the counter.

"You should invite them over for dinner again," Claude says. "I'm sure Sophie is getting closer to making it through the evening without fainting from my presence."

I laugh. "I hope so. It's getting a little ridiculous." My smile fades after a few moments, though. "And… my mom called again."

He looks sideways at me. "Oh?"

I bite my lip and nod. "I finally blocked her. It wasn't doing me any good, seeing her name pop up every few months."

He pulls me against him and presses a kiss to my forehead. "Good. I'm proud of you."

Dinner is quiet and delicious as always. Claude is finally getting better at cooking normal portions, too. When we're done eating—and him drinking—I clean the dishes. Of all the adjustments to our new life together, I think letting me help around the apartment has been the hardest. Even now he fidgets as he watches me, twirling rings around his fingers like he's physically suppressing the urge to come do it himself. But as I've told him a million times, sometimes I want a chance to take care of him, too.

Maybe the discomfort of that isn't the only thing making him restless tonight, though, because when I'm finished, he clears his throat and takes my hand, giving me a serious look.

"I want to show you something," he says.

"Okay..." I follow him into the bedroom, and pause as I see the paintings crowding the room. Even now, Claude has been hesitant to show me his work; he usually has his art put away by the time I come home, and I've always respected his privacy.

But now, it's all laid out for me to see. A dozen different paintings I haven't seen before—all of them of me.

A lump grows in my throat as I look from piece to piece. Me curled up in a chair reading, me lying in bed with my face slack in sleep, me in the shower with droplets of water cascading down my face. Some of them are suggestive. A few are downright lewd. But most just capture me in moments of day-to-day life, relaxed and unassuming.

The portraits are realistic. They have the same flaws I see in myself: the chip in my front tooth, the uneven squint in my eyes when I smile, the same imperfect face and body I see every day. Yet it isn't like looking in the mirror. I look different in Claude's hand, from Claude's eyes. I look...

"Beautiful," I whisper.

Claude's arms encircle me from behind, his chin resting atop my head. "Yes," he says, and I can hear the smile in his voice.

"This is amazing, Claude." I lean back against him, still unable to take my eyes off the portraits. "What are you going to do with them?"

"Well, that's up to you," he says. "I have toyed with the idea of doing an exhibition, after I help Lady Elizabeth organize her next one. But are you alright with me sharing them with the world?"

"I..." I turn over the idea in my head, imagining it. A gallery full of pictures of me. Once, I would've shied away from the idea immediately, afraid of what it might mean. But now...

I point. "*That* one is definitely not seeing the light of day."

Claude's laugh vibrates against my back. "Oh, no. That one's for me."

"But the rest..." I bite my lip, surprised at my own daring, and how the idea of these portraits in a gallery makes my chest fills with warmth. "The rest you could share."

Claude spins me around and lifts my chin with a finger, searching my eyes. "Really?"

I smile. "Really."

His smile grows. "*Mon coeur*," he murmurs. "I love you."

"I love you too." More than I ever would've thought possible.

"Now..." He slowly lowers himself to his knees in front of me, looking up with a familiar mischievous grin. "Time for dessert?"

And now, as every time before, Claude makes love like he makes art: his touch careful and incisive, his beauty almost painful to behold.

Acknowledgments

Many thanks to:

My developmental editor Sarah Chorn and copy editor Claudette Cruz ("The Editing Sweetheart").

My cover designer, Mayhem Cover Creations.

My beta readers, Jennifer and Medgai.

The Romance Author's Writing Group and Indie Authors Ascending discords.

My family, my partner, and my friends.

And lastly: thank you, readers, for your support for this series!

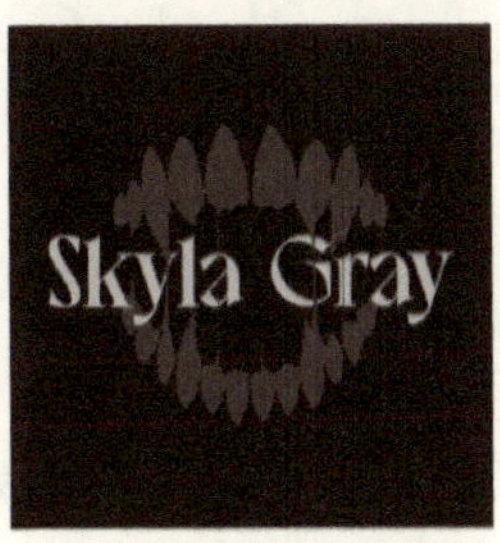# About the Author

Skyla Gray is a romance author fond of all things scary and steamy. When not writing, she can usually be found gaming, cooking, or binge-watching horror movies. She lives in Arizona with her partner and an absolute rascal of a dog.

Sign up for my newsletter for monthly updates and free bonus shorts!

You can connect with me on:
🌐 http://skyla-gray.com

Subscribe to my newsletter:
✉ https://skyla-gray.ck.page/e838b44108

Also by Skyla Gray

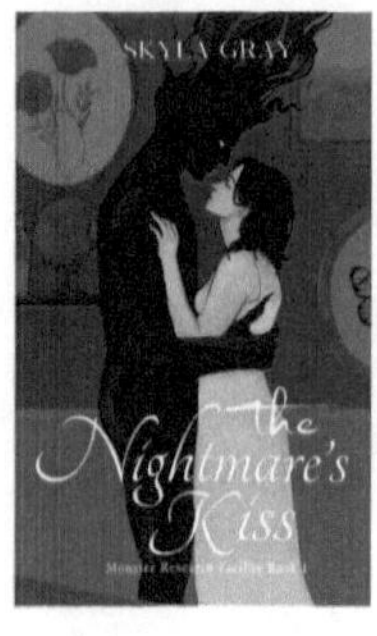

The Nightmare's Kiss
How can a living nightmare bring such sweet dreams?

Mara Vance never thought her "useless" psychology degree would lead to studying an actual monster. Subject X-13, aka "The Nightmare," is armed with sharp teeth, claws, and a constantly shifting form… yet Mara finds the huge shadow creature as intriguing as he is terrifying.

But as Mara studies him, she soon realizes that the Nightmare is far more intelligent than her shady superiors say he is. And every night, she indulges in twisted fantasies about the same monster. What happens in her dreams stays in her dreams – right?

Everyone says he's nothing more than a monster. But when dream and reality collide, Mara must decide how much she's willing to trust him – and herself. Will she risk setting him free, or will she lose him forever?